B FOR BUSTER

ALSO BY IAIN LAWRENCE

THE LIGHTKEEPER'S DAUGHTER

GHOST BOY

LORD OF THE NUTCRACKER MEN

THE HIGH SEAS TRILOGY

The Wreckers

The Smugglers

The Buccaneers

B FOR BUSTER

IAIN LAWRENCE

DELACORTE PRESS

Published by
Delacorte Press
an imprint of
Random House Children's Books
a division of Random House, Inc.
New York

Library of Congress Cataloging-in-Publication Data

Lawrence, Iain.
B for Buster / Iain Lawrence.
p. cm.
Summary: In the spring of 1943, sixteen-year-old Kak, desperate to escape his abusive parents, lies about his age to enlist in the Canadian Air Force and soon finds himself based in England as part of a crew flying bombing raids over Germany.
ISBN 0-385-73086-1 (trade) — ISBN 0-385-90108-9 (GLB)
1. World War, 1939–1945—Aerial operations, Canadian—Juvenile fiction.
[1. World War, 1939–1945—Aerial operations, Canadian—Fiction.
2. Air pilots—Fiction. 3. Bombers—Fiction. 4. Interpersonal relations—Fiction.
5. War—Fiction.] I. Title.
PZ7.L43545Bae 2004
[Fic]—dc22 2003017345

The text of this book is set in 12-point Garamond Number 3.
Book design by Trish Parcell Watts
Printed in the United States of America
June 2004
10 9 8 7 6 5 4 3 2 1
BVG

For Alysoun, my terrific fire-walking, board-busting sister

EUROPE IN 1943
10
4
5
6
TOKYO
CHUNGKING
1 BALTIC SEA
2 NORTH SEA
3 ENGLISH CHANNEL
4 CANADA
5 CHINA
6 JAPAN
UNITED KINGDOM
WHITBY
SETTLE
TOPCLIFFE
HARROGATE
LEEDS
YORKSHIRE
LEICESTER
HIGH
WYCOMBE
CHELMSFORD
LONDON

7 United Kingdom
8 Germany
9 France
10 Russia
11 Denmark
12 Netherlands
13 Belgium
14 Poland
15 Italy
16 Sicily
17 Lampione
Kakabeka
Germany
Kiel
Peenemünde
Hamburg
Berlin
R. Elbe
Krefeld
Gelsenkirchen
Bochum
Essen
Wuppertal
Remscheid
Düsseldorf
Cologne
München-Gladbach
Mannheim
Nuremburg
Aachen
R. Rhine

B FOR BUSTER

CHAPTER 1

I LEFT A TOWN where fewer than a thousand people lived. I traveled half the world, in the middle of a war, to get away from there. By the spring of 1943, when I finally arrived at a lonely airfield among the hills of Yorkshire, it seemed I had gone as far from Kakabeka as the moon was from the earth. But the first thing I saw when I walked through the door of the sergeants' mess was a guy I knew from home.

He was standing beside the piano, and I saw him only from the back, but I knew right away it was Donny Lee. No one else had hair as red as that, or ears as wide as those. No one but Donny looked so much like a clown from the back.

I thought of running away, but there was nowhere to go. I wanted to hide, but I couldn't. Lofty and Ratty and Buzz had come in behind me, filling the door of the Nissen hut. I just stood with my duffel bag in my hand as Donny turned toward me.

Just then, for a moment, I thought that it wasn't him after all, that it was someone older by many years. His face was a man's, with wrinkles and lines and dark blotches below his eyes. He couldn't be the boy I had seen just two years before, grinning as he climbed on an eastbound train. But his head started back in surprise and his mouth opened wide, and it was Donny, all right. He shouted across the crowd of airmen, "Hey! It's the kid from Kakabeka."

"Donny!" I said. I dropped my bag and pushed away from Lofty and the others. The tin hut was full of smoke and noise, of laughter and a dreadful singing. I pushed my way through groups of fliers, desperate to reach the piano, to get to Donny before he blurted out my secret.

He kept shouting in a voice that was too loud, as though he had gone deaf as well as old. "It is!" he cried. "It's the Kid. It's the Kakabeka Kid!"

He had never called me that at home, and I wished he would stop it now. He was too much older and wilder than me, and we'd never really been friends. But now he threw his arms around my shoulders and hugged me like a brother. He turned me round and introduced me to his crew.

In all of England only Donny knew the truth about me, and I was sure he'd tell the others. But all he said was that we'd gone to the same crummy school in the same little town. He said that he had been my hero, which wasn't exactly true. Then he steered me behind the bar and backed me into the corner made by the storage room.

"Hey, Donny," I said. "How many ops have you got?"

He didn't even answer. He pinned my shoulders to the wall and asked me, "What are you *doing* here?"

"What do you think?" I said.

"You stupid kid." He thrust his face near mine, and his voice was angry. "You're only sixteen."

If he had said it any louder, *everyone* would have learned the truth right there on my first day. But all the sergeants were busy with their bottles and their glasses, not even looking at me anymore. Lofty and little Ratty, still in the doorway, were gawking round the hut like tourists at a zoo, while Buzz just looked as half-witted as ever.

Donny lowered his voice, but didn't back away. His breath smelled of beer; his eyes seemed strange. "Go home," he said. "Tell them you lied and you want to go home."

"You're nuts," I told him.

"Do it." He pushed me again, so hard that the wall rattled. "Now. Before it's too late."

He grabbed my sleeve and twisted it round my arm. He stared at the blue patch where a fist held a sheaf of lightning bolts, then down at the cloud-shaped badge of a warrant officer. "Man, oh man," he said. "You must have told some beautiful lies."

He was right; I'd told some good ones. I'd invented years of school and made myself an orphan. The only real things in my life anymore were the patch and the badge, and I was proud as a peacock to have them. I yanked the cloth from his fingers.

"Does your old man know you're here?" asked Donny.

"I doubt he knows I've *gone,*" I said. "It's only been eight months." I tried to make a joke of it. "But just wait till he sobers up, eh?"

Donny stared at me so intently that I looked away, down at his tunic and tie. I saw a pair of wings on his chest, and my single one didn't seem so grand anymore. I envied Donny; I had wanted so much to be a pilot.

"I should tell them," he said. "I should go to the CO right now and—"

"No! Donny, don't." I raised my voice too high, and it broke into an embarrassing squeak. Faces turned toward us; conversations stopped. Over by the door, Lofty frowned at Buzz, then started walking toward me. I put my hand on Donny's arm and begged him, "Please don't tell. Nobody knows the truth."

He looked suddenly sad, and I saw how really deep his wrinkles were. He had aged like a dog, seven years for each of the two since I'd seen him. Just then—half angry, half sad—he looked a lot like my old man.

"What's wrong with you?" I asked.

"You'll get the chop," he said.

"I won't."

"You will. It's always the sprogs who buy the farm."

"Well, not me. Not *us.*" I tipped my head toward the door. "Lofty's the best there is. And anyway—"

"All right, Kid." He straightened up; he took his hands away. "Come and see me when you change your mind."

"You won't tell?" I asked.

"No. You're on your own."

"Then swear," I told him. "Swear to God."

He shook his head. "You'll fly an op or two, then beg me to get you out."

"Just do it," I said. "Swear."

And he did. I made him cross his heart and spit on his hand. Then he waved me off, with the same flick of his fingers that would have chased the deerflies back at home. "You'd better totter along and see Uncle Joe."

"Who's that?" I asked.

"The CO. He likes to meet all the sprogs."

Air force words were like music to me, but that one I hated. It made me blush, even though it was true; I *was* a sprog, a greenhorn.

Donny turned his back and disappeared into the swirl of blue just as Lofty came out of it. He was the tallest bloke I'd ever known, and I really felt like a kid as I looked way up at his face. Because of his height, and because he was almost twenty, I had always thought of him as an adult. But now, compared to Donny and the sergeants in the mess, he looked a bit silly, like an actor in a school play, only *trying* to look older.

"That chap," he said. "I say, was he binding you, old boy?" Lofty was Canadian too. He had been in England no longer than me, in the air force just a month or two more. But he talked like an old hand, trotting out the airmen's slang whenever he could, and he sometimes mumbled through his nose, trying to sound more British than the Brits. "What was that he called you? Kaka *what*?"

"Beka," I said with a sigh. "Kakabeka, okay?"

He had never heard of the place. I had told him and everyone else that my hometown was Port Arthur. He laughed and said, "I'll just call you Kid."

Everybody did, from that day on. My real name was forgotten, and I became the Kid or Kak or Kakky. But sometimes I was Kaka, and then I cursed that Donny Lee.

Lofty and I, and Ratty and Buzz, stood by ourselves in a corner. We listened to bits of conversation and snatches of song, and it was like hearing echoes from our training unit. All that fliers talked about were searchlights and flak and who had bought the farm. We nudged each other and pointed at the battered old sofas and the battered piano, a baby grand. It was missing one key and one leg, and it was propped up at its narrow end by a paperback book and a bomb. I wasn't an expert on pianos, but I thought it was a twenty-pounder bomb. I was glad when an adjutant whisked us off to meet the commanding officer.

He took us down a cinder path to the buildings that were grouped below the control tower. Waiting there for us, sitting side by side on the steps, were Simon and Will, the only officers in our crew. Both lieutenants, they'd been housed in the separate officers' quarters at the other side of the airfield, an enormous building—a manor or something—that I imagined was swank as could be. But I smiled to see their bicyles, a pair of old crates no better than the ones we'd left behind at the old squadron. They were parked in the usual heap by the path, a pile of rusted metal and bent spokes.

The adjutant slipped into the building and right back out. He sent us inside. "First door on your left."

Right away I liked Uncle Joe. He wore his Irvin jacket of leather and fleece, and his flying cap, both so scruffy that he looked like a puppet that had been stuffed too long in its box. He didn't get up from the chair behind his desk, and when we saluted he scowled. "Stop that nonsense," he said. "Sit down like proper people."

His furniture might have come from the mess. The legs of his wooden chairs were splinted together, as though the medics had been practicing on them. His little sofa oozed bits of white stuffing. Wedged in its corner, picking bits of fluff, sat an old guy, quite thin, all bent up like a big insect. Uncle Joe pointed at him. "Here's your flight engineer," he said. "Been waiting for a crew."

There was a lot of nodding all around. Ratty nipped up and shook the fellow's hand. "Pleased to meet ya, Pop," he said.

I felt sorry for the old guy. A pained expression came to his face, and I imagined that he didn't think of himself as very old, though he must have been at least thirty-five. It seemed he had just gotten his new name, and he didn't look any happier with it than I had been with mine.

The CO talked for an hour, telling us all about his squadron, the Four-Forty-Two. "Not the best," he said. "Not the worst. Just another lot in the Canadian Group." He went through everything in the same fashion, telling us the best and the worst of all his machines and pilots and men. Then he looked through a stack of paper and gave us *B for Buster,* an old Halifax Mk1 that was right down there with the worst. "It's an old crate, but it's got the gubbins," he said. "Prove yourselves and you'll get a top-notch job. I don't let the sprogs prang my best buses." I grinned like an idiot at his magical language.

He leaned back, his hands behind his head. "Now tell me about yourselves."

It didn't take long. Six of us had met only three weeks earlier, at an operational training unit on the coast. We had stooged over London for a couple of nights, to get a taste of the searchlights, and we'd done a bit of gardening in the North Sea, sowing the mines that fliers called vegetables. But we hadn't even been shot at yet. Four of us were Canadian: Lofty had sold shoes in Vancouver. He wanted to be a bush pilot when he got back to civvy street, like Wop May after the Great War. Will had been studying law at the University of Toronto. He was a great poet, but he didn't tell that to the CO. Buzz, our mid-upper gunner, had hammered railway spikes in the Rockies, and we all thought of him as nearly equal to his hammer in the brains department. Ratty was American, with a past nearly as mysterious as mine. He had gone to Canada in 1941 to volunteer for the air force, but none of us ever learned how he'd spent more than a year in flying school. Everyone loved Ratty; he was small and strange and funny. Simon was Australian, with a booming voice and a tangle of gingery hair. He had told us once, in his normal shout, "I was a gadna down unda," and I'd spent a week wondering if a "gadna" worked with kangaroos. It took me that long to figure out his accent and learn that he was really a gardener.

"And you?" asked the CO, nodding at me. I rattled off my usual lies about my poor dead parents and how I'd worked myself through high school. I nearly brought a tear to Uncle Joe with all my nonsense, and I saw sheer pity on the old guy's face. No one in the room—scarcely anyone in the world—knew that I had a drunken old logger for a dad, and a mother who cowered from him nearly every night but loved him in the mornings.

It was well after dark when we finished. All I wanted was to dash out and look at *B for Buster.* But Uncle Joe sent Will and Simon up to the officers' mess and called for an orderly to lead the rest of us to our Nissen huts. "Hop them round to the iron lung," he said.

It was quite a hike, across the apron and over an empty pasture. In the distance we could see the Halifaxes, their black-painted bodies kind of swallowing the moonlight, but their cockpits and their turrets glowing silver and blue. They looked wonderful to me, like a flight of great birds come to rest for the night.

"Which one's *Buster*?" I asked. "Huh? Which one?"

The orderly kept walking. "Who cares?" he said. "They all look alike in the dark."

I felt as small as a squashed bug. Then Pop grunted. "Cor," he said. "You need spectacles, mate. Old *Buster*'s the third from the left." I thought, *I'm going to like the old guy.*

We were taken to a hut that looked just the same as all the others. The beds inside were arranged in two rows as straight as graves. Smack in the middle, like a monument in a churchyard, stood a hulking black coal stove. None of the beds had people in them, but it was easy to see which were vacant just by looking at the walls. There was a nearly solid display of pinup girls and snapshots. At the end of the hut was a picture of Kakabeka Falls, and I knew that Donny slept below it. But here and there, above beds, there were empty spaces where the walls were speckled only with pinholes. I chose the one closest to the door, flinging myself across it with a cry of "Mine!"

It was a dumb thing to do, for someone who was always trying to seem older. But I did a lot of things like that, to the amusement of Lofty and the others. They thought I was a bit wild, a bit stupid, maybe. Buzz's deep laugh brayed through the hut. Then Pop broke into a sprint and flung himself on the bed nearest the stove. "Mine!" he shouted, acting like a kid.

I thought it was lucky that there were five of us and five empty beds in one hut. But Ratty figured out the truth. "Hey," he said. "Who do you think slept here last?"

"Some other crew, I guess," said Buzz.

"Yeah, and what happened to *them*?" asked Ratty. "They got the chop, didn't they? They must have done; no lie."

That was his second favorite expression: "no lie." It

was as though he thought we doubted everything he told us. But I stretched out on my bed, and I knew he was right. Mine and all the others were empty because a bomber hadn't come home. Our beds didn't only *look* like rows of graves. That was exactly what they were.

CHAPTER 2

WE WALKED ACROSS THE field at dawn, with our parachutes and our yellow Mae Wests. We didn't bother with our fur-lined clothes; we wouldn't be going high enough to freeze to death on an afternoon in May. We walked in a row, with Lofty in the middle, and I felt like Doc Holliday stepping out with the Earps. I swaggered, and swung my chute.

But I forgot about cowboys as I got close to the bombers. They were huge, fantastic things, with little men working underneath them. Their black wings, wet with dew, reached a hundred feet from tip to tip. Just the wheels were nearly as tall as a man, and they towered up from those—on their struts and engine pods—with their long noses thrusting out even higher. At their very top their canopies sparkled, as high above me as third-story windows. I wished I could sit up there, in the pilot's "front office." The nearer we came, the more our heads tipped back to see them, until my cap fell clear off my head. I picked it up and jammed it on again, embarrassed to think I'd been caught at a silly game. Desperate to look like Uncle Joe, I had hidden in the lavatory and torn the stiffening wire out of the cap. I'd crumpled the cloth, and now the darned thing was too big. But no one even noticed. They all gawked at the bombers as we strolled toward them.

The little men—the erks—that bustled round seemed like the keepers of fabulous beasts. They passed in and out of the shadows, behind the tail fins, under noses. They swarmed over the wings and round the wheels.

I couldn't walk as slowly as the others, or wait the extra minute to see our *B for Buster.* I started running, first with my head down in a sprint, and then with my arms spread out and my parachute swaying, my feet dancing me along in spirals and hops. I swirled in among the erks, and they all stopped working to watch me. Two were tightening bolts on a wheel; another tapped at a tail fin. One was high on the wing, crouched like a gargoyle, and I smelled the petrol that he was pumping into the tanks, and saw how the fumes shivered and shook him.

I stood beside the fuselage, below the little window that was fitted in where I would sit, at my own desk with my own wireless and all the controls. I grinned at that small opening, imagining myself staring out of it, looking down through miles of sky at a land like a toy-train world.

Above my window, tiny white bombs were painted on the metal in columns and rows. I counted them, and saw that *B for Buster* had flown forty-four ops already. That was good, I thought. She knew her business. Farther forward, at the nose, a mule was painted on the metal.

Head down, heels up, it kicked at a frightened little Hitler. But Hitler had no legs, and the mule, no ears. The metal was patched in those places, the painting never redone.

Lofty and the rest came sedately, but grinning as well. They stood in their row right under the nose, and *Buster* towered above them. Lofty said with a nod, "She's a pretty good bus," as though this wasn't his first one. Then we took a walk around her, and one of the erks came, too, the chief of the bunch. He said his name was Sergeant Piper—just like that—"I'm Sergeant Piper," he said, as though his mom had named him Sergeant. He carried a clipboard, and he pointed at all the metal plates that were newer than the rest; he told us how each had come to be there. He talked about night fighter cannons, and flak, and eighty-eights. He pointed at a wingtip and said a tree had whacked it once. "Silly bloody tree," he added. "So the pilot said."

It seemed that *Buster* had healed herself from a thousand wounds, her metal plates regrowing. Up and down the fuselage, on both the wings and right across the double tail, the scars stood out in strips and squares.

"She seems a bit unlucky," said Buzz.

"No lie," said Ratty. "Wheezy jeezy." His number one expression.

The erk had a smear of oil on his face. He rubbed at it with the back of his hand. "Well, there's truth in that," he said. "Yes, there's truth in that, all right." And he spat on the ground.

He was a funny erk, a sort of *middle* guy. He wasn't old

or young, not tall or short, not thin or fat or mean or nice. In every way he was somewhere in the middle.

Lofty squinted down at him. Lofty was so tall that he looked down at just about everybody. "There's no such thing as luck," he said.

"That so?" said Sergeant Piper. "That so, is it?"

"Yes, it is," said Lofty.

"Well . . ." The erk rubbed at the oil. "Seems to me there is, all right. Yes, seems that way to me."

"Then you're wrong, old boy," said Lofty in his British whine. He turned his back and pointed to the starboard tail fin, a mass of new metal. "What happened there?"

"It got shot up," said the erk.

"Silly bloody bullets?"

Sergeant Piper grunted. "Well, I don't know, you see. There was no one left to tell us." He looked at the oil that he had smeared now to the back of his hand. "Only two came back. We used a fire hose to wash out the rear gunner, and—"

"Wheezy jeezy," said Ratty, our rear gunner.

"The flight engineer died in the cockpit," Sergeant Piper continued. "He was a goner before anyone reached him."

"What about the pilot?" said Lofty.

"Wasn't there," said Sergeant Piper. "No pilot. No wireless operator. No navigator." He ticked them off on his stained fingers. "No bomb aimer. No mid-upper gunner. Gone. All of them gone. The flight engineer landed the bus. Beautiful landing, too." He shook his head. "A real daisy cutter."

It was a chilling story, if I thought about it. The entire crew now dead, but the kite still here and ready to go again. We stood with our fingers at our chins, staring at the tail, and I—at least—wished the erk had kept the story to himself. Pop was frowning, and Ratty looked a little frightened.

The erk shook his finger at Lofty. "Now, wouldn't you say that that was bad luck, *old boy*?"

Lofty glared back. His nostrils opened and his eyebrows narrowed, until he looked a bit like a dog getting ready to growl. Then he laughed and said, "What a load of rubbish."

"You think so?" asked Sergeant Piper. "Is that what you think?"

They studied each other for a moment. Then Sergeant Piper nearly smiled. He held out his clipboard, and Lofty signed the Form 700, which said he was taking responsibility for the kite. *Buster* belonged to the erks, and we could only borrow it, signing it out for each flight like an enormous library book. Sergeant Piper spat again, then walked away under *Buster*'s nose.

"Impossible fellow," said Lofty. He made himself British in the worst way, all puffed up with a funny pout on his face, his eyes bulging. "Im-*poss*-ible!" Then he shook himself. "Come on, boys. Let's take a look inside."

I went like a kid to the fair, but Pop held me back. "Let Lofty go first," he said quietly. "He's the skipper; she's his ship."

I stepped back, and Pop smiled. "That's a good lad," he said.

We climbed through the door on the starboard side, down toward the tail. Will followed Lofty, and Simon followed him. Then Pop nodded at me. "Up you go," he said, and I put my knee on the sill and hoisted myself into the fuselage. I went forward, climbing uphill through the tunnel above the bomb bay, past the little toilet and the two bunks, through the flight engineer's narrow compartment. Beyond the bulkhead, on the left, Lofty was settling into his seat. I stepped down to the nose, into a smell of leather and petrol and kerosene.

Right at the front, Will was hunched over his bombsight, holding the button on its twisted cord as though he imagined himself on a bombing run. Simon was at his navigator's desk, facing the starboard side. I slid to my left and dropped into the seat by the little square window. I twiddled the knobs on the wireless.

We put our helmets on, buttoned our oxygen masks, and plugged into the intercom. Lofty called out our names. Then he said, "Right. Let's get this bus in the air."

There seemed a hundred gauges that had to be checked, a thousand buttons and switches to press. Finally the engines were started, and the four airscrews buzzed in big gray circles. The erks pulled the chocks away. We taxied to the runway, talked to the tower. Lofty said, "Hang on."

The throttles opened; the noise was nearly deafening. We rushed forward, and I felt myself pressed against my seat. Fields of green went shooting past my window. The tail lifted; Ratty said, "Oo-oop!" as though the bounce had made him airsick. We shimmied left, then right; we lurched and bubbled. And up we went, free from the ground, banking in a turn.

"Shazam!" I cried into the intercom.

Someone laughed, and I knew it was another stupid thing I'd done. I slapped my helmet and called myself an idiot. *Quoting Captain Marvel. What a fool you are,* I thought. But, still, it was the way I felt, that I could—like Captain Marvel—use the wizard's spell to change myself from a boy to a hero. In the bomber, in the sky, with my wireless and all, I really did gain the powers of the six gods that I summoned with that cry. I was Solomon, Hercules and Atlas, Zeus and Achilles and Mercury all rolled into one. I whispered to myself that magical word made of their initials. *Shazam!*

We flew toward the west, two thousand feet above the ground. Farms went by, and villages, and little carts and horses on the roads. We wheeled and turned, dipping into valleys. We flew so low across the hills that we mowed the grass along the crests.

The kite tilted. Will whooped like a cowboy as the ground zoomed up toward him. Then Ratty did the same as it fell away behind, and the words "jolly rovers" popped into my mind, and a picture of sailors laughing. We were like that: like sailors in the sky. I felt warm inside, as happy as I had ever been. Suddenly it didn't matter at all that I was too clumsy to ever be a pilot; it was good enough to go roving in the sky.

My life right then was nearly perfect. If a genie had appeared in *Buster*'s cramped nose and offered me three wishes, I would have taken only one: to be older by two or three years. It was a curse to be young.

The rest of the crew—like all the crews—stuck together as though they had magnets in their clothes. They liked me well enough, or I thought they did. But I had to keep myself apart, from a fear of being discovered. I knew that I stood out too much when the others started drinking or gambling, or just talking about all the things they'd done. On the outside, in my uniform, I looked old enough; I looked nearly the same as them. But inside I was shy and awkward, sometimes loud and stupid, and often felt that I didn't fit in. Even my voice still squeaked now and then. I had to *pretend* to shave, sometimes nicking my skin—with a grimace and a quick flick of the razor—to raise a drop of blood. Each night I was terrified as I slipped into bed that someone would see my nearly hairless body or, worse, the part of me that so often stood at attention no matter what I was thinking.

In the air, though, I never had to worry. Hidden at my desk, just a voice on the intercom, I was equal to them all. They needed me then, all right. I was the ears and the mouth of *Buster,* and without me they were deaf and dumb.

We flew over Harrogate and on toward Settle. Puffs of clouds floated by, shining in the sun like steamy parachutes. I wished I had a glass bubble around me, as the gunners did, and the bomb aimer. Only Simon could see less than me; the navigator had no window at all.

I pushed the button for my intercom. "Skipper, can I come up?" I asked.

"Be my guest, old boy," said Lofty.

I went and stood beside him. I leaned on the side of his seat and watched the clouds race toward us. They looked solid from the cockpit, like giant cue balls sliding through the sky. I loved the way they tore apart as *Buster* went ripping through them, and I muttered, "Bam! Kapow!" as they shredded open. I felt the giant bomber shake and lurch, and I heard the thrumming of the airscrews, a roar that was always with us. I saw the sunlight flashing on the metal wings, the feathery streams of our vapor trail, and I felt like Buck Rogers racing through space in a fabulous ship. "Roaring Rockets!" I said, my voice drowned out by the engines.

I wished that my friends from Kakabeka could see me. I wished that my *dad* could see me, and know that I had done better than him. Already I had gone farther and seen more than he ever would, and one day I would go home covered in medals, and I would walk past him on the street and pretend that I didn't even know him. That would make him feel sorry, I thought, for all the things he had done, and I planned for that day, but dreaded it, too. The war had made me special, and I didn't want it to end. My secret hope was that I would still learn to fly, and then—at the end of the war—the air force would give me a Spitfire as a kind of reward, and I would go barnstorming all across Canada.

Lofty adjusted the pitch on the number one engine. He worked the lever, then tapped a gauge. He was always moving, pushing the column back and forth, pressing his feet at the rudders. His head tipped and nodded to watch the sky, and I watched *him,* almost green with envy.

Whenever we flew, I imagined Lofty passing out or something. I imagined everyone panicking, but me staying calm, rushing up to take the controls, sitting in that fabulous chair in the great "front office," surrounded by switches and dials. I could take her down, I thought; I could land the bus.

Lofty made it look so easy. He flew old *Buster* as low as he could, then as *slow* as he could, with the wheels down and the flaps down and the bomb doors open. He had to run the engines flat out to keep her going like that, and he shouted the airspeed, and it was so impossibly slow that everyone whistled and clapped. Except for Pop. "She'll stall," he said. "You'll put us in a spin."

But Lofty laughed and kept the throttles open, and flew the kite more slowly than she was meant to fly. "Eighty-five knots," he said as *Buster* rattled like an old car. "Eighty, boys. Look at that!" Then, finally, a wingtip dropped and down we went in a dizzying turn.

We flew for two hours, hoping that a flight of Hurricanes would come along and launch a mock attack. But the sky was all ours until we headed home, and Lofty sent me down to my wireless.

I poked through my little space, peering into the corners and under the seat. Then I looked up and saw, penciled on the ceiling, the first lines of the poem that all of us knew. I smiled to see it written there, and read it over and over, louder and louder, until I shouted it out against the din of the engines.

Oh, I have slipped the surly bonds of earth
And danced the skies on laughter-silvered wings

I thought it was the best poem ever written. It said better than anyone possibly could—except maybe Will—what was in my heart and why I flew.

I stood up and looked more closely. The letters were small and tidy, printed on very faint lines drawn by a ruler. I wondered who had bothered to do that, to get the poem as perfectly arranged as a sampler in a kitchen. How many times had he looked up and read the words?

Then I wondered where he'd gone and what had happened to him. Was it true that the last person who had sat here had vanished? What had happened that night in the dark hull of *B for Buster*?

I shivered, then laughed. It was like a campfire story that could chill you through the hottest flames. I didn't want to think about it then, as we flitted across the fields to home.

CHAPTER 3

ON THE TWENTY-NINTH of May, Lofty went on his dickey flight. It was only a fifth-wheel sort of business, "a passenger trip," as he called it himself. But we were green with envy when he climbed into the truck with his escape kit and all his gear, and headed off to Uncle Joe's own kite. I wished they sent everyone as second dickey, but only the pilot ever went. He would wedge himself into the folding seat beside the pilot's, and watch the CO fly the crate.

We gathered at the tower to wave at Lofty, feeling foolish that we were staying behind. The only other ones who were waving were the girls of the Women's Auxiliary Air Force, and the bookish types who never flew, who seldom left their offices. The Royal Chair Force, Ratty called them.

We watched the bombers taxi from dispersal. They separated from a great tangled mass into a stately parade, with the air shaking from their engines. They rumbled through the hazy twilight like a fleet of battleships heading out to sea. Uncle Joe was the first off, and a thrill went through me to see his black bird thundering along the runway. The tail came up just as it passed us. We waved, and I tried to look for Lofty in the glass pulpit of the cockpit. But in an instant he was fifty yards beyond us, and we were clamping our caps to our heads as the propwash gusted by, smelling of smoke and petrol.

The rudders were pushed over, the flaps down. The Halifax hurtled along in that blistering sound that was better than music, such a blur of tires rumbling and cylinders popping and airscrews turning that it was impossible to sort out any one part of it. The sound vibrated in my chest and roared in my ears. Then the kite lifted up, and I felt my breath snatched away to see such a magnificent machine become weightless and free. It soared over the hedge and over the field, and the throttles gurgled back as it banked to the right. The wheels were rising, the flaps pulling in. It seemed to be changing, becoming a creature of the sky. The orange light of the setting sun flashed from the wing and the belly, from the little globe of the rear gunner's turret. I blinked to knock away the tears that came bubbling up at the beauty of it.

We watched the rest of the aircraft taking off, but we left the waving to the WAAFs and the Chair Force. We put our hands in our pockets, and ducked our heads to keep our caps on. Even I tried to be the picture of nonchalance. We were airmen, after all.

The bombers were off to Wuppertal, and it would be hours before they came back. Will and Simon drifted away to the place where only officers went. I imagined long tables covered with fancy food, knives and forks of the finest silver. It seemed strange that they got all of that just because they had finished at the top of their classes in training. Everyone did the same job, but for the rest of us it was back to a hut where the furniture was broken and the air always smelled of cigarettes. We found it nearly empty, the wireless set blaring out dance tunes. We settled in a corner where a pair of wicker armchairs faced a sofa. Pop took the sofa, stretching out on his back. Buzz settled into one of the chairs, and Ratty folded into the other the same way he fit himself into a rear turret—with his knees drawn up until they nearly touched his chin. I perched on the end of the sofa, by Pop's smelly feet.

"I wish we were flying," said Buzz.

"No lie." Ratty peered up from his chair. "You know where I want to go? More than anywhere?"

"Yeah. Berlin," said Buzz. "You only told me a million times."

"The Holy City," said Pop, already half asleep.

"That's why I joined up, you know. To see Berlin. No lie."

Buzz searched through his pockets until he found his crossword puzzle, the only one he ever did, the same one that he had torn from the Sunday *Telegraph* on his first day in England. Why he didn't get a new one, I didn't know. If he was waiting to finish that one, he would be a geezer before he was done. He had written and erased so often in the little boxes that the paper was gray and thin. I had heard the clues a hundred times, each one a little riddle on its own.

"Here's one," he said. "'Southern Canadian becomes

embarrassed? No, he's terrified.'" He drew his lips open, and tapped his pencil on his big front teeth.

I groaned to myself. They would go at it for hours, the two of them, and never find an answer. Ratty would ask, "How many letters?" Buzz would count them aloud. Ratty would say, "You got any?" And Buzz would say, "No, not yet." For weeks I had watched them do this, and they *still* hadn't found more than three answers.

"How many letters?" asked Ratty.

I went outside. The sun had set, and the runway flares had been extinguished. There were high clouds covering most of the sky, with only a band of pale stars above the southern hills. The airfield was utterly dark, heavy with a sense of emptiness, a silence where I wasn't used to one. I heard memories of noise: the rumble of the bombers, the laughter of the airmen. I walked across the runway and didn't see *Buster* until she suddenly loomed above me, against the sky, with her enormous wings spread wide.

I went right around her, reaching up to touch the airscrews, the rudder fins and ailerons, the panels of the rear turret. I stood and gazed at the hugeness of her, then opened the door and climbed inside.

I could see absolutely nothing. Though I stood only a few feet from the rear turret, I couldn't tell if its doors were open or closed. I had to grope my way forward, passing under the black holes of the upper turret and the astrodome. Even in the cockpit, with walls of glass around me, I could only barely see the levers and controls. Farther on, one deck down, the entire nose was as dark as a cave. I sat in Lofty's seat. I put my hands on the column, my feet on the rudders.

There was no ground below me, no runway or buildings, nothing to be seen at all except the southern horizon with its humps of hills. It was easy to imagine that I was flying. And suddenly I was high over Germany, slipping through the darkness. I held the column, and heard in my mind the drone of the engines. Then a night fighter came swooping in from ten o'clock high, and I banked to the left, climbing to meet him. He zoomed past, so close to the cockpit that I ducked my head. Then I rolled us right over, pulling back on the column, and we went spiraling down in a corkscrew. I felt the kite shaking, but I held it steady. I leveled out at a hundred feet and dashed along above the ground, weaving past trees and houses, over hedges and under wires. "Pilot to navigator," I said. "Pilot to navigator."

And I heard his voice; I really did.

I heard it in the darkness, in the silence of the bomber. It was faint and tinny, a breathy whisper through an intercom that wasn't plugged in. It was a terrible voice, full of worry and fear. "What's the course?" it asked. "What's the course for home?"

I bolted upright, my hands jerking from the column. I listened to the silence, to my own breaths. Then I looked behind me, down the empty length of the fuselage. "Ratty?" I shouted. My voice rang through the metal tunnel. "Ratty, you there?"

It was something he would have done, scaring me with whispered voices. But no one answered.

"What's the course?" whispered the voice again. It echoed in the fuselage. Another answered, "Two-one-niner. Steer two-one-niner."

My skin prickled all over. From my head to my feet I felt touches of ice.

To the south, the spidery crescent of the new moon came riding up the hills. Its silver glow fell through the canopy and the Perspex in the nose, and I saw the navigator seated at his desk. He was there but wasn't there; he was the gray and silver of the moonlight, the blackness of the shadows. He was a collection of shapes. But I saw the leather on his helmet and the sheepskin at his collar. I saw the light shining on his rubber mask as he slowly turned his head.

I bounded from the chair and went clanging through the bus, nearly panicked by the noise I made. What sounds were hidden in my thudding and my banging? Was the navigator clomping up the steps? Were the buckles jangling on his boots? Was he shouting at me in his ghostly voice, "Where the devil are we?"

I reeled from wall to wall, half crouched, half running past the struts and past the beds. I tumbled through the door. I fell, got up, and fell again. Then I scrambled away like an animal, my hands just paws on the ground. But fifty feet from *Buster,* I stopped and pulled myself together. Sounds and moonlight; that was all that had scared me. I had heard creaks of metal, maybe crows on the roof. I hadn't heard voices, and I hadn't seen people at all.

It was easy to tell myself that, but harder to believe it. Crows didn't fly at night. But I had never doubted that ghosts were real.

I made myself turn back and look at *Buster.* I half expected to see the gunner in his upper turret, the bomb aimer peering out, white-faced, from his bubble. But there was only the machine, huge and empty. *Nothing there,* I told myself. *Nothing there.*

I backed away from *Buster,* then turned around and ran across the field. I never stopped until I reached the huts.

Ratty and Buzz looked up as I stumbled in, but only for a moment. They were used to seeing me running places, barging in through doors.

"He's terrified," said Buzz.

"Who?" I said.

"The Southern Canadian," said Buzz. "I bet that's important. Hey, Kak, what's a six-letter word for *terrified?*"

They were still at their crossword; they were still on the same clue. But the sofa was empty.

"Where's Pop?" I asked.

"He just *popped* out," said Buzz. He shook with his horsey laugh.

I stretched out on the sofa, trembling inside, wishing I had never gone to see stupid *B for Buster.* I heard my mother's nagging voice: *"Well, you got just what you deserved. That should teach you,"* Mother always said.

I stared around the walls, at the painting of King George VI, at the dartboard on a wall riddled with tiny holes. The dance music ended on the wireless, and a posh sort of voice started reading the news. Back home in Canada, the government was rationing meat. The American army was beating the Japs on Attu Island, way far away in Alaska. I couldn't have cared less.

I rolled on my back and looked at the curved ceiling, then down along the blackened pipe that twisted toward the coal stove. I saw the light shining on it, and it looked like an arm, like a tentacle, groping toward the ceiling. *Buster* was jammed with pipes like that, with hoses that snaked in every direction. That was all I'd seen, just a bunch of wires and pipes and hoses. I laughed from relief.

"What's so funny?" asked Ratty.

"Nothing," I said.

"Popped out," said Buzz, without looking away from his crossword. "He just got the joke."

He made me think now, with that stupid joke. I lay on the sofa where Pop had been and wondered if there wasn't another explanation for what I'd seen. Maybe there really had been a person in *Buster*'s dark nose. "Where did he go?" I asked Ratty. "The old guy?"

"Wheezy jeezy, I don't know."

"You think he went out to see *Buster*?"

"Why?"

I shrugged, as though I had no idea why *anyone* would do that.

"Maybe he's pretending to fly," said Buzz. "Bet he is. I bet he's sitting in Lofty's seat, pretending to fly the crate. He's crazy, that guy. Just like a kid sometimes."

I was sure I was right. He was probably *still* out there, sitting in the doorway and laughing at his joke. Maybe he was just where I'd left him, waiting to scare me again. "Let's go and see." I leapt from the sofa. "Let's surprise him."

Ratty frowned, looking more like a rat than ever. "No," he said simply.

I went by myself. I stepped out of the hut, onto the grass, and stared across the field. *Buster* stood in the moonlight, black on black, looking sinister and not quite real. I didn't go any closer.

Metal squeaked behind me; a breath grunted in the darkness. I smelled birds and rotten straw. And out of the night came Dirty Bert, pulling a bomb trolley. He had a pigeon on his shoulder, and he walked in a hunch, like a half-crazy old pirate.

Every squadron had a pigeoneer to care for its flock of homing birds. In every bomber, on every op, a pigeon went along. It carried a metal cylinder strapped to its leg, and would fly home with a message if the kite was forced down. At our Operational Training Unit the pigeoneer had been a smart young man who had always dressed as though on parade. He had raised the birds as a hobby in peacetime, and had asked to look after the loft. He kept it as clean as a kitchen, and when he wasn't tending pigeons, he was tuning instruments on the bombers. But here at the Four-Forty-Two, the squadron's pigeoneer was a dismal man.

He was known as Dirty Bert. He lived in a hut adjoining the loft, and everywhere he went, he carried the smell of birds. Day in and day out he wore the same blue coveralls, crusted with mud and droppings. His entire life was spent caring for birds, and washing latrines.

I was sure he would pass me by. He rarely spoke to anyone, nor anyone to him. But he called out as he trundled toward me, "Good evening, sir."

No one ever called me sir. I was only a warrant officer, no more than a glorified sergeant. I actually looked behind me to see if there wasn't a *real* officer there. But Bert was talking to me.

"Lovely night, isn't it, sir?" he said.

"Yes. It is."

"Not flying tonight, sir?"

"No."

He swung his bomb trolley round in a circle, not even grunting at the effort. It was a massive thing, meant to be hauled by a tractor. But Bert just pulled it by hand. "Having trouble with the motorized, sir," he said.

"The what?"

"The motorized loft, sir." He tugged the trolley forward, pushed it back, looking like an oversized boy with an oversized wagon. Bert was one of the biggest men I'd ever seen, with hands the size of boxing gloves. His barnyard smell made me sneeze.

"Bless you, sir," he said.

I sighed. "You don't have to call me sir." He was so much older that it made me feel ridiculous, as though we were playing a childish game.

"But you're an officer, aren't you, sir?" asked Bert.

"Just a WO."

"Ah." He nodded. "Well, it's one and the same to Percy, sir."

I didn't understand.

"The pigeon, sir." He pointed a thumb toward the bird on his shoulder. "Ol' Percy tipped me off, sir. 'E stands at attention whenever 'e sights an officer. Must 'ave seen your badges, sir."

I touched the tiny thing on my sleeve. "In the dark?" I asked.

"Oh, darkness doesn't bother Percy, sir. 'E 'as the eyes of a—" Bert leaned toward me and whispered, "Of a *cat,* sir." Then he winked, and nodded, and a little spiral of white droppings fell from his wedge-shaped cap. He touched the pigeon's breast. "Best bird in the loft. That's Percy, sir."

The little pigeon puffed itself up at the touch of Bert's finger. It opened its wings and cooed with a funny little muttering sound. Its pink feet twitched on the man's shoulder.

"Would you like to 'old 'im, sir?"

"No," I snapped.

I could see I'd hurt Bert's feelings. I suddenly felt sorry for him as he stooped down to his trolley to fiddle with something that didn't need fiddling with. I knew how he felt to be dismissed like that. I said, "You see *B for Buster* over there? That's my kite."

"That so, sir?" he said a bit coldly.

"Have you seen anyone near it?" I asked. "I thought there was a guy inside."

"Like a ghost, you mean?" said Bert.

It shocked me that he came so close to the truth so quickly. I stared at him, but he didn't look up.

"You must see a lot of them, sir," he said, still down by his trolley. "There, but not really there. Faces that you knew." The pigeon fluttered across his bent back, from his left shoulder to his right. "You see them at breakfast, don't you, sir? And at night? In the corners of your eyes. And when you look, they're not there?"

"No," I said. "I don't."

"'Ow many ops 'ave you flown, sir?"

"None," I told him. "Not yet."

"Oh, I see." He stood up, his legs straightening like the struts on a landing gear. If Lofty stood on a step he wouldn't have been as tall as the pigeoneer. "Well, sir. Not to worry, sir, I'm sure."

"I wasn't really *worried,*" I said.

"It's the night, sir," said Bert. "And this place, sir, with its 'ills and its ruins and such. You'll get used to it, sir."

I felt angry at him then. He was talking as though I knew nothing, as though I was the greenest of sprogs. Then I realized that he was mostly right, but I wouldn't admit it to him. "I've flown lots," I said. "Hundreds of hours. I fly bombers, not *pigeons.* I know what I'm talking about."

"Yes, sir," he said. "You're quite right, sir."

It angered me more that he would agree with me so easily, just because he had to. I wished he would move along, but I saw that he could never leave his precious trolley. So I stood there beside him so that he wouldn't think he'd driven me off. Then the bird made an odd little sound, and stiffened on his shoulder, and Bert said, "'Ere comes another one, sir."

"Another what?" I asked.

"An officer, sir."

Out of the darkness came Simon, the Australian, his shoes tapping as he stepped from the grass to the tarmac. "G'day!" he shouted. Everything he said was a shout. "What are you doing out here in the never-never, and all by your lonesome, too?"

It was as though Dirty Bert wasn't even there, and again I felt sorry for the miserable pigeoneer.

"Fetch the others," said Simon. "Tell them the boys are coming back."

He went off again, and old Bert just stood there with the pigeon on his shoulder. I said, "I'd better go."

"Right you are, sir," said Bert. "Good luck to you, sir."

I didn't know why he wished me luck, but I didn't think about it then. I ran to the mess to get Ratty and Buzz, and Pop was there again. He looked at me with such a friendly smile that I was sure he hadn't tried to frighten me in *Buster.* "Where were you?" I asked.

"Writing letters," he said with a shrug. "Why?"

"They're coming back."

Ratty and Buzz leapt up from their chairs. Pop grinned and slapped my shoulder. Then we all ran out to watch Lofty coming home.

The airfield was suddenly alive. Trucks and tractors bustled through the darkness. Erks headed off to their dispersals, the Chair Force to the tower again. The flares were lit along the runway.

We gathered below the tower, a crew without a pilot. We listened to a distant drone that grew steadily louder and closer. Then the first Halifax thundered past above us, flashing its recognition signal. Someone asked, "Is that Lofty?"

I was pleased that I could read the Morse better than the others. I rattled off the signals as each black machine passed overhead and banked to the right. Buzz was counting: "Seven, eight, nine."

The bombers started landing, one by one. They dropped from the sky with their airscrews set at fine pitch, their engines throttled back. Tires shrieked as they touched the ground, exhausts spluttered and growled. Each bomber rolled away, to merge again into the darkness, and the next one came, and the next.

"Thirteen, fourteen," counted Buzz.

"There's Lofty!" I said.

His machine didn't join the circuit with the rest, but

came straight in, wobbling above the field. It sounded kind of ragged in a way.

"He's got an engine out," said Pop.

The Halifax flew along the runway, its wheels six feet above the tarmac, as though Uncle Joe had to force it from the air. Then it touched in a shower of sparks, in a rending of metal. Something banged and clattered along the ground as sparks flew up like balls of fire. The broken bits fell away, and the bomber rumbled on along the runway.

There was a gap then, in the landings. A truck went out, and men with torches, and the bombers circled round and round. Then a twisted chunk of metal was carried from the runway, and Buzz started counting again as the rest of the squadron came in. Or most of the rest; one never returned.

The ambulances went out with their bells ringing. Canvas-covered trucks brought the airmen from their bombers, and Lofty hopped down from the back of the first one.

He seemed the same as ever, strutting in his gangly walk, smiling his old grin. In most ways he *was* the same old Lofty, but his eyes were somehow different. They didn't sparkle anymore.

That same morning Lofty bought a pipe, and he smoked it once. His face turned green and he coughed his guts out, and we never saw him light it a second time. But he kept it in his mouth, puffing and whistling through the stem. Once in a while he even took it out to tap it on a chair or something, as though to tamp his tobacco down.

He never talked about that first op. We gathered from the others that it had been the usual sort of business, with searchlights and flak, and fighters here and there. Nothing outstanding; nothing alarming. But Lofty had changed. He had become more serious. He reminded me of Donny.

CHAPTER 4

OPS WERE CANCELED FOR a while, as the weather darkened over Britain. Behind blankets of cloud, the moon shrank to a sliver, then grew again. We cursed the clouds and the weather over Europe. Black nights were perfect for flying, but we were socked in, and stood down.

We toured round the countryside on clattery old bicycles, played baseball with the erks, and partied in the mess at night, when all the games were rough and wild. We joined in the songs about searchlights and flak, as though we'd already flown twenty ops. We grumbled all the time. We had come to fly, but were bored to tears.

The wireless news didn't help at all. We were pleased when the Japs fled from Attu, when a U-boat was sunk in the Atlantic. But we really perked up our ears when we heard that the crew of the *Memphis Belle,* the first of the big American Flying Fortresses to finish a tour of duty, were given their tickets home.

Ratty listened to that last bit of news without a single joke or even a hint of a smile. He looked almost angry, and I could tell what he was thinking, that he might have been a part of that crew—a hero already—if he hadn't hurried up to Canada in the months before Pearl Harbor. Poor Buzz looked as worried as a dog. He always dreaded that Ratty would go away one day to fight with the Mighty Eighth, lured by the huge Forts and the glamour of flying in the sunlight. The Americans bombed Germany in the daylight, in bombers that bristled with guns.

In cloud-covered Yorkshire, the only one flying was Donny Lee. And he did it on the ground; Donny was the only pilot who owned a car. It was a Morris, a tiny thing with seats for two but room for seven standing. He raced around the Yorkshire hills, with his navigator balanced on the fender, his rear gunner on the bumper, facing backward. He drove that black heap to Inverness and all the way to London.

In the second week of June, the weather cleared. On the ninth, a Wednesday, Donny kicked me from my bed early in the morning. "Get dressed," he told me. "I'll take you for a spin."

I could hardly believe my luck. No one but his own crew ever went flying in the Morris. But he and I went rocketing out through the gate and down the road in a plume of dust. Donny drove east through that land of grass and sheep and scattered villages. He threw the black Morris round the curves, and wound it up when the road ran straight. The air gusted round the windshield, the engine howled, and the leather seats baked hot as pitch. With every shimmy and every pothole I heard bottles jingle in the boot.

We crossed the River Swale, shot through Busby Stoop and Thirsk, then climbed into the Hambleton Hills.

They were really nothing but hummocks; only Englishmen would have thought of them as hills. I had seen *buildings* higher than the Hambletons. But to the locals, they were the Himalayas of hills.

In a moment we were parked at the summit. Donny fetched a couple of bottles out of the boot and offered me one. I shook my head; I didn't like beer when it was *cold,* and this was hot and shaken. When he rapped the bottle on the fender, the cap flew off like a bullet, and a geyser of foam spewed out. He slurped it up as it spilled along his fingers.

We sat side by side on the running board, on the shady side of the Morris. Donny scuffed his heels in the grass. He looked up at the sky. "How's Kakabeka?" he asked.

"I'm fine," I said.

"Not you." He laughed. "You twit. The town, I mean."

"Probably the same," I said.

"You miss it?"

"No."

He took a mouthful of beer and gargled with it. Then he swallowed and spat. He just stared off across the hills with a strange, sad look on his face.

"What happened to *Buster*?" I asked.

"Huh?"

"*B for Buster.* I heard that—"

"Oh, yeah," said Donny. "Seven went out, two came back, and both of them were dead. It was crazy."

"Why wasn't the pilot there?"

Donny shrugged. "He bailed out, I guess. Maybe he thought he was the last one left. Maybe he panicked. We'll never know, Kid."

"Who was the wireless operator?"

"You got me." Donny shook his head. "No, I don't remember."

"Why not?" I asked.

"Hey, there's twenty-four kites, Kid. Seven guys to a kite." His voice rose, and there was real anger in his eyes. "I just don't remember all the guys who got the chop, okay?"

"Okay," I said.

"They were sprogs."

"Jeez, Donny."

He popped his finger in and out of the bottle. He finished the beer in one long gulp.

"If you don't want to fly, you don't have to," he said.

"What?"

"You don't *have* to fly," he said.

"But I want to," I told him. "Whatever happened to *Buster,* it—"

"Takes guts, though," said Donny. "Takes more guts to stay on the ground than it does to get into the crate. But guys have done it. They've refused to go."

"But I *want* to fly," I told him again.

"It's not like they shoot you for it," said Donny. "Some guys say they do, but they don't."

I didn't understand why he'd brought me so far to talk about this, and then to ignore everything that I said. It was as though he was talking only to himself. He opened the other bottle and shoved it to his lips as the foam came out. His cheeks swelled as fat as a chipmunk's. Then he swallowed, and grimaced. He said, "Who cares if they call you a coward?"

I didn't know what to say to him. So I only stared back, and I saw again how old he looked. In the morning, in the sun, he seemed worse than ever. His eyes were shot with red, his skin all pale and waxy.

"Uncle Joe would understand," he said. "You could always go to Uncle Joe and tell him you're afraid to fly."

"I'm *not* afraid," I said.

"Uncle Joe would understand."

A wasp came and buzzed around the bottle. It landed on the neck, crawled up to the top, and went round and round in a slanted walk. Donny didn't even shoo it away. He just lifted the bottle. The wasp took off, did circuits round Donny's head, then settled back on the bottle as he lowered it again.

"I dream," he said. "Awful dreams."

"Like what, Donny?"

"Kid, you don't want to know."

Then why did you tell me? I thought.

He handed me the bottle. I didn't want the beer, but I took it, wasp and all. I set it down on the grass, on its side, and let the beer dribble out in a dark brown stream.

Donny leaned sideways, against the curve of the fender. Painted on the door beside him were rows and columns of little white animals—shrews and moles and cats—that he had mowed down in his mad driving and recorded there like the bombs on a Halifax. He stretched along the fender, his red hair resting on the metal, and closed his eyes. "The bank's on the corner, right?"

"Huh?" I said. I thought he'd gone nuts.

"In Kakabeka. The bank's on the corner, and the bakery's beside it."

"Yes," I said.

"It always smells of bread there. They put cakes in the window. And those strips of flypaper that look like raisin bread. The window's gooey down here." He waved his hand back and forth at the height of his knee. "'Cause the kids get fingerprints all over it. And snot."

I smiled. "That's true," I said.

"Then the drugstore, eh?"

"Yes."

"Mr. Taylor keeps the door so clean you can never tell if it's open or not. You have to feel for it, or you crack your head on the glass." Donny stretched his hand out, groping like a blind man. "Then you go inside, and it always smells of bug dope."

"Floor polish," I said.

"No kidding? I always thought it was bug dope."

He walked us right through Kakabeka, in and out of every store. He seemed to come awake—or alive—

shaking off whatever it was that was wrong with him, and he rambled on about things I'd forgotten, and things I'd never known. But he grew terribly sad as he talked.

"I miss it like crazy sometimes," he said. "I hated living there—I couldn't wait to get out—but I'd sure like to see it again."

"You will," I said.

"I don't think so, Kid. I don't think I'll ever see Kakabeka again."

"Why not?"

He smiled to himself, hardly a smile at all. He turned his head on the fender, squashing his big flap of an ear. "You're such a kid," he said.

"And *you're* such an old man, Donny."

I didn't mean to hurt him with that, and I would have taken it back if I could. He *was* an old man, and I saw in his eyes that he knew it. And then, angry, he talked to me as only an adult would. "Kid," he said, "I should have told them. That first day. I should have marched you right off to see Uncle Joe and told him you were only sixteen."

"Yeah?" I said. "You and whose army?"

Then he laughed, because that was such a stupid thing to say. Donny Lee could have picked me up and *carried* me to the CO. He could have *tossed* me half the distance. He laughed, then kicked out his leg, knocking my feet from the grass. I fell against him, and a moment later we were rolling on the summit of the Hambletons, over and over, back and forth, pummeling and laughing.

But the game lasted no longer than a moment. Donny pushed me away, and stood up. He wasn't a boy anymore.

We drove down the east face of the hills, then circled back through a string of tiny villages until we reached the Swale. Donny stopped the car, and again he opened the boot. He took out a roll of canvas and rubber. He set it on the grass at the river's edge, pulled a string, and the bundle exploded and became a boat.

I was horrified. It was a life raft from a Halifax.

"What are you doing?" I asked.

"Don't you want to go fishing?" he said.

We launched the boat in a shady pool. Donny tossed in a couple of bottles, a chocolate bar, and oranges. We fished for trout with the hooks and line that were packed in the raft's little kit. We didn't catch any, but I didn't mind. We just drifted down the river, past muskrat dens, under dangling willows. He called me Huckleberry Finn ("Pass me that orange there, Huck"), and I called him Tom Sawyer.

We let the current take us down to Topcliffe; then Donny paddled with his hands to nudge us up against the bank. He took his car keys from his pocket. "Go fetch the bus," he told me.

I was stunned. No one but Donny *ever* drove the Morris. "Go on," he said, jangling the keys.

"I can't," I told him. "I don't know how to drive."

"Now's your chance to learn," he said.

"I'm too young."

"Jeez, Kid. Who cares?"

But I had never been as daring as Donny. So I guarded the raft as he went hiking back along the river. I lay on my back on the warm rubber, holding on to a willow branch as I felt the tug of the stream.

I never figured out why Donny took me fishing. Maybe he meant to prove that he wasn't entirely a grown-up, that he still had a bit of the boyish wickedness that had let him stand at the very edge of Kakabeka Falls, closer to the brink than any kid ever stood. But it was his last day as a boy, and nearly his last altogether.

CHAPTER 5

EVERY MORNING AT BREAKFAST the loudspeaker switched on. There was a click and a buzz, then the deep thump of a finger being tapped on a microphone somewhere. And then a voice came on—the lovely, whispery voice of an English WAAF. "Good morning, gentlemen," she always said.

A silence filled the room with the first click from the speaker. Talking stopped, and eating stopped, and row after row of airmen became as still as photographs.

The WAAF cleared her throat. She always did, and I always imagined her fingers, thin and white, lifting up to touch her lips.

Everyone was listening, and no one moved. They *never* moved before she spoke again. Our whole days depended on the next thing she would tell us. I wanted her to say that we were "on" for the night. I was sick of being stood down day after day—more than a week since Lofty went flying. I wanted her to say that we were on, that I would be heading off to Germany.

I looked at little Ratty and saw he had his fingers

crossed. Lofty was putting his hand in his pocket. Two tables away, Donny Lee's head of clown-red hair was bent over his breakfast.

The WAAF, like an angel, said, "You are on for tonight."

I cheered. I shook my hands in the air like a boxer; I shouted, "Hooray!"

I was the only one who did. Ratty was grinning, and Will had a thumb cocked up. Buzz and Simon and Pop all looked as happy as clams, but I was the only one in the whole room who cheered. Lofty took his hand from his pocket, and his pipe was in his fingers. He popped it in his mouth and smiled at us, but his new, dark eyes seemed hollow.

At every other table, all around the room, there was one long groan followed by a lot of muttered voices. There was a lot of staring, too, all aimed in my direction. Donny Lee went scurrying to the door like a guy with his hair on fire.

"Well, chaps," said Lofty, "I'll take a squint at the list. See if we're flying." He puffed on his empty pipe as he wandered away.

All around, plates were being pushed aside and breakfasts left unfinished. But we kept tucking in at ours, hoping that *Buster* was on the list, trying to guess where the night would take us. We were the only ones left in the room when Lofty appeared in the doorway again and told us, "Shake a leg, chaps. We're on."

The hours seemed endless. We flew circuits and bumps from ten to noon, ate a lunch and stooged around, then went in for briefing. It was my first time in the hut, and I felt like bounding across the benches to claim a seat at the front. But I forced myself to go slowly, swaggering instead, with my worn-looking cap pushed back, nodding hellos to people I didn't know. I thought I looked like Billy Bishop, but a wave of titters came from behind me. I wanted to sink through the floor, until Lofty looked up and smiled to see me.

There was a stage at the front of the room, a row of chairs and a lectern, an enormous curtain at the back. More than a hundred airmen stamped to attention as the officers came in, then sat again with a squeal of benches and a shuffling of feet.

The CO stood at the lectern in his leather jacket and crushed cap, looking the way I had only tried to look. He made a joke that wasn't funny. I laughed loudly, though no one else laughed at all. Then he pulled a cord, and the curtain slid open.

The room filled with voices and mutters. "Good God," said a gunner. "It's Happy Valley again."

A pair of red ribbons started at Yorkshire and bent their way south, turning here and there, to end at Düsseldorf in the valley of the Ruhr. It didn't look like a long way on the map. The ribbons passed over the North Sea, over Holland, then dodged into Germany with a sudden turn. "Piece of cake," I told Lofty.

He didn't answer.

We got the weather report from a white-haired meteorological officer, a little fellow so short that he might have been the eighth dwarf. The crews called him

Drippy because he nearly always predicted rain. But tonight, he said, the skies would be mostly clear. He sniffed and sat down, and a parade of officers followed him. We got the news—the gen—on signals and timing and routing. Nearly eight hundred aircraft would be converging over Düsseldorf, so we had to be sure that we kept at the proper altitude and headings. The intelligence officer tapped a pointer on the map to show us where we'd meet the flak and searchlights. His stick went *tappa-tappa-tappa* across half the stupid map. I said, "Sir! You should tap where there *isn't* flak." Again, my laugh was the only sound.

I cringed inside myself, and didn't look up until the briefing was finished. Then the pilots and the navigators swarmed toward the front, and gunners drifted off. I joined the mob of wireless operators lining up to collect a list of frequencies on a bit of paper called a flimsy.

I kept to myself until supper, then joined *Buster*'s crew in the dining hall. I could smell the eggs and bacon, and went drooling to my table. Only the operational crews got eggs; to me they were something like medals.

A WAAF brought one to me. In her little blue suit she leaned over my plate and served me from a spatula. "There you go, love," she said.

I could hardly turn my eyes away; they nearly popped from my head. Right in front of me, beautiful and smooth, as white and soft as cream, was the first real egg I'd seen in more than a month. But my second would be waiting when we came back from Germany, so I ate this first one in two big bites. All around the tables people were joking about the eggs, asking each other, “If you get the chop, can I have yours at breakfast?”

We ate quickly, then collected our escape kits and our parachutes. We changed into flying clothes—into clobber, we called it. The gunners lined up to plug into the electricity and test their heating systems, and there was a smell of hot wires and scorched leather. Then the sun was going down, and we waited on the lawn for the truck to take us out to *B for Buster.*

Dirty Bert came along with his bomb trolley. It was stacked with pigeon boxes, and each of the metal crates had its end open, the round lid clipped to the side of the box. Inside, behind the flaps of the cardboard linings, the pigeons cooed and scratched. Bert doled them out to the “wops”—the wireless operators—so I got in line with the others.

The wops ahead of me took the boxes without a word, without even a nod to Bert. I tried to do the same, but he held the box too tightly. My hands slid right off it, and I staggered back, surprised. Then, head down, I went at him again.

“'Allo, sir,” said Bert.

I tugged at the box.

“I saved Gilbert for you, sir,” he said. “Gibby's a fine little bird. I think you'll like 'im, sir.”

The box still wouldn't budge. Gilbert had his head so far through the hole that I was afraid he would peck me on the wrist. The guys behind me were muttering and pushing, trying to hurry me along. I looked up at Bert and saw the friendliest smile I had ever seen in the air force.

"You'll watch 'im, won't you, sir?"

"Yes," I said. "All right, I will."

"Good luck to you, sir." He winked. "'Appy flying."

"Thank you," I said.

The box came easily then. I carried it away with my face red from the shame of talking to Bert. The pigeon clattered and cooed, until I was sure that everyone was staring at me. I shook the box and told the bird, "Shut up!" The more I shook, the more he squawked, the stupid thing.

I thought of shoving the box underneath a fuel bowser and telling Lofty, when he asked, "Gee, I didn't see any pigeon." But when the truck came to take us out to *Buster,* it was too late. Lofty shouted, "All aboard! Women and children and pigeons first."

He was just showing off for the lady driver, who turned around in her WAAF cap and tittered at me as I held the pigeon, like a kid with a giant lunch box. "Don't eat him, now," she giggled. All the way across the field I thought of clever, withering things I should have told her.

Sergeant Piper was waiting under *B for Buster,* with his gang of erks around him. He greeted us in a way that was friendly and rude at the same time, with a wisecrack about sprogs. Then he stood at the tailgate, catching our elbows as we tumbled down. Gilbert fluttered and squawked as I leapt to the ground. "Careful with that, boy," said Sergeant Piper, as though it was a bomb that I carried. He had a big wrench in his hand, so I only glared at him.

We carted our gear to *Buster*'s door. Everyone had a flask of coffee and a paper bag full of sandwiches and oranges and chocolate. We climbed in and lugged it all to our places. As I stepped down from the cockpit to the nose I squinted at the pipes and hoses and tried to see in them my phantom navigator.

There was no *feel* of ghosts. I knew the sense of haunted places: the witch's house in Kakabeka; the gloomy meadow just above the falls, where an Indian princess had flung herself into the river. They were clammy places, even in the sunshine. *Buster* just felt empty, like any old machine.

I stowed my parachute away and strapped the pigeon box in place. As I reached inside to take out the food and water cans, the pigeon tried a breakout. "Get back," I said, giving him a poke.

From up and down the kite came thuds and bangs as others stowed their things. We examined everything from the bombsight in the nose to Ratty's twin guns in the tail, then went out to lie in the grass and wait.

The sun was nearly down, the moon not risen yet. The tiny blackflies—midges, the English called them—swarmed around in swirling clouds. Dew had settled on the grass. Ratty and the others who smoked got out their cigarettes and puffed circles at the sky. Buzz lay stretched on his side, digging with his fingers at the soil.

I couldn't sit still. I tingled all over with the excitement of flying, and I sat up and lay down and sat up again.

Lofty and Pop went walking around *Buster,* tugging at

the trimming tabs, patting at the wheels. Sergeant Piper went with them, his hands in his pockets, talking like a car salesman about every little thing. The three of them bent down to look at the tail wheel, and I saw a flash of silver at Pop's throat. He was wearing a crucifix that I hadn't seen before.

It was for luck, I thought. He wasn't the only one who carried something with him. Little Ratty had a rabbit's foot that he had brought from the States. He had hung it round his neck for his very first flight, on the Canadian prairies, in one of the canary-colored trainers we knew as Yellow Perils. He had never climbed into an aircraft without it. Will had a picture of a girl tucked in his helmet. We all knew she was his wife, and we all knew he kept her picture there, though he was always very secret about the way he slipped it into place before a flight. Simon, somewhere, had a white handkerchief that smelled very faintly of perfume. Buzz carried nothing with him, yet he never flew without a charm, and he was busy digging in the grass now to find one.

I had a ray gun. It was just a ring—a kid's silly ring—such a stupid thing to carry that nobody knew I had it. It was buttoned in my tunic pocket, and it would stay there until I was alone in the darkness, bent over my desk where no one could watch me.

Only Lofty had no lucky charm, and no belief that he needed one. He had smiled at the stinky handkerchief, and chuckled at the rabbit's foot, and he certainly would have howled at my ray-gun ring. It wasn't stuff like that, he'd said, that had kept us alive through our training, while so many others had bought the farm. "You don't need *luck,*" he'd told us. "You've got *me.*"

I patted my pocket. The ring was still there.

"Hey!" cried Buzz, suddenly sitting up. "I found one." He held up his trophy, a tiny four-leafed clover.

Ratty applauded; Will made a wolf-call whistle. Buzz wedged the clover into his flying glove, up to the tip of his trigger finger. By the end of the flight it would be a green smudge, like a bug squashed on his skin.

We spent half an hour loafing around on the grass before Lofty signed the 700. Then we climbed aboard for another half hour of waiting in the kite. The sun had warmed the black metal, and *Buster* was oven-hot. I sweated in just my jacket and my trousers, and pitied the gunners bundled in their leather coveralls. At seventeen thousand feet their sweat would freeze into ice. So would Lofty's. He was such a great guy that he kept the hot-air outlet aimed down toward me and Simon instead of at himself. I would always be warm.

Gilbert squawked. I rapped on the box, but he squawked even louder. Then Simon shouted at me, "Why's that bird throwing a wobbly? If he doesn't shut up, he'll come a gutser."

I didn't know exactly what Simon meant, but it sounded awful. I banged on the box and told the pigeon to be quiet. It bashed around, then settled down. And through my window I watched the darkness close in. The other bombers stretched away in staggered rows. The closest one was *E for Eagle,* and I could see the pilot in his cockpit, a black dot against a sky that wasn't much lighter. Sergeant Piper and the other erks stood around their trolley. They leaned back with their arms crossed, digging their toes at the grass. They looked bored and impatient, like people waiting too long for a bus.

Then at last we got the word. It started at Bomber Command in High Wycombe, filtered down to Group, down to the squadron, and at last to the airmen.

Lofty cleared his throat. "Right. Let's get this bus in the air," he said.

CHAPTER 6

"SWITCH TO GROUND." That was Lofty, his voice coming through the intercom.

"Switch to ground," said Pop.

"Landing gear locked."

They ran through their checklist, the old guy sounding bored. He had been a mechanic long before the war began, and he still had that slow, mechanical way of thinking.

The erks bustled below me. Others wheeled the trolley into place, then stretched out the cable to plug into the fuselage. Every moment brought us closer to the op, and every moment was harder to wait. Other bombers were being readied in just the same way at just the same time—dozens and dozens and dozens of them—at every airfield in every county in all of England. But it seemed that the entire air force, from Bomber Harris down to the lowest erk, had only one task right then—to get old *B for Buster* airborne.

"Master switches on. Tanks one and three, switches on," said Lofty.

"Switches on," echoed Pop.

"Propeller fully up. Gills open."

A pair of erks walked the first propeller around, grabbing the blade tips to roll the engine over.

"Ignition, number one," said Lofty. "Booster on. Coils on."

The outer engine whined. The propeller blades turned and stopped, turned again, then spun in a blur as the engine caught. Number two was started, three and four, and they ran in a ragged, shaking roar until Lofty got them synchronized. He backed the throttles to let the engines idle.

"Compass set to on," said Lofty. "Ground battery disconnected. Switch to flight."

Our lights came on, gleaming on the ground. Along the row of bombers, others sparkled red and green and white.

"Door closed," said Pop. "Ready to taxi."

"Roger that. Switch on, clutch in, gyro out," said Lofty. "Right, let's go."

Will passed by my station on his way to the cockpit, and I looked up to watch him lower the second dickey seat and settle in at Lofty's side. He would work the throttles and the pitch levers, letting Lofty put all his strength into the rudders and the column. I heard a rasping sound below me, and saw an erk come running out from the wheel, dragging a chock on its bit of rope. The engines quickened, and we rumbled forward.

Lofty steered a weaving path along the perimeter, then swung quickly onto the runway with a burst from the starboard inner. We rocked forward as the brakes went on.

There was still a chance we wouldn't be flying. At any moment the op could be canceled, the bombers sent back to dispersal. *Hurry up,* I said under my breath. *Just get us off the ground.*

"Elevator tabs, two divisions," said Lofty. "Rudder neutral. Fuel cocks, Pop?"

"All switches set," said Pop.

"Flaps down thirty. Gills open one-third."

We waited for the flare. My stomach churned from excitement.

"Hang on," said Lofty. "Full throttles, Will."

The engines howled. *Buster* shuddered and lurched forward, veering to the left. For a moment I clutched my belts, but Lofty got us straightened out, and the ground blurred below my window, faster and faster.

"Throttles locked," said Lofty.

"Okay," said Will. He started calling out the speed. "Forty knots. Fifty knots," he said. "Sixty knots, Skipper."

The tail came up. "Oo-oop," said Ratty. No one laughed; we'd heard the joke on every training flight since April.

"Seventy knots. Eighty," said Will. "Ninety knots, Skipper."

B for Buster hurtled down the runway, the engines at a high pitch, the metal vibrating, the wheels thundering on the tarmac.

"Ninety-five. One hundred, Skipper."

"Are we there yet?" asked Ratty.

And all the thunder and the shaking stopped. We were flying, the ground below us falling away. The end of the runway went by, and then dark fields split by a silvery web of old stone fences.

"Climbing speed," said Lofty.

"Okay, Skipper."

"Flaps up ten."

"Flaps up, okay," said Will.

"Wheels locked. Undercarriage up."

"Okay, Skipper."

Hydraulic motors hummed. *Buster,* half-alive, cranked up her wheels and her flaps. Her four-engined heart beat loudly and fast from the effort of hauling herself from the ground. Then the undercarriage thudded into place, and the wind whistled through the canopies.

"Cruising speed," said Lofty.

The engines settled to a steady, hurried thrum. The huge Halifax leaned in a turn, the nose high, the deck and my table slanting steeply. I had to lunge to catch my pencil as it rolled toward the edge, and I saw the pigeon in its box, its head poking through the round hole in the flap. Will came down from his perch on the folding seat and poked me in the side. He pointed up with his thumb, telling me to look.

I twisted backward in my seat. Peering up through the passage, I saw Lofty there—his whole right side—his leg thrust toward the rudders, his arm reaching for the column. I saw, very dimly, the bottom of his cap brim and the bulge of his oxygen mask. He had his pipe in his mouth, jammed in the rubber.

Will leaned down. He pried up my helmet flap and bellowed in my ear. "Good old Lofty, eh?" Then he went smiling to his bombsight.

"Skipper, your course is two-one-oh," said the navigator through the intercom.

"Two-one-oh, roger," said Lofty. We tilted farther.

It was wonderful to fly. I felt sorry for the erks, and for everyone else who labored on the ground—for all the farmers and the villagers and the people in the cities who had never slipped those bonds of earth. Flying was the one thing that had brought all of us together, that kept us apart from the poor slobs below. I was better than them. I was an airman, a flier, a rover of the air.

"It's a beautiful night," said Will, in his place again at the bow. Surrounded by glass, lying flat on his stomach, he could *feel* that he was flying. "There's kites all around us, all turning and weaving. I can only see their navigation lights, and they look like hordes of fireflies. And there's moonlight on the river, and stars floating. It looks magical. As though the Milky Way has fallen on the ground."

"Gee, all I see's a river," said Ratty.

"And there's a farmhouse, a chink of light between the blackout curtains. It's the only thing on the ground, and it looks so lonely, one light in all the dark and nothing. It looks like God's house, that's what it's like." Will was a poet. It was why we sometimes called him Shakespeare. He wrote things down but hardly ever showed them to anyone, and never read them aloud. "We're going to pass right over it," he said, "and—

there—I can look right down the chimney and see the fire in the hearth. Just an instant. Just a glimpse."

I set the frequencies on my wireless. I fitted the screwdriver into the slot and turned it back and forth to match the numbers on my flimsy. It was a chore I had done so often, on so many flights, that I found it hard to believe that I was doing it now on the way to Germany, astride a belly full of bombs. Then I grinned inside my mask to think that I was already on the battlefield, fighting in the boundless world of Superman and Buck Rogers, on a fabulous field that stretched in all directions and rose from the earth to the heavens. I imagined the people below turning their faces to the sky, telling each other, "Look! Up in the sky! It's a bird, it's a plane. It's—the Kakabeka Kid!"

I tightened my curtain. I leaned into my corner and, hunched by my desk, pulled the ray-gun ring from my pocket. It was a crummy thing that didn't shoot rays, or anything else. But it stood for the Space Patrol and all my heroes, and I always felt a tingle when I put it on. When I was small I had worn it on my thumb, and I'd had to clench my fist to keep it from falling off. Now it barely squeezed onto my little finger. I had owned that ring for years and years.

"Skipper, steer one-five-six," said Simon.

"Roger. One-five-six," answered Lofty.

We joined with fifty other bombers and all flew south together. Our lights went out, and those of the others, and we traveled through the blackness. I drew the curtain round my desk and covered up my window. The little goosenecked lamp made a pool of light on the wireless.

"Seven thousand feet," said Lofty.

The plane shivered as we passed through someone's slipstream. The engines quickened for a moment, then settled back to their steady drone.

"Twelve minutes to the coast," said Simon.

"Roger," answered Lofty.

We passed ten thousand feet. "Oxygen, boys," said Lofty. I tightened my mask and connected to the system. The air had a taste of rubber, but I thought of it as the breath of *Buster.*

"Hey, Kakky, how's the bird?" asked Simon.

I didn't bother to look; I knew that he'd be lying like a lump on his belly, maybe sleeping and maybe not. No matter how high we flew, it didn't seem to bother the pigeon. At eleven thousand feet, a man would conk out in a minute or two, but pigeons kept breathing at twice that height. I hadn't known it at first. On one of our training exercises, at fifteen thousand feet over the North Sea I had shone my torch into the pigeon box and seen the bird standing up. I'd shouted, "Holy smokes, the pigeon's awake!"

Simon laughed again now. I aimed my tiny ray gun at him through the curtain.

I couldn't listen to the wireless and the intercom at the same time. I kept switching back and forth between them, listening on the wireless for any recalls or news about wind shifts, then catching bits of talk on the intercom.

"Crossing the coast," said Will. "There's the surf. A silver thread."

I turned off my lamp and peered out through the little window. I could see nothing down there, but I didn't like the thought of empty water. It would be so cold, so dark and heaving.

"Okay to test the guns, Skipper?" That was Buzz, his voice sounding excited.

"Roger. Blast away, boys."

I heard the whine of the powered turrets, and I felt the hammer of the guns. The bit of sky that I could see lit up with bursts of tracer curving off in all directions. It was sudden and short, and then there was only the darkness again. But the flashes glowed on my eyelids, sparkling white and orange every time I blinked.

We carried on across the Channel with the engines booming. I couldn't see very far ahead, not at all behind or straight below. I didn't like looking out at nothing but a black emptiness, so I covered the window again, switched on the light, and sat and waited. I looked up at the rudder cables and the hoses, then down at the deck, imagining the bombs nested in their bay below it. To my side, by the window, the paint didn't exactly match where two metal plates met at a riveted joint. I touched the place, wondering which bit was new and which was old, and then what had happened on *Buster* the night that a dead man landed the plane. I thought of the voice I had heard, or imagined, calling out for the course for home. Then the same coldness touched me again, and I knew it had been a mistake to start thinking like that.

My intercom crackled. "Searchlights ahead."

"I see them, Will," said Lofty.

"Flak now. Just starting up."

Lofty didn't answer. There were two clicks from his intercom, and we droned along toward the enemy coast, jinking left and right, now dropping fifty feet, now rising so much more. Lofty never used the autopilot; he kept us moving through an empty sky the way a rabbit flits from hole to hummock to dodge the hawks above it.

"It's beautiful, really," said Will. "Terrible, but beautiful." He sounded dreamy and wondering. "It's like a fence of light, like rows of swords all waving back and forth. The flak is bursting high—big orange balls—and the tracers are flying through it. They look like flaming onions, all right. It's quite a show. It's— Oh, Geez, someone bought it there. A ball of fire, like a meteor."

I had to see for myself. I put my head through the curtains and looked toward the nose. Simon was shrouded at his desk; I couldn't see him at all. Will was stretched out atop his Perspex, above a glow of light, as though he flew along like Superman. The searchlights swung, the tracers soared, and the flak puffed in sudden, scattered bursts, as though they had blown holes right through the night to show the day behind it. It was like watching, all at once and from up above, all the fireworks that I had ever seen, and watching them in silence. Our own engines drowned out all the sound. But there was nothing beautiful there; my first look at the enemy scared me half to death.

The searchlights weren't at all like the ones we'd seen

at London. Those had turned and reeled like dancers, but these jabbed at the dark; they hunted through it. They seemed alive, and cruel.

I saw the bomber going down—or another. It passed across the Perspex with its streaming tail of fire. For a moment it glowed in the searchlights, and I saw that one wing was sheared off in the middle. A parachute blossomed from an upper hatch, then wrapped itself around the tail, and a little speck of a man squirmed and writhed on the end of the cords, dragged behind the bomber. Wrapped in flame, the Halifax went hurtling toward the ground, pulling that poor doomed man behind it.

"Unsynchronizing," said Lofty. He fiddled with his levers to set the engines at a ragged roar. The single deafening note became a fluttering *oom-ba-oom* that was meant to fool the lights that sought us out by sound.

Then I heard the flak—or *felt* it—faint, hard pops that ripped the air apart. I was too scared to look away. The lights seemed to slide toward us, spreading out and stretching higher. We jinked along, up and down, left and right, but straight toward a wall of light, and it didn't seem possible that we could fly right through it. The Perspex bubble glowed a silver white, and the colors of the flak washed across the panes. They flickered on the metal walls, orange tongues like a fire catching.

I gripped the edges of my desk. I was absolutely terrified.

The flak knocked us sideways. It hammered us down and tossed us up. The kite reeked of exploded shells as we lurched through shattered air. Everyone was shouting all at once, and poor old *Buster* groaned and rattled.

Then suddenly everything was quiet. We were back in the darkness, in our cloak of night. I thought hours had passed, but it had been only moments. We had crossed just one belt of flak. We weren't even close to the target.

CHAPTER 7

THE OP PASSED LIKE a nightmare, in a series of visions that were too frightening to be real. Now we were growling through the darkness, now being hurled across the sky. With *Buster* tipped on its side, I looked through my little window, three miles down at the valley of the Ruhr. I saw smoke in the moonlight, oozing along over factories and buildings, across a silver ribbon of the river. I saw target markers tumbling in a cascade of crimson and green. And everywhere were the searchlights, weaving back and forth, flailing across the sky like the legs of a terrified spider.

They didn't seem at all like beams of light. They were solid things that would knock us from the sky if they touched us. They were the death rays that even Superman was scared of.

"Ten minutes to the target," said Simon.

"Roger."

A band of searchlights guarded Düsseldorf, slashing at us with those white-hot rays. And from their middle rose a single blue one that never moved, that stood erect like a column in the air. The night fighters would be swarming toward it, wheeling round that pillar of light.

"Hello, hello. The welcome wagon's here," said Lofty. A light washed over us. I heard a shell go whistling by and the *whump* of another exploding ahead. I smelled the powder, and felt the kite shiver as we flew through the shattered air.

"Bomb doors open," said Lofty.

The whistle of air that was always with us became a terrible scream. I huddled in my little space, with my eyes closed and my teeth locked.

"She's all yours, Shakespeare," said Lofty.

"Okay, Skipper."

Here we go, I thought. For the next minute and a half we could do nothing but fly straight across the target at a steady speed and a constant height. Forget the search-lights; forget the flak and the fighters; just put the bombs on the target or the op wouldn't count.

I couldn't stop shivering. I held my head and closed my eyes, and with every lurch and shake of the plane I was afraid that something had hit us, that our wing was shearing off. I kept thinking of that man snagged to his falling machine, and I was certain that the same thing would happen to me. Yet Will sounded nearly as calm as Lofty. He lay on his glass floor, looking straight down at the searchlights, straight into the gun barrels, but there wasn't a hint of fear in his voice. "Left, left," he said. Then, "Right a bit. Steady, Skipper. Steaaaady."

I wanted to get out of that machine. I felt that I *had* to get out before it was too late.

"Left, left."

Flak exploded beside us, then above us. A terrifying rattle sprayed across the fuselage, and I screamed into the intercom, "We're hit! We're hit!"

Ratty shouted, "Where?" and Buzz cried, "Corkscrew. Go!" Then Lofty hollered, "Shut up! Everyone shut up!" He said, "It's just cartridges. Empty cartridges." They were spewing from the turrets of the bombers up above us.

"Steady," said Will. "Left, left. Steady now. Steaaaady."

There were bombers all around us, covering acres of the sky. I prayed that one of *them* would get the chop instead of us—that *all* of them would get the chop so long as we were safe.

Lofty clicked on. "Kid, get ready with the flash."

"Roger, Skipper." My hands fumbled with the buckles and connections. My legs wobbled as I climbed to the cockpit. I closed my eyes and groped through it, not wanting to see all of the sky through those greenhouse windows. I stepped down toward the flare chute and bumped right into Buzz's legs. His shoulders were above me, his head in his turret.

When I got to the chute I plugged myself back into the oxygen and intercom. I took a flare from the holder, and waited for Will.

Come on, come on, I thought. The fuselage was a horrible place to sit out the minutes. A dark and lonely tunnel, it stretched back to the tail, where a door led to Ratty's rear turret. The coldness ran right to my blood and my bones. I was afraid that my fingers would freeze, and that I wouldn't be able to drop the flash at the right time. When the bombs fell away they would start our camera running. If I released the flash too soon or too late, it wouldn't light up the ground for the picture. I was afraid that if I messed up, we would have to do the op all over again. *Come on, Will.*

I listened to his voice guiding us on. I opened the chute, and heard air whistle through it. *Come on.*

"Bombs gone!" he cried at last.

B for Buster leapt up a hundred feet. Lightened from the load, the enormous thing floated up like a feather on a breath of air. But still we flew straight along as our bombs hurtled down. I held the flare in the mouth of the chute and started counting the seconds. When I got to eight I dropped the flash and slammed the little door.

"There's flares popping off all over," said Will. "Great explosions on the ground. They look like boils at first, then they shatter into pus. There's a clot of smoke ten thousand feet high."

The air buffeted against us. I felt the blasts of the bombs, as though fists pummeled at the wings. The air-frame creaked, then banged, and I was certain that the old bus was about to crack open. But at last we tilted to the left, and went down in a spiraling dive.

"Bomb doors closed," said Lofty.

I staggered back to my wireless to send the signal that we'd bombed the target. This time I dared a glance from the cockpit. I looked down at a land of fire and smoke, and saw that the peaceful place we'd come to had been turned to a horror. The stream of kites was still passing the target, the bombs still bursting.

When I plugged in at my desk Ratty was babbling through the intercom. "Look at it burn," he said. "Wheezy jeezy, look at it, will you? We gave it a pasting, eh? We plastered that place. No lie."

I saw him in my mind, glowing red from the fires on the ground, a little demon hunched in his ball of glass. Helmeted and masked, plugged into air and heat, he was a part of the plane. We all were. *Buster* kept us breathing and *Buster* kept us talking. We were only the nerves of a metal monster.

But we had leveled out, and were flying for home. I breathed again, and smiled again, and blinked out tears that came for no reason except that I was still alive. I tuned in England on the wireless and tapped out a message on the key. Somewhere miles and miles away, in a little room with lights and people, someone listened to my dots and dashes and put a tick on a bit of paper to count another load of bombs.

"Skipper, your course is zero-zero-niner," said Simon. It came out "noiner" in his Australian accent.

We flew toward home. There was flak near the border, and again at the coast, but it didn't seem so bad anymore. I just trembled and sweated until it was past. And then the Channel seemed almost friendly.

Ratty told a long joke about two farmers and a nun. Buzz thought about his crossword clues. "Hey, is there another word for an orange?" he asked.

We started descending before we crossed the English

coast. Gilbert poked his head from his box, blinking around with his stupid eyes. I felt a twinge of guilt to think how I'd promised to look after him but hadn't given him a thought. So I got out my water bottle and gave him a drink in his little tin. Then I unbuttoned my mask, took a sandwich from my bag, and shared tiny bits of the bread.

Will saw distant combats—brief spurts of tracer—but no fighters came on our tail. I ate an orange and a chocolate bar as the gunners kept their watch. Our engines droning, we slipped along above fields and cities, over the little Yorkshire farms. And we landed well before the sun was up.

Our flaps were down, our undercarriage locked. Will, in the second dickey seat again, called out the height and speed as Lofty kept us aiming for the flare path.

"Sixty feet, one-ten," said Will. "Fifty feet, one hundred."

We flitted past the pigeon loft.

"Forty feet, one hundred."

"Throttles back," said Lofty.

The wheels shrieked once as they touched the runway, then hummed along the ground. The nose came up and the tail wheel settled. We coasted past the tower, past the offices, and swung hard right onto the taxi strip.

The erks were waiting where we'd left them, as though they hadn't moved in the hours we'd been gone, or as if those hours were really only seconds. With big sweeps of their arms they guided Lofty into place, then threw down the chocks and swarmed around the bomber. One of them found a shrapnel hole pierced right through the wing, and they all rushed over to see for themselves. They shook their fists toward us as they grinned from ear to ear.

Lofty and Pop shut down the engines, and the silence was amazing. We rose from our places, stretching our shoulders and necks. I took the pigeon box and followed Simon through the bomber, over the struts and out through the door where we'd entered.

The air was magnificent, so cool and fresh. It tingled on my face where the rubber mask had turned my skin all hot and clammy. I tore off my helmet and shook the sweat from my hair, and it was the most wonderful thing in the world to be standing on grass again. Lofty and Pop went for their circuit round *Buster,* nodding and pointing for the erks, and the rest of us settled on the ground, sitting on our parachutes because there was thick and beautiful dew on the grass. The ones who smoked got out their cigarettes again.

"Well, that's *one,*" said Ratty. "Twenty-nine to go."

He didn't exactly laugh; no one did. They grunted at him, and someone threw an orange. But all my joy in being alive suddenly ended with Ratty's words. We had flown one op, just one crummy op, and I couldn't imagine going through the same thing over and over again for twenty-nine more.

It had seemed so easy at first. Even that morning it had been a lark. Fly thirty ops and take a rest. Fly thirty more if you like. Or move to something else, and then go home with a row of gongs across your chest. I had seen myself going home the hero, waving the flag and selling war bonds. I'd thought I would barrel-roll my Spit across Quebec and Ontario, and fight off the girls who would clamor around me. Well, so much for that. Already my dream was shattered, my hopes destroyed. They didn't give out gongs for being afraid.

The bombers taxied past us, nose to tail, like a parade of elephants. We watched them emerge from the dark and slide back into it, and there was the smell of exhaust and the throaty sound of engines. But the place beside ours, where *E for Eagle* had started, stayed empty. The erks there stood in an awkward-looking group, like the only boys at a dance who had no partners to be with. They looked up at the stars, then kicked the grass and shuffled back and forth.

They were still there when the truck stopped to give us a lift across the field. By then they were looking at their watches, and their shoulders were starting to slump.

Nobody talked very much as we rode across to the huts. Lofty and the rest went in for their guzzle of eggs and bacon. I carried the pigeon box and followed the smell of birds down toward the tower where old Bert was waiting with his trolley. There was already a stack of the yellow boxes on it.

"'Allo, sir," he said. He even saluted. "Did you 'ave a good op, sir?"

I wasn't sure what to tell him, but I didn't want a pigeoneer to know how scared I'd been.

"Wasn't *too* bad, was it, sir?" he asked.

"No," I said. "Not really."

"Glad to 'ear it, sir." He beamed at me, then took the box and hoisted it close to his face, the hinged end open. He made a kissing noise, and Gilbert's head came out through the flap. They touched each other, lips to beak, the bird and the pigeoneer. "And 'ow was Gibby, sir? Not a problem, was 'e?"

"No."

"Never is. Not this one." Bert clucked his tongue. "Pretty Gibby." He smacked his kisses again, and the bird stretched out its neck. It warbled in its throat with a funny little cry that I had never heard before from any bird.

"I know, I know," said Bert. He piled the box on the trolley, gave the bird a little tickle, then eased its head through the flap and closed the door. He turned to me. "Lots of searchlights, sir? Flak was 'eavy?"

I tried to make a joke. "He told you that, I guess."

"In 'is little way," said Bert. "Yes, sir. If Gibby comes 'ome uneasy, singing 'is little worry song, I know it's been tough on 'im, sir."

"I *was* a little bit scared," I told him.

"No shame in that, I'm sure," said Bert. "The first op scares the willies out of people. For some blokes it's too much. They see the flak and the fires, and they never get over it. The pigeons are the same way, sir. I've seen some go bonkers their first time up."

I felt a great relief just then. If even old Bert knew that ops were terrifying, maybe there was nothing wrong with me.

No other wireless operators were coming with their boxes, so I didn't mind lingering for a while, in the dark, with the filthy pigeoneer. I moved toward the trolley, hoping to find a place to sit, and nearly stepped on a pigeon that was loose on the ground. It startled me with its sudden flurry of wings, and went whistling past my face to perch on the pigeoneer's shoulder.

"Ah, Percy," said Bert. "Poor old chap; 'e's probably been standing at attention down there all this time, 'oping we would see 'im."

I leaned back on the boxes. "Do you always let him fly around?"

"At night I do," said Bert. "Safe enough at night. 'E's my little pet, old Percy."

The pigeon cooed, a happy sound.

"Is everyone 'ome, sir?" asked Bert.

I shook my head, and his face went pale. "Who's missing, sir?"

"*E for Eagle* isn't back," I told him.

"No!" He actually staggered sideways. Percy fluttered away, flying a circuit and bump to land again in the same spot. "Not that one, sir. There must be some mistake. That's Jesse, sir. Twenty ops. *Twenty* ops, sir."

I was surprised that Bert knew any of the fliers. I said, "Was he a good pilot?"

"Not the *pilot,* sir. The pigeon! Jesse Owens, fast as fire, sir. Nearly as fast as Percy. That black Morris that races about, that little car? Jesse can outrun it, sir. Like it was standing still. Jesse can—" His big, square face collapsed. *"Could,"* he said. Jesse *could."*

His fists suddenly clenched. "You bastard!" he screamed. "Don't you see what you're doing? Don't you care?"

"Who are you shouting at?" I asked.

"At 'im!" Bert pointed at the air. "The man upstairs!"

He was so big that he scared me. He was like the giant in my old storybooks, gentle one moment, fierce as God the next.

Just as suddenly, he was himself again. He hung his head, flicked a white spiral of droppings from his sleeve, and sighed. "I'd better be off, sir," he said. "Before they 'ear me down in High Wycombe. I'll get the pigeons 'ome. Get my letter written. I always write to the breeder, sir, when a pigeon gets the chop." He saluted again, and slouched off to the front of his trolley. "You 'ave a good sleep, sir," he told me.

I started back toward the huts, but Bert was still talking. "I'm going to fly them tomorrow," he said. "Would you like to come, sir?"

He caught me by surprise. If Lofty or Will had asked me that, I would have had to be wary, careful to make sure that I could fit into whatever we did or wherever we went. But with the pigeoneer, I found, I didn't have to worry about being so young. I just smiled and told him I would. "I'd like that a lot," I said. "Thank you."

We moved apart, but Bert kept talking, his voice growing louder with every step. "That is, of course, if you're not on, sir. If you're on, then it's off." He laughed. "Do you see what I mean, sir?"

"Yes!" I shouted. It hadn't occurred to me that I

might be flying the next night as well. I started to run, at first to get away from Bert, and then to get away from the fear that came surging through me. I ran and ran, until the patter of my shoes was like a hammering of guns. It wasn't even morning yet, and the last thing I wanted was to climb into *Buster* again before the day was finished. I needed rest, I thought; I needed sleep.

But first came debriefing. We sat in a little room and told the Chair Force everything we'd seen. After that, I had a tuck-in of eggs, and when I finally got into bed I found that I couldn't sleep at all. At the other end of the hut, an airman tossed and muttered in his bed. Then he cried out, piercingly and loud. And I saw him bolt upright in his bed, his arms flailing.

It was Donny Lee.

CHAPTER 8

WHEN I WAS STILL in school I read a story about a boy who had to choose between two doors. Behind one of them was a beautiful princess who would love him forever. Behind the other was a tiger who would kill him.

I didn't remember anything else about the story, only those two doors and the boy's terror as he stepped forward to open one of them. But in the morning, at breakfast, I knew exactly how he felt.

I stared at my plate and waited for the loudspeaker to come on, for that English WAAF to tell me if I would fly or not. It was strange, but I dreaded that moment more than I dreaded the flying.

Ratty was tucking in as though he didn't have a care in the world. He was talking to Buzz at the same time, in a voice louder than anyone else's. Bits of brussels sprouts bubbled round his teeth as he talked about his home, a little farm in the dust bowl, and how he had watched it blow away in a cloud of soil when he was six years old. "All that smoke we saw last night?" he said. "It was just like that. No lie. I saw that smoke, and I thought of the Krauts watching their houses blow away."

He laughed as he stuffed his mouth full of potatoes. "We moved into a cardboard box. No lie. We did. My folks and three kids, we lived in a shack made out of cardboard."

"I guess you could sell that to the Krauts just now," said Buzz.

"Yeah, I guess! No lie," shouted Ratty.

For once I wasn't the one who drew attention, the one who got the frowning faces turned toward him. But Ratty, of course, didn't even notice. "None of you guys lived in a goddamned box," he said. "I could put my finger through the wall. I could pick up my whole friggin' house."

"Could you shut your flap?" asked Lofty.

The loudspeaker hummed. Every head rose, as though the airmen were a herd of grazing cows looking up at a gunshot. Even Ratty went silent.

"Good morning, gentlemen," said the WAAF.

My fork trembled in my hand, rapping on the tabletop. Poor, stupid Buzz must have thought that I was trying to beat a drumroll because he started his own, with his fingers thrumming on the table edge. He grinned like the idiot that he was.

The WAAF cleared her throat. She tapped on the microphone, and it sounded to me like a door latch turning. Then her angelic voice warbled through the speaker. "You are on for tonight."

Ratty held up his thumbs. Buzz finished his drumroll

with a flourish, with a cymbal tap on his drinking glass. Already Lofty was shoving himself back from the table. He had his pipe in his hand, and he popped it in his mouth as he stood up. "Well, chaps," he said. "I'll take a squint at the list. See if we're flying."

It was exactly the same as the day before, down to the very same words. I had a strange feeling that it *was* the day before, that I was living it all over again. I dropped my fork, but my hand still trembled. I put it up to my forehead, and then down to my knees, where it bounced and jittered on my trousers.

"You don't think they'd send us twice, do you?" I asked. "Not twice in a row."

"You frightened?" asked Buzz. He was leering.

"No." I wouldn't admit to that. "I had something to do. I was supposed to go and see . . ." I let my voice fade away.

"Who?" asked Ratty. "Not a bird, you mean?"

I thought he was making fun of me because of the pigeons, but it was worse than that. Birds, to the British, were girls.

Buzz laughed like a chuckling horse. "Look at him blush! It's true; the kid's got a bird."

They went away howling, but jealous as well, with a bit of spite in their jokes and their stares. I doubted that either of them had ever held a girl hand in hand. As much as they boasted about the things they had done, it was all talk, and everybody knew it. It was just a lot of flak.

I didn't even bother to go and see the pigeoneer. I just sat in the sunshine and stared at the hills. They were yellow humps with sick little clusters of trees, like the backs of mangy dogs. In Canada, they would have been covered with pines, but I wouldn't have even seen them for the forest all around me. I could have walked for miles and never seen the sky.

I got homesick sitting there—for a home that I'd hated. I wished I had never left it, that I had never heard of the air force. I tried to *take* myself back, willing my body and soul over the thousands of miles to the forests and the tumbling waters of Kakabeka Falls. Like Donny had done that day in the Hambleton Hills, I walked through the town, and I saw the people as clearly as if I really were there. But they didn't see *me.* I was like a ghost strolling along.

Then all that vanished, and I was looking not at the hills but at the bombers ranged across the field. I thought of climbing into *Buster* and flying through the searchlights, watching the shells come floating up, seeing the bright flashes of bombers exploding. The more I thought about it, the more I dreaded the coming night.

Over to my left a baseball game was starting. To my right was a group of laughing fliers. Straight ahead, Donny Lee went by, with all his crew packed into the little Morris. They looked like seven dolls stuffed into a child's toy. And in the middle of all this I trembled by myself.

I wasn't a whiz at math, but I knew the odds, and they had never seemed so dismal. If I was going to fly every night, and if every night about five percent of the bombers bought the farm, then I had no chance at all. If

I lived as long as twenty-one ops, I was breaking all the laws of averages, all the rules of numbers. It was impossible, mathematically, that I would ever get home to Canada. Within a few months or a few nights—maybe this very night—I was bound to get the chop. I had always been sure it would happen to some other guy, but now I knew it was going to be me.

Then Lofty came ambling up, and the whole crew was at his heels. They were carrying parachutes, all laughing at some joke that Ratty must have told. He had a wicked grin on his face as he hurried along between Buzz and Pop. Lofty puffed through his pipe.

"'Allo, 'allo," he said in his English way. "We've been looking for you everywhere."

"Are we on the list?" I asked.

"Roger that," he said. "Get your chute, old chap. We're going to take the crate for a spin. Make sure it's all tickety-boo."

"When?" I asked.

"Right now. So shake a leg." Lofty clapped his hands. "Chop, chop."

It was a bad thing to say, but he didn't even know it. He looked at me with his new kind of smile that showed his teeth but didn't glitter in his eyes.

I ran to the parachute hut and all the way back, only to find that the six of them had gone ahead without me. I raced across the field shouting, "Wait up! Wait up!" I felt awfully sorry for myself as I panted up among them, and immediately worse when I saw Bert trudging toward us all.

Buzz pointed and laughed. "Here comes old feather-head."

Even Pop chuckled. "That crazy old bird," he said.

Bert bobbed up and down as he walked, as though there were springs on his shoes. He had his pigeon riding on his shoulder.

"That's the dirtiest guy I ever saw," said Buzz.

"Look at his shoes," said Lofty. Of course he always noticed people's shoes. "I say, they've got to be fifteens."

They crushed the grass as Bert started running. I was tempted to join in with the others and laugh and mock the man. I was tempted, too, to tell them there was nothing wrong with Bert. But I only kept walking, and turned my head away to study the farthest bomber, hoping that—somehow—Bert wouldn't see me.

It didn't work. "'Allo!" he shouted. "'Allo, there, sir!"

"Who's he talking to?" asked Lofty.

"It's off, sir," shouted Bert. "Sir, it's off!"

"Eh? What's off?" said Lofty. "Is he nuts?"

"Sir!" Bert's arms were pumping, his head up high. The pigeon bounced on his shoulder like a little jockey, stretching its wings as Bert's whole body rose and fell.

"Jeez, I can smell him from here," said Ratty.

So could I. The odor of birds, like sour vinegar, was in his clothes and his boots and his hair.

"Who the hell does he want?" asked Lofty.

I tossed up my hands. "Me," I said. "He wants *me,* okay?" They all gawked as I stopped walking.

Ratty made the connection. "*That's* your bird?" he said.

I nodded.

"A *real* bird? No lie?"

"I was supposed to take them flying," I said. "All of them." Stupid Buzz—he still didn't understand—asked me, "Huh? Take 'em flying? In *Buster,* you mean?"

"Wheezy jeezy!" Ratty howled.

I said, "No, not in *Buster.* We were going to take the pigeons out and let them fly home."

Buzz didn't have a clue what I was talking about, but I didn't explain any more. The rest of the crew kept going as I turned away to meet old Bert. He came thumping up beside me, and little Percy stood at attention on his shoulder.

"You shouldn't have come out here," I said.

"No bother, sir." He was red and winded. "I wanted to tell you that it's off. The flight, sir."

Percy warbled and cooed on his shoulder. "Why, 'e likes you, sir," said Bert. "I told 'im I was going to see you. 'Appy? Oh, 'e wanted to come."

I looked at the pigeon. Its head was turned away, but its eye seemed to look right at me.

"Oh, 'e wants a tickle, sir," said Bert. "Give 'im a little tickle, sir."

I felt stupid, but I did it. I reached up and touched the pigeon's neck the way Bert had done. I thought it would feel as soft as a kitten, but it was rough and sort of starchy.

"There. Look at 'im gloat, sir," said Bert, almost gloating himself. But sure enough, the pigeon did seem happy. It made its warbling sound again as the muscles pulsed in its neck. I took my hand away and wiped my finger, secretly, on the back of my trousers.

"We'll fly them tomorrow instead," said Bert. Then he added, "So long as you can, sir, of course."

"You mean if I make it home tonight?" I said.

He smiled. "Oh, I'm sure you'll make it 'ome, sir. I meant if you don't 'ave something better to do. But if you'd rather be somewhere else . . ."

"No, I'd like to fly them," I said.

"Then tomorrow it is." He waved his huge hand, then went off in his awkward run toward the pigeon loft. Half a mile he'd come, and half a mile he had to go, but he didn't seem to mind.

I sprinted to catch up with the others. I got to *Buster* just as they did, as Sergeant Piper came around from the tail. Lofty asked him, "What's the news, old boy?"

The sergeant told us how much fuel we would carry, and what sort of bombs, then scratched his head and told us, "It's Germany for certain. Happy Valley, that's my guess. That's what *I* think."

I wished I hadn't hurried. I didn't want to know any sooner than I had to just where the target was.

High on *Buster*'s side, a new bomb—the forty-sixth—had been painted below the cockpit. Small and white, it was the start of a new column, a fresh stick of bombs beginning to fall. There was a patch over the little hole that flak had punched in the wing.

We climbed aboard and started the engines. It was only a test flight, I told myself, to calm my nerves. I was glad that Lofty was the careful sort who always took a test flight. The kite smelled of the kerosene that the erks had used to wash it down, and I hoped it was the oily smell that made my stomach churn. But that sick feeling stayed with me through the flight and after it, through all the hours of the day. It grew worse with the waiting.

In the sergeants' mess, the wireless set spilled out the news of our raid, and the damage we had done to Düsseldorf. A British announcer counted the lost bombers against the Germans killed like scores in a football match, then cleared his throat and said that President Roosevelt was urging the Italian people to rise up against Mussolini. He said Russia was celebrating a bombing raid against the Germans.

But I had nothing to celebrate as I worried through the afternoon. Three times I joined the crowd lining up to use the latrine, and my fear only grew. It was almost too much to bear when I sat down in the briefing hut, squashed between Buzz and Will. I closed my eyes when the curtain shivered and started to open, hoping that Sergeant Piper was wrong, wishing for a target that was closer and safer than Happy Valley.

I heard the curtain rattle on its rail. A deep groan rose from the airmen, from all of them at once. I looked up, and I saw the red ribbons on the map twisting down to Bochum, right to the heart of the Ruhr, to the cluster of cities where the flak would be strongest. It was the black cave where the night fighters lived. My fear came suddenly, like an icy hand squeezing at my bones.

A thin whistling started beside me. I leaned forward

and saw that Lofty—next to Will—had taken out his pipe. He crossed his long legs, tugged at his trousers, and winked at me.

I didn't know how he could be so calm, how everyone could except me. They looked at the map with blank stares, as though they were only watching another boring lecture about security or lice. No one seemed the least bit worried.

The intelligence officer got up and tapped at the flak with his pointer, the sound as steady as a clock. Drippy, the met officer, showed us the weather map and told us that it would be cloudy over Germany. We would go in above the overcast, and I was relieved to think that we'd be hidden from the searchlights. But all along the benches, the airmen coughed and sniffed and scuffled their shoes, as though they were disappointed that they wouldn't be seeing the target.

Lofty leapt to his feet when the briefing ended. He got us into a little huddle in the middle of the room. He put his right arm on my shoulders, his left on Simon's, and he told us—with his pipe in his mouth—"Cheer up, chaps; it won't be so bad."

He must have been talking to me. No one else seemed sad or glum.

"So long as we all keep awake and do our jobs, there's no worries tonight." He looked at each of us, eye to eye, then tightened his arms and drew us into a smaller circle. "No mistakes, okay? If *one* of us messes up, *all* of us get the chop."

We looked sadder when he finished than we had before he started. Simon was the first to break away from the circle. Then Ratty followed him, and Pop wandered off, and I didn't mind being left alone. I wanted to talk to Donny Lee, to tell him that I'd changed my mind.

CHAPTER 9

DONNY LEE WAS SITTING on his bed, with a collection of little things spread across the blanket. He was picking them up one by one, holding them for a moment in both his hands, then setting them back on the gray wool. He had a wallet, a pocketknife, a photograph or two. He had them arranged in a row.

He looked at me as I walked down the aisle between the beds. "Hi, Kid," he said.

I thought he was sorting out the things he could take on the op. We weren't allowed to carry wallets or train tickets, or anything else that might show where we came from. We weren't allowed to take a single thing that a German spy could take from *us* and use to blend himself into England.

Donny picked up his knife. "You want this?" he asked.

"For keeps?" I asked.

"Sure."

I couldn't believe it. He had owned that knife for years and years. I had watched him slice the blade through the bark of a pine tree, carving his initials inside a heart.

"Don't *you* want it?" I said.

"Don't need it," he told me.

"Well, thanks, Donny. Thanks a million." I took the knife and opened the blade. It was sharp and shiny.

"Anything else you fancy?" he asked.

His hands moved across the bed, palms up, the way a storekeeper would show off things on display.

"Why? What are you doing?" I said.

"Moving out."

"Where to?"

He smiled sadly. "I don't know, Kid; not for sure. But I won't be coming back."

"Don't say that, Donny."

"It's true," he said. "I can feel it, Kid. As soon as I woke up, I *knew* it. I'll get the chop tonight."

"It was just a dream," I said. "I heard you shout. You were only dreaming."

"I was *dying.*" He panted a little laugh. "You want my wallet?"

"No," I said. "I don't want anything." I threw the knife back, and it bounced across his blanket. "I don't even want to talk about this."

"Hey, it's okay, Kid," he said. "There's nothing I can do to stop it."

His calmness upset me. If he knew he was doomed, he should have been more scared than I was. He should have been trembling or crying or *something.*

"Don't go tonight," I said. "Just say you won't go."

"Come on, Kid." He started gathering his things, putting them all in one little pile. "If I don't go, I'm a coward. They'll mark me down as LMF and—"

"What's that?" I asked.

"Lack of moral fiber."

It sounded silly the way he said it, as though his body—or his soul—could tatter and unravel. "So what?" I said. "Who cares?"

"*You* did," he said. "I told you I could get you out, and you told me no."

"I've changed my mind," I said.

He laughed. "Don't bind me, Kid."

"It's true," I said. "I'm scared now, Donny. I'm really scared."

He didn't understand. He thought I was scared for him, and not for myself. He got his little pile together, then stood up and put his hands on my shoulders. "Don't be frightened," he said. "Don't worry about me. I've seen so many guys come and go. So many, Kid. I think they're waiting for me somewhere: for all of us. It's like they'll meet a train or something, and I'll be on this one and maybe you'll be on the next. In the end, we'll all be together, I think." He leaned toward me. "Kid, I've *seen* them."

"Who?" I asked.

"Them. They come back."

He touched his teeth, ticking his fingernails across them. He took one more look at his bed, at his wallet and his pictures. "Let's go," he said. "You can watch the fun."

He led me from the hut, outside and along the path.

He looked down at the ground and up at the windows, here and there at everything we passed, as though he knew he was seeing it for the last time. At the sergeants' mess, his fingers caressed the door handle before he went inside.

The room wasn't full, but there was still quite a crowd sitting around in the old wicker chairs or standing at the bar. Lofty was there, his pipe in his mouth, reading the front page of a newspaper. Buzz was frowning at his tattered crossword, and Ratty—at the bar—was playing shove-ha'penny with himself, dashing back and forth to catch his coin as it teetered at the edges. Donny went straight to the piano. He stepped onto the bench, up to the keys with an unmusical jangle, and up again to the piano's top.

In most places he would have drawn some attention. In almost any place at all it would have seemed unusual for a fellow to climb onto a piano that was propped up with a bomb. But the sergeants' mess was pretty wild, and no one even looked.

Sunlight from the window shone on his bright red hair. He did a little soft-shoe in the center of the piano, but no one looked at *that.* Then he pulled his car keys from his trouser pocket and held them up above his head. Still nobody looked.

"Who wants the bus?" he asked.

"Donny, don't!" I said. He could give away his knife, but I hadn't dreamed that he would ever give away the Morris. "Please, Donny."

He stared down at me—straight down from the

piano. "I'm okay," he said. "Don't worry, Kid." He shook the keys, and the sunlight sparkled on them.

"Who wants the bus?" he said again, louder than before.

All over the room, the sergeants looked up. They put their papers down, their magazines and drinking glasses. I saw Lofty watching, and Buzz and Ratty, and maybe twenty others altogether. There wasn't one of them who hadn't fancied that sleek black Morris. But none of them said a word, as though they couldn't believe that anyone would give away that treasure.

"Come on," said Donny. He shook the keys, and they jingled in his fingers. "Doesn't anybody want the bus?"

They must have seen the sadness in his eyes. They must have known that he was serious. Seven sergeants came suddenly leaping from their chairs, and Lofty was among them. They ran toward the piano and made a little mob around it, shouting out, reaching for the keys.

Donny laughed; he was pleased by that. He walked a circuit round the piano as the sergeants' fingers brushed against his knees. "A list!" he cried. "We'll make a list. Write your names on the chalkboard, and the first one gets the Morris."

The seven went off at a rush. "Go, Lofty, go!" shouted Buzz. And Lofty hurdled tables and wrestled with a gunner; then all of them were crowded in the corner by the blackboard.

"No shoving, now," said Donny Lee. "You might all get a turn if you're lucky."

The sergeants struggled. "Lofty! Lofty!" shouted Buzz,

and others chanted different names. They laughed and cheered the seven on as they battled for the chalk, as they flung themselves like blue waves against the wall. Their arms reached up; their legs kicked out. When at last they fell away, Lofty's name was sixth. At the top of the list was the navigator from *J for Jam,* a big and burly fellow.

Donny stepped down. He hung the keys on the nail beside the blackboard, where he hung them every time he flew. "First guy gets it," he said. "Then the next, and the next."

He came and stood beside me, flushed and happy—truly happy. "They'll remember this for years," he said. "For years and years. In every mess in every squadron they'll talk about the guy who stood on a piano and gave away a car."

I saw that was all he wanted: to be remembered, to be famous in a way. He could easily refuse to fly that night, be marked as LMF and wonder forever if he would have got the chop or not. Or he could give away his lovely Morris and go off on his op, to catch that train to a different place. And even if he was wrong, and he came home, people would remember.

He seemed his old Kakabeka self, his cares stripped away. He told me, "Kid, if you ever want out, go and see Uncle Joe. Go talk to him, okay?"

"Why won't *you*?" I asked.

"We're different," he said. "You can do it, but I can't. Kid, I gotta go."

I thought he wanted to be by himself for a while. So I said, "Okay. I'll see you later, Donny."

But he laughed, and I realized he'd been talking about his op, that he had to go on that. "Yeah," he said. "I think you will, Kid." Then he turned around and nearly ran from the room.

He went and wrote a letter, as it turned out. He wrote a letter to his mom, then left it with his other things, in a tidy pile, so that it wouldn't be any bother to the fellow who would have to come along and pack it all in a box. That was what bothered me later, thinking how he'd told me that he *had* to go, as though he hoped I would talk him out of it.

I didn't try hard enough. In the end, I let him down. I watched him run from the sergeants' mess, and I saw him only one more time before the op, as he climbed into the back of the truck that would take him out to his bomber. He stopped halfway, with one leg hooked over the tailgate. He waved at me, one-handed. He said, "Hey, Kakky. Look after yourself." Then he winked. "I'll be seeing you, Kid, okay?"

"You're coming back," I said.

He shook his head, and I got angry. "Then don't tell me that," I said. "Don't jinx me, Donny."

It was a terrible op, worse than the first one. We nearly collided with another Halifax high above the sea. Nobody saw it in the utter blackness until our wings were overlapping. Then we veered across the bomber stream, shaken by the propwash of aircraft that seemed invisible.

Gilbert rustled nervously in his pigeon box as we crossed the enemy coast. He fluttered from side to side in there, so violently that a little feather drifted out through the hatch. I looked around, wondering why, and saw through my window that the clouds I'd thought would hide us were worse than no clouds at all. The searchlights splashed across their bottoms and turned their tops into glowing sheets as bright as movie screens. And I thought of the night fighters above us and how, to them, we would stand out against those clouds like a cockroach crawling on a pure white floor.

Our turrets whined round and round as the gunners watched the sky. But they didn't see the night fighter that pounced from above. The tracers suddenly flickered past, and Ratty cried, "Corkscrew left!" But Lofty didn't react; he flew us straight and level. "Corkscrew! Corkscrew!" Ratty shouted. The kite shook from our own guns, and at last Lofty sent us cartwheeling through the sky. We plunged into the clouds and went tearing right through them, nearly out of control. My arms were pinned at my sides, my feet to the floor. We came hurtling out into the searchlights and flak, plummeting down in a tight spiral. Pop shouted at Lofty. "Pull up, pull up!"

And down we went.

I saw the ground spinning fast, a pinwheel of searchlights and tracers and flak. Someone vomited, and the reek of it came oozing through my mask. Ratty, in the tail, kept crying out, "He's still behind us!"

The wings thumped. The rudders creaked. *Buster* came shuddering out of its dive with its nose high, its wings tipped over. I felt the airspeed falling off; I heard the shriek of wind fade to a whisper. "Watch it!" said Pop. "You'll stall her now."

Slowly, *Buster* rolled over. My window faced the ground and now the sky. My stomach filled with butterflies as *Buster* tipped and rolled, then tumbled again through the night. We fell a thousand feet to our right, a thousand more to our left. Then Lofty brought the nose up and hauled us round in a swooping turn.

He set the throttles; he set the trimming tabs. And up we climbed toward the clouds, back on route to Bochum. I shone my light into the pigeon box and saw the bird lying on the floor, twitching like a dog in a dream. I gave him water, and he settled down a bit.

Our engines growled; the deck was slanted as we climbed. Then Lofty, breathing heavily, came on the intercom. "Will. You okay?" he said.

"Okay, Skipper," said Will.

He was the one who had thrown up, dizzied by the motions. He was crawling now across his splattered Perspex, cleaning up as best he could.

"Simon?" asked Lofty.

"Here, Skippa," he said in his Australian way.

"Kak?"

"Yes," I said. My voice cracked in a high tremble.

"Pop?"

"Right here."

"Buzz?"

"Here, Skipper."

"Ratty?"

There was no answer from the tail.

"Ratty?" asked Lofty again. "Ratty!" he said more loudly.

"Roger," said Ratty. He sounded frightened. "Skipper, I'm okay."

We carried on and bombed the target. It was a nightmare over Bochum, with the clouds lit up, and the night fighters floating bright white flares above us. We never saw the buildings we were hitting, only the flashes of the bombs and the reddish glow of a spreading fire. We bombed on sky flares that drifted, red and green, through the canyons of the clouds.

Then I dropped the photoflash. We took our picture and turned for home in the bomber stream. Lofty kept us jinking left and right as we flew a weaving, droning course.

An hour after midnight, somewhere over Gelsenkirchen, Donny Lee and all his crew vanished from the sky.

CHAPTER 10

THAT MORNING I DREAMED that I was falling. I went spinning through the sky, and a fiery earth went round and round below me. It looked exactly as the ground had looked from *Buster*'s window, but in my dream I fell alone, without the kite around me. I spun through empty air, through darkness, feeling that I was floating instead of falling. I tried to run, and woke up kicking at my blankets, clutching my pillow to my chest like a parachute. I was thumping at it desperately, trying to tear it open.

It all seemed so real that it took me a minute or more to shake the dream away. I had to make myself remember that *Buster* hadn't really broken up over Bochum, that we had come safely home before dawn. I remembered the surge of the engines as we floated over the hedge, the little shriek of the tires touching the runway.

I even heard Ratty's voice, his laugh. "That's two. Just twenty-eight to go."

I stayed in my bed, in the gloom of the hut, thinking of Donny Lee. I tried to picture the boy I'd known in

Kakabeka, but all I could see were searchlights sweeping, and the gleam of his bomber in the sky.

We had seen it happen, on the homeward trip. The searchlights had coned him over Gelsenkirchen. There had been bursts of flak all around him, but they didn't seem to hit his Halifax. It rolled on its side and went corkscrewing down, and the searchlights flailed as they tried to find it. But the whole black sky was empty.

I lay trembling in my bed. Lofty patted my shoulder on his way from the hut. So did Pop a few minutes later, and Buzz and Ratty after him. They just touched me and kept on going, and I squeezed my pillow and closed my eyes.

When the room was empty, I got up. Three of the beds were utterly bare, stripped of blankets, pillows, and sheets. The boys who had slept there would never be back. Everything they had owned had been packed into boxes, and even the boxes themselves had been packed away.

I didn't know what had happened to those boxes. Maybe there was a room somewhere, maybe off in Hangar D, where all the boxes went—seven that night, seven the night before—filled and folded shut. I could imagine them piling up in some secret, hidden place. And I could imagine another stack of boxes still unfilled. There were two dozen bombers; there must have been scores and scores of boxes waiting somewhere.

I went to breakfast, dreading the moment when the speaker would crackle. But the others just sat and stared at nothing, and I wished that I could be so calm.

At last the WAAF came on. I wondered where she sat and what she looked like, if she was smiling or if her eyes were filled with tears. "Good morning, gentlemen," she said.

Lofty took out his pipe. Ratty's eyes nearly closed; his hands tightened into fists.

I found that I didn't really care what she would tell us. If we didn't go flying that night we'd go the next, or the one after. *Just get it over with,* I thought.

"You are stood down for tonight," said the WAAF.

The sound from the airmen was like one huge breath let out. Someone laughed. A bit of toast went soaring across the room. The joy I felt surprised me. I felt incredibly free, as though tons of weight had been lifted from my back.

Lofty leaned forward. "I think we should raid the Merry Men," he said. "You up for an op, Ratty?"

The Merry Men was the local, down in the village five miles away. None of us had seen it, but we'd heard the talk of what a wonderful place it was. "Sure," said Ratty. "I want to get blotto."

Buzz and Pop both wanted to go. Lofty said he'd tell Simon and Will. He tapped his pipe on the table, put it back in his pocket. "We'll take off at eighteen hundred," he said. "You coming, Kid?"

I had gone to a bar only once, and gotten so sick that I'd sworn I would never drink again. If I went and sat there, not drinking or smoking, they might see how young I was. If I stayed behind, they might *know.*

"Kid?" asked Lofty.

"Well, I'll try," I said.

"Try?" Buzz almost leered. "What's the matter with you, Kid?"

I could see my whole world of little lies about to collapse. But Pop stepped in and saved me. "He's probably got something better to do," he said. "We'll hope to see you there, if you make it."

They went off in a group, each of them feeling through his pockets to count his money. I went the other way, down toward the pigeon loft, and old Bert seemed overjoyed to see me. He called out when I was still yards away, "Well, 'allo, sir! I wasn't expecting you so early, sir."

He was plucking weeds from a small garden. On his shoulder stood Percy, stiff-necked, wings at his side. "Stand easy, now," said Bert. He gave the pigeon a shoot from the garden. "I grow their greens 'ere, sir," he said. "They like their greens."

He took me into the loft, and I was sorry that I had waited so long to see it. Warm and bright, it thrummed with a sound that took me straight home in my mind. The cooing and the clucking of his birds made me think of the great flock of pigeons that roosted under the railway bridge at Kakabeka. Then, they were pests, only targets for stones. I had never killed one, but I had sure tried hard enough.

The pigeons swarmed around my feet, nudging like cats at my trouser cuffs. It was kind of creepy, but I liked it.

"Don't squash them, sir," said Bert. "Mind where you walk, now."

The loft wasn't as dirty as I'd thought it would be. Buckets and bags were stacked in one corner, along with bales of straw. Clipboards bulging with papers hung from a row of nails. There were troughs of water on the floor, roosts and nesting boxes everywhere. I waded through the pigeons, laughing as they scurried away in a mass of feathered backs. Only one bird was still on the perches, standing right below the wire mesh that made the roof.

"What's that one doing?" I asked.

Bert sighed. "She 'asn't moved a muscle all this day," he said. "She 'asn't moved since lights-out yesterday."

"Is she sick?" I asked.

"She's sad," said Bert. "She misses old Ollie something terrible, I think."

"Where's old Ollie?"

"From *L for London,* sir."

That was Donny's kite. "My friend was the pilot," I said.

"Then I'm sorry, sir," said Bert. "I'm sorry as can be."

He looked it, too. He looked suddenly miserable, and tears nearly came to my eyes. Just looking at him made me want to cry myself.

"There's not a 'ope in 'eaven, sir," he said. "Ollie could 'ave flown from Berlin by now. I fear the worst."

"I think the flak got them," I said.

"The flak?" Bert looked shocked as well as sad. He raised his head to the wire roof, and all the veins in his neck stood out. But instead of shouting at his man upstairs, he nearly whispered. "Damn you all to 'ell." He didn't want to frighten the pigeons, I saw, as he gazed down at their backs. "They always know, sir. See how Ollie's mate is pining away? Why, she's even letting the babies starve."

He made me kneel among the birds and look into one of the nesting boxes. Percy leaned forward from his shoulder, peering in along with Bert. There were two babies inside, purplish blobs with oversized heads and enormous eyes. "The one on the left," said Bert, " 'e looks just like Ollie, sir."

Poor Ollie, I thought. The baby was clumsy and ugly, too awkward to stand. It just sat there, trembling all over.

"They're goners, those babies," he said. "If she doesn't pull out of it."

"Can't you feed them?" I asked.

"Not all day and all night, sir," he said. "I 'ave to keep up with the work. I 'ave to sleep."

"No one's flying tonight," I said. "I could come and feed them."

"Bless you, sir," said Bert. "That would 'elp a lot."

He showed me how to do it. He got a medicine dropper and a can of milk, and let me hold the babies as he dribbled trickles down their throats. Their eyes swiveled, their throats pulsed, and they seemed to bloat with the milk they drank. Then they flopped down in the straw and went to sleep.

I had thought we would fly the birds in the sunshine,

but Bert said we would have to wait until twilight. "They're night flyers, sir," he told me. "You don't train 'oming pigeons to fly at night, then turn around and fly them in the day. Not that you'd know, sir."

We fed and bathed the pigeons, did the paperwork in triplicate, then tinkered with the motorized loft that was parked behind the building. Like a hillbilly's shack stuck on the frame of an old truck, it had cages on the sides and space below them for the boxes. The bonnet was open, and an old sack of rusted tools was set down by the fender.

The wrenches were so rusted and the motor so old that we worked for hours to loosen one bolt. Bert's hands got bruised and cut, but he didn't complain. He just went doggedly on, whistling "Roll Out the Barrel" between his quiet cries of "Ouch, sir!" and "Ooh, sir!" as the wrenches kept slipping.

We gave it up when the sun was close to the hills. Bert said we'd use the trolley instead. So we snatched up pigeons and stuffed them into boxes, and when the trolley was full, we each took a side of the handle. But it was Bert who did all the pulling. He grunted once, then put his weight on the handle and got that heavy cart rolling so quickly that I had to trot beside him just to keep up. We trundled down a path that became a lane that wound its way between the hills.

Five miles from home, when the sun and moon went down nearly together, we stopped to let the pigeons loose. Bert took them from their boxes one at a time, held them just so, and tossed them into the air. Each rose in a spiral, its wing feathers whistling, until it found its direction and flew off toward home.

Bert paced them slowly so that they couldn't follow each other, and I lay on the grass looking up at the stars coming out.

"Do you like to fly?" he asked suddenly.

I wasn't sure what to tell him; I didn't really know Bert very well. But right then, all alone with him in an empty land, I thought that I could tell him most anything I wanted.

"I like the *flying,*" I said. "I love to fly."

"But you don't like dropping bombs? Is that what you mean, sir?"

"Oh, I don't mind that," I said. I'd hardly even thought about it. "I don't care what happens to the bombs. It's all the rest. The searchlights, the flak. The fighters. I don't like people shooting at me."

Bert laughed softly. He launched his pigeon and went to get another. "Would you like to toss one, sir?" he asked.

"Sure," I said.

He showed me how to take it from the box, and how to keep it still between my hands. I could feel the nothingness of its feathers, and the metal band around its leg. Then Bert held my wrists and pushed them up and pulled them out. And the bird came loose. The wings swept up; the feathers splayed. They whistled down, then up and down. The tail shifted once for balance. The legs drew in like aircraft struts, the feet swinging forward.

"Fly home!" shouted Bert.

We each brought out another pigeon. We sent them off with that boost they didn't really need. We shouted, "Fly 'ome!" and watched them spiral high above us, into a bright and glittering sea of stars. We fetched two more.

"I get scared," I told Bert. "I think of flying, and I get scared."

"Everyone gets scared, sir," said Bert.

"They don't get *terrified,*" I told him.

"Oh, I think they do, sir," he said. "I think you just don't see it."

It annoyed me that he would say a thing like that. "How would you know?" I asked. "You don't understand. You don't know what it's like in the air."

"Quite right, sir," he said. "I'm sorry, sir."

I felt awful then. Bert huddled over his pigeon, stroking it with his thumbs, as though I'd given him a whipping. I hated that a grown man had to agree with everything I said just because I said it.

"Fly home!" he cried halfheartedly, tossing up the pigeon. He was such a huge man that he looked clumsy no matter what he did. He almost hopped from the ground, and I felt the sod tremble when he landed. But Percy didn't move from his shoulder. Then up went my own pigeon, and I took another from its box.

"You see, sir," said Bert without looking at me, "it's

like the birds. If it was thundering and lightening now, they would still fly 'ome. But some wouldn't like it very much. They're scared to death of lightning, sir."

"But all of them would go," I said. "That's what you mean?"

"Yes, sir," said Bert. "It's what they're trained to do. Like Ollie, bless 'is little soul. Fifty miles an hour, through sun or storm, 'e was never bothered by the weather, sir." Bert blinked, then scowled at the air. "Damn you!" he shouted at the man upstairs. And suddenly he was calm again. "But in the loft, in the lightning, Ollie was a shaky little jelly."

I stared at the pigeoneer. "But what if lightning scared him so much that he *couldn't* fly home?"

"Wouldn't 'appen, sir. Not to good birds like 'im and Percy. They want to get 'ome so badly that they keep on going, scared or not. That's courage, sir."

"No," I said. "Real courage is not being scared."

"Oh, no, sir. Pardon me." He tipped his head, as though saluting. "*Real* courage is carrying on though you're scared to bits. It's doing what you 'ave to do. Birds are scared of lightning; men are scared of dying. Anything else wouldn't be proper, sir. But we all 'ave to carry on. Every living thing. Men and birds and fish and worms, we all just carry on."

"Except for me," I said. "I can't."

"You can, sir. You 'ave to."

"No, I don't," I told him. "I could go to the CO tonight and say I won't go flying anymore."

Bert sighed. "You *could,* sir. Yes, you could. But you might be sorry, sir." He tossed his pigeon. "You might find everything changed if you did. All your 'opes and all your dreams. You might be sorry all your life."

"As if you would know," I said.

"You're quite right, sir."

The last pigeon to fly was Percy. Bert took the little bird from his shoulder and held it like a treasure, as though somehow he could hurt a pigeon by letting it fall. He turned a full circle, looking all around. It was such a clear and perfect night that we could see the hills for miles around. "Any 'awks about?" he asked.

"Awks?" I said.

"No, sir. 'Awks, not awks."

Hawks, he meant, poor Bert. "Not that I should worry, sir," he said. "Percy would give them a run for their money. Fastest pigeon I've ever seen, sir. Seventy miles an hour, maybe more, and nothing ever stops 'im, sir."

He lifted Percy to his lips. They kissed each other, and old Bert grinned. He held out his hands, ready to fling the bird up. Then he stopped. "Would you like to toss 'im yourself, sir?"

I didn't see how one pigeon could be any different than the others, but Percy clearly meant a lot to Bert. So I took the bird, closed it in my hands, and felt its tiny heart thumping against my palm.

"Give 'im a good, clean toss, sir."

I bent forward, holding Percy at my waist. Then I straightened, lifting my arms, and opened my hands above my head. "Fly home!" I shouted.

Out came Percy. His tail spread wide, and his wings stretched open. They *whirred,* so quickly and so strongly that I felt his propwash as he leapt from my fingers. He shot straight up, then banked to the right. He turned only half a circle, and off he went toward the loft, into that white sea of stars. In a moment he was gone.

"Look at 'im go," said Bert in a whisper. He moaned to himself, then dabbed at his cheek with his big sausage-sized fingers. He took hold of the trolley and turned it around. Then he looked up the hill. "'Ome," he said. "'E's already 'ome, sir."

We took a longer route back, climbing slowly up a flatter hill. At its top, silhouetted against the sky, stood the wreck of a Halifax. I gawked at the ragged bits of metal, the double tail rising up like a strange, twisted cross. I said, "Let's go and look inside."

"No, sir," said Bert.

He kept walking, but I dashed ahead to see the wreck. I went right to the nose, over a pile of shattered Perspex. I squinted in the faint light to see what was painted there, on the fuselage. It was a white knight, warped by the twisted metal. In his armor, with his lance, he was riding a bomb instead of a horse; his visor was open, and his face was a skull.

"When did this old crate go down?" I shouted.

Bert didn't answer, if he even heard me. He trudged past with his trolley, and I ran to catch up. I said, "When—"

"Months ago now, sir."

I could imagine the horror in that aircraft, in the split

second after the ground came into view. I imagined the bomb aimer holding up his arms to protect himself. I imagined the glass shattering, the metal crushing as everything folded up toward him in a fraction of a second.

"Did you know the fellows?" I asked.

"I did, sir." Bert's trolley wheels rumbled on the path; I wasn't even pretending to pull. "The Captain's still inside."

"The pilot?"

"The pigeon, sir. Captain Flint. Solid gray from end to end."

The wreck unnerved me, but fascinated me, so I kept looking back at the grim silhouette. It didn't seem fair that a crew could die just a couple of miles from home, smashing into the ground in safe little Yorkshire. Were they laughing when they hit? Were they celebrating another op that was minutes from being over?

"Damn you!" shouted Bert.

I tried to force myself to turn away from the ruined kite; I really didn't want to see it anymore. I didn't want to know that a fellow could die at any time, not only over Germany. But I kept glancing at the twisted metal, and I wondered how long that thing would stay there. Would it stand forever on that Yorkshire hill?

We towed the trolley back to the loft. Bert dropped the handle to race inside, anxious to count his birds. He lit a lantern and shone it around. Out of the shadows, Percy came fluttering to meet us, landing first on Bert's shoulder, and then rising again to settle on mine.

"Well, well," said Bert, laughing. "Look at that. 'E likes you, sir."

To me the pigeons on the floor were just a swarming mass of gray and green. But Bert watched them—his finger pecking as he counted—and then announced, "Yes, sir. They've all come 'ome."

From the highest perch, the lonely pigeon was watching. She had pulled out some of her tail feathers; they lay now on the floor beneath her. The rest were huddled close together, the way the sergeants filled the mess. They were making sounds I hadn't heard before, a doleful sort of crooning.

"Do you 'ear them, sir? They're singing, sir," said Bert.

"Pigeons don't sing," I said.

"Oh, they do, sir. When they come 'ome, they sing. It always sounds sad like this. I think they're singing, in their own sort of way, ''Ere's to the next to die.'"

I was sure he was pulling my leg, and I grinned at him foolishly.

"No, it's true, sir," he said with a solemn nod. "They always know when their number's up."

CHAPTER 11

I MISSED THE OP to the Merry Men by only a few minutes. I dithered for a while, wondering if I should go or not, then took a bicycle from the tangle beside the Nissen hut. It was bent and broken, like all the others, with twisted handlebars and warped wheels. But I climbed aboard and went flat out down the lonely roads.

At the edge of the village I heard the others up ahead. Their bicycles squeaked like a swarm of rats, and they laughed and shouted as they pedaled along. In the starlight I could see that Lofty had his helmet on, the goggles over his eyes. His long legs were splayed sideways to keep his knees from hitting the handlebars, and he had to sit bolt upright, like a squire on a horse. The old guy rode behind him, and a little bit to the side, in the same position he would take in *Buster.* But Ratty and Buzz and the rest zoomed and circled like Spitfires, and now and then there was a shouted "Corkscrew!" followed by a clattery collision.

I gathered speed and bounced them from behind. I hurtled between Simon and Buzz, and just as I came up to Lofty, I spat out sounds like machine guns. He lifted from his seat, veered wildly to the right, and pranged into a thornbush. Pop, the good wingman, nearly followed him in. Then I was past, cackling away, and they were shouting behind me, "Who was that? What moron was that?"

They were angry at first, until they saw it was me. Then they said they weren't surprised at all, and we all untangled Lofty and carried on together.

We didn't park our crates at the Merry Men; we *piled* them. We tossed them down at the door and headed into what I thought would be a place full of girls and jitterbugging crowds. But the pub was dank and dreary, with a low ceiling and a clag of pipe smoke that lowered visibility to half the length of the room. The only people there, apart from the publican, were a few old farmers and sheepherders, all bundled into one dark corner. They moved only to lift their pints or to mutter at each other through shaggy mustaches sodden with beer. The way they glowered, they must have thought of us as a murder of crows, squawking and unwelcome. After an hour I had had enough, and I went outside to wait for the others.

The sky was clouding over, the village dark and quiet. I stood for another hour or so, and then one lamp came on, in a window high in the vicarage. It was a round window and a yellow light, and I was so used to the blackouts that I was amazed just to see it.

A second hour passed. Only Will emerged, bleary-eyed, disheveled, and drunk. He stood on tottering legs and relieved himself against the wall. Then he turned around and looked up. "Gosh, look at the moon," he said. "It's full; it's beautiful, isn't it?"

I didn't tell him it was only the vicar's window.

"Hail, Master," he said, and held up his hands like a pagan praying. He staggered sideways. "Hail, Master," he said again. Then, "Come on, Kak."

I felt silly, but I raised my hands, and looked up toward the window.

"We are your servants, O Master Moon," said Will in his poetical Shakespeare voice. "We do your bidding; we set our lives by you. We are your minions."

I liked that. Even if it was only a window, I liked it. I was a minion of the moon.

"O, Master," said Will. "In your shadow we take to the air; in your brightness we keep the ground." He stretched his hands even higher, as though he hoped to touch it. "Watch over us on this and every night. For you decide if we live or die."

Then he laughed. He dropped his hands and staggered again, as though he had knocked himself over. "What are you doing out here, Kak?" he asked.

"I don't like beer," I said. "I don't like smoke."

"I thought you didn't like *us,*" he said. "You're always by yourself, Kakky. You don't join in enough."

Well, he was only drunk, and you couldn't believe anything a drunk might say. A drunk could tell you, "Son, I'm proud of you," then turn around and belt you one across the chops.

"Come back inside," said Will.

"I can't," I said. "I have to feed the baby birds."

He coughed and belched. "Well, hang on a sec. We'll all be leaving soon."

He went back inside, and I waited again. But the only person who came out through the door was one of the farmers. I heard the airmen laughing, a crash of glass; then the door swung shut and the farmer shook his head. "Bloody Canadians," he said to me. "Why don't you just go home?"

"I sort of wish I could," I said.

But he didn't care. He went plodding down the narrow street, muttering to himself. I didn't wait any longer at the Merry Men. I took a bicycle from the heap and pedaled down the dark road, squeaking through the night.

Halfway to the airfield, a car's headlights flashed around a corner and came racing toward me. They were faint and yellowish, narrowed to slits by their wartime hoods—like a pair of tin cans stuck to the car. But the car came on at breakneck speed. I moved over to the ditch and watched the Morris hurtle along, Donny's black bus with its new crew aboard. The driver—the burly navigator from *J for Jam*—drove it madly, with the gears screaming and the passengers screaming, too, as they clung to the windshield and the boot and the running boards. It shot past, and I saw the glimmer of the little white animals that Donny had painted on the port-side door. I didn't feel sad for him then. I actually smiled to think that he'd be happy to see his car being driven like that, just as he had driven it himself.

I pulled my bike onto the road, and didn't stop again. I went through the gate and along the runway, down to the pigeon loft. Then I lit the lantern and huddled by myself, squeezing drops of milk into the throats of little birds that couldn't even stand by themselves.

The mother still sat on the high perch by the trap. She had shorn her tail of almost all its feathers, but hadn't moved from her waiting place. All around me the other pigeons slept, and cooed, and I felt calmed by the sound, by the warmth. Only Percy was awake. He'd come bounding from the darkness in such a frightening rush that I had almost beaten him away before I'd realized who it was. Now he lounged on my shoulder, nuzzling at my ear, and I gave him a drink from the dropper.

I talked to him, in the darkness. I told him that I was terrified of flying, but that I still hoped to get used to it. I told him, "I do love to fly. It's great, you know." Then I laughed. "Of course you do; you're a bird. Isn't it swell to go flying?" He rubbed his head against my neck and made a musical little murmur. "I just wish I wasn't so frightened," I said. "But I don't know how not to be."

Percy had no answer. How could he? He was just a bird, and I suddenly felt ridiculous telling my worries to a pigeon. I put the dropper back in its place and found a spot among the feed bags where it wasn't too dirty to sit. Percy came down from my shoulder and nestled in my hands. I lay back to hold him for a moment, to think everything out in the bird-mutter sound of the loft. But I fell asleep, and dreamed again of falling.

It was just as real and as frightening as the last time. I plummeted through the sky, spinning end over end. Then I started to run in the air, and tumbled instead. I saw the stars go by, blurring with the fiery ground. When Bert shook me awake and I opened my eyes, I was looking up through the trap, and I *saw* the sky and the stars and thought my dream was real. I was sure that I was falling, that any moment I would smash into the ground.

"Sir!" shouted Bert. But I struggled and kicked; I started to scream.

"Sir, it's all right!" shouted Bert.

He pressed me down into the feed bags. He held me still and said, "Shush, shush, now," and the dream faded away. I looked around the loft, at all the birds with their eyes shining in the light of Bert's lantern. He put his hand on my forehead.

"What were you dreaming?" he asked.

I shook my head; I didn't want to tell him.

"Well, you're safe, sir," he said. "You're on solid ground now, sir." He stamped at the floor to show me how solid it was, though he sent the pigeons scrambling. "You see, sir? It's over now."

He knew that I'd dreamed myself above the ground. I didn't know how, but he did.

"You did a fine job with the babies, sir," he said. "They'll be fit as fiddles soon enough."

He bustled around in his filthy coveralls, shoving bunches of straw into nesting boxes. Percy was gone from my hands, and I couldn't see him. But the lonely pigeon hadn't moved.

"You've got a friend now, sir," said Bert. "You've got a little guardian angel, like."

He pointed above my head, and I twisted round to look. Percy stood there, balanced on a bucket rim.

"It was Percy that woke me up," said Bert. "All 'is flapping and 'is squawking; it gave me a turn, sir. I thought there was a—F-O-X, sir," he said, spelling the word. "Then I came running, and I saw you in a blue fit. It was like you wasn't breathing, sir."

"But where were you?" I asked.

"In my room, sir." He pointed backward with his thumb. "Just behind the loft 'ere."

"Well, thank you," I said.

"Thank Percy, sir."

I held my hand up, and Percy hopped onto my knuckles. He seemed to weigh nothing at all, as though he was just a balloon covered in feathers. I brought him down to my chest, and he tickled my lips with his beak.

"You'll never have a finer friend than Percy," said Bert. "You know 'e 'as the eye-sign, sir?"

"Does he?" I said. I didn't know what the eye-sign was, but I thought I should sound impressed.

Bert brought the lantern and crouched beside us. "Just look at 'is eyes there, sir. See 'ow they shine? See 'ow 'e's got a 'alo inside 'im, sir?"

The light from the lantern flashed across Percy's face. "Look close, sir."

I had never peered into a pigeon's eyes, or into the eyes of any bird. But Percy turned his head aside, as though to give me a better look, and I saw a beautiful walnut-colored ball with a black pupil gaping in the middle. And all around the black was a pinwheel of gold, bright as sparks. It *was* just like a halo.

"That's the eye-sign, sir," whispered Bert.

"Does it hurt?" I asked.

"Oh, 'ardly, sir. That's the mark of a great pigeon. A truly great pigeon, sir." He raised the lantern higher, and it lit his own face as well, in a glow that made him look saintly. "A bird with the eye-sign will find its way 'ome no matter what. Nothing can ever stop it."

The light glistened on Percy's feathers; it filled his eye with liquid gold.

"Percy's father was bred for racing. His grandpa, too, and don't he take after them both?" said Bert. "A thousand miles would be *nothing* to 'im. Rain or snow, 'e wouldn't mind. There's not a single thing in 'eaven or earth that would ever keep Percy from coming 'ome."

"Does he ever fly in the kites?" I asked.

"No, sir." Bert pulled the lantern back and put it down, and the shadows drew around him. "I can't risk losing 'im, sir. Not on ops. Percy's a breeder, sir."

"But he's got no mate," I said.

"I'm waiting for the proper girl to come along," said Bert. "For a girl with the eye-sign, see?" His voice fell to a whisper. "I'm thinking maybe it's going to be one of those babies, sir."

"Really?"

He nodded. Then he touched his nose. "But mum's the word, sir."

I got up from the feed bags and brushed at my clothes. There were pigeon droppings round my ankles and my heels, and I felt disgusted at first to see them. But then I smiled at the thought that I was perhaps becoming a little bit like Bert. It made me think of someone stripping off Batman's cape and finding underneath not Bruce Wayne, the millionaire, but just a lowly servant.

The sky grew light as I worked with Bert. He told me stories of the pigeons, and of their parents and their grandparents, tales the breeders had passed along. He made me look at Gilbert, and told me how an ancestor of that chubby little bird had saved the lives of a regiment in the Great War. "The men were pinned down," he said. "The Germans were shelling them 'ard. They sent a pigeon, but it got shot down. They sent another, and lost that one, too. Then they 'ad just one left, and it was '*is* granddad, sir. It was Gibby's grandpa."

I listened, leaning forward.

"They tossed 'im, sir. And up 'e went, spiraling over the trenches. There were shells exploding, bullets flying. One of them winged the bird, and 'e fell and splattered in the mud. But up 'e got, and off 'e went again, dodging through the bullets, sir. 'E 'omed in seventeen minutes, and the British aimed their guns and knocked out the German artillery. It saved them all, sir. It saved the regiment."

"Jeepers," I said.

Bert rambled on about other birds in other lofts. He knew dozens of stories that sounded like wild adventures but were absolutely true. Pigeons had brought help to airmen forced down in Europe, to kites ditched in the

Channel, and to others lost on the moors. He told me of one bird who had flown fifty ops when his bomber was forced down nearly four hundred miles from the airfield. The bird went for help. "And 'e 'omed in eight and a 'alf 'ours," said Bert with awe in his voice. "Percy now: 'e would 'ave done it in five and a bit." And he winked.

I could have listened all day. The pigeons, to me and everyone, had been a bit of a joke all along. It had seemed ridiculous that we went flying in great machines jammed with men and tools, only to rely—in the end—on a bunch of feathers and a bird's brain, on a grown-up egg. I had imagined the scientists, those brainy boffins, laughing at the idea of us carting pigeons everywhere we went. But now I saw the birds differently, and I thought I had found a sort of home in the pungent loft, a sort of eccentric uncle in the mocked-at pigeoneer.

CHAPTER 12

FOR EIGHT DAYS WE didn't go flying. The war went on in little spurts, so distant that it might have been just a radio play on the wireless. The Flying Forts of the Mighty Eighth took a pasting over Kiel. The Italians surrendered the island of Lampione to the British, and the Chinese pushed back the Japs on a drive toward Chungking. But for us there was nothing but waiting.

On eight mornings I dreaded the words that would come from the speaker, that would open a door on the beautiful lady of restful days or on the frightening tiger of ops.

I came to hate that WAAF. When the week was finished, I despised her. I no longer saw her as young and pretty, but as a crone with snakelike arms, who took delight in torturing me. Every night I had my dream, and every morning I woke with a fear of flying and a fear of waiting. One seemed as bad as the other.

There were endless parties in the mess. All the sergeants crashed about in the mad piggyback battles of Horsey, until there wasn't an airman standing. Then they shifted to the wilder game of Tank, where crews of four picked up the sofas and went charging at each other down the length of the hut, meeting in the middle in a crack of furniture and bodies flying. The parties were hardly less dangerous than the ops.

A new crew arrived to take the place of Donny's. The sprogs moved into the empty beds and tried as hard as they could to fit in with the crowd. But I spent the days at the pigeon loft, watching the babies grow. When Bert was there, I listened to his stories about heroic birds. When he wasn't, I told my troubles to Percy. And somehow the telling of them made them a bit easier to bear.

Then on the twenty-first day of June, the WAAF told us, "You are on for tonight." I realized right away that I'd been wrong. Flying was much, much worse than waiting.

We were sent to Krefeld, back to the valley of the Ruhr.

In the setting sun we lay on the grass under *Buster*'s wing. We all looked up at it, then down at our watches; this last bit of waiting was the hardest. It didn't make it easier that the midsummer days were so long. With all of Britain set to double daylight saving time, it would be well past ten when the sun disappeared, and nearly midnight before twilight ended. Less than two hours later the moon would rise, lighting us up for the German fighters.

Ratty looked at his rabbit's foot, Will at his picture of his wife. Pop had his crucifix, Simon his scented handkerchief. Buzz was crawling around, searching for another four-leaf clover. I got out my ray-gun ring, slipped it on, and cupped my other hand across it.

Foolish. As soon as you hide something, somebody notices. It was Sergeant Piper, trotting behind Lofty, who looked down and said, "What have you got in your hands, boy?"

"Nothing," I said.

Suddenly *everyone* was looking at me.

"Nothing?" he said. "Seems to me you've got something. Seems that way to me."

I shook my head.

"Then open your hands. Show me, boy."

He couldn't make me. I outranked him—in that useless, technical way. But I couldn't argue with *any* grown-up, let alone Sergeant Piper. I spread my hands apart, palms up, hoping no one would see the wiry loop of the ring. To me it seemed as big as a doughnut.

Sergeant Piper grunted. He moved his foot until it touched my hands. I didn't know what he was thinking, maybe that I'd stolen one of his precious little tools and was somehow hiding it in a sort of magic trick. He said, "Turn them over, boy."

And I did.

Ratty burst out laughing. So did everyone, except for Buzz.

"What the hell is that?" asked Sergeant Piper.

It looked ridiculous. The little plastic barrel was aimed at him, and I wished that it was real, that it could melt him into a pool of slime.

"It's a ray-gun ring!" cried Buzz. There was only one way he could know that. He must have had a ray-gun ring himself. But even Buzz would have been smart enough to leave it home in Canada. "Kakabucka Rogers!" he cried. "Hey, Buck!"

"That's so funny I forgot to laugh," I said.

"You gonna vaporize the searchlights? Huh?" He rolled onto his stomach, laughing in his mindless way. I was sure he would go on and on about my ray-gun ring until Lofty sent us into *Buster.* But he found his lucky clover then, and forgot all about my ring. Buzz could never keep track of more than one idea at a time. "I got one, boys," he cried, pulling up the sprig. "A four-leaf clover. Look at that!"

Lofty said, "Let's go."

We got up and piled aboard. I hauled myself through *Buster*'s door, my legs suddenly as weak as spaghetti. My hands sweated so much that they stuck to the pigeon box as I stowed it away. We took our places, went through our checklists. We started the engines. "Rear door locked," said Pop. "Ready to taxi." I had never felt more trapped.

The erks pulled the chocks away. Sergeant Piper raised a thumb, then scurried off as the engines raced and the airscrews growled like tigers.

We taxied down to the end of the runway, right behind old *J for Jam.* We called up the tower to test the wireless. A WAAF said, "Read you five by five. Strength niner."

Lofty turned us onto the flare path. He put on the brakes and let the engines idle.

Will was sitting beside him in the second dickey seat. "There goes *Jam,*" he said.

I heard its engines race. *Buster* quivered in the prop-wash, and a hail of grit blew across our blister.

"Gosh, look at him wobble," said Will. "Lofty, what's he— Holy crow!"

The explosion shook me in my seat. The blast of light glowed in my window, then the shock rattled the whole bus and sent my pencil rolling across the desk.

"What happened?" I said. Everyone was asking, and the intercom was choked with our voices. Bells clanged and jangled as a fire truck and a meat wagon went racing down the runway.

"They just fell," said Lofty. His voice was higher than it should have been. "They took off and they just—" He sounded as though he was shaking all over. "They fell."

I couldn't see from my window. But the light of the fire shimmered on the wing and made yellow halos of the port-side airscrews.

"They got a hundred yards maybe," said Will. "No more than that, eh? Then they tipped over and went straight in. Rolled to the left and went straight in."

We sat twenty minutes there, next in line, before our flare went up. Then we started forward. We swung to the left. "Christ!" shouted Lofty. He swung us back too far; the engines sounded crazy. Then we ran straight again, gathering speed, and the tail lifted up.

"Oo-oop," said Ratty, his same old joke, as though he thought it would be bad luck not to say it.

The ground fell away. Our landing gear started rising,

our flaps pulling in. I saw the wreck of *J for Jam,* the firemen standing like black dots before the flames, shooting rainbows of foam that tore into streaks as they arced toward the burning metal.

It was a terrible start to an op. Lofty puffed through his pipe all the way to Germany. We droned through searchlights and flak. We saw the flaming onions of the tracer shells flinging up at the stream, and we saw two bombers go down, riding rivers of fire. And then—fifty miles from Krefeld—one of our engines conked out.

The change in sound was sudden, alarming. A shock seemed to run through me and set my heart pounding, and the old guy started yelling. Pop almost never raised his voice, but now he shouted at Lofty. And a whole series of memories flashed through my mind: our first flight in a Halifax; the instructor feathering an engine, and Lofty not knowing how to react. I remembered the instructor taking the controls, and how he had explained it all later on the ground, telling us how dangerous it was to lose an engine if you couldn't figure out which one had quit. "You have to think it out," he'd told Lofty. "Don't act too fast." If you did, and guessed wrong, you would put the crate into a spin, and you'd be lucky if you ever got it out.

"Port!" the old guy was shouting.

I didn't know how Lofty could know what he meant. Had a port-side engine quit, or was Pop telling him to turn to port? They were opposite things, and if Lofty guessed wrong we were finished.

"Port! Port!"

Rudder cables creaked through their pulleys above me. The kite wallowed and tipped. We started turning, and the sky disappeared in my window, the ground rushing up to fill it. Sixty feet behind me the rudders were swinging over, and out on the wings the ailerons lifted and dipped. I braced against my desk, waiting for *Buster* to stall herself into a spin. But she leveled off, and I tasted rubber in my lungs as I took a deep, shaking breath. Lofty had guessed right.

For a minute or two we flew along on three engines. The nose was pointed up, but we didn't climb much higher. *Buster* banked and leveled, banked again, as though she wanted to turn, but Lofty wouldn't let her. Then his voice came calmly through the intercom. "I say, chaps. What do you think? Go on or go home?"

We were minutes from the target. We had come all the way from Yorkshire and had just nine more minutes to go. I didn't want to carry on with three engines, to cross the city at twelve thousand feet—below even the Wimpies—with all the other Hallibags a mile above us and their bombs whistling down like metal hail. But if we turned back, our op wouldn't count. We would have to wait all over again, on another night for another target, and I feared that even more.

Pop wanted to press on; Buzz, to turn back. When Lofty took a vote, it came out a three-three tie because I was too frightened to speak.

"Kak?" asked Lofty. "What do you say, Kid?"

I knew my voice would tremble. I leaned out from

my desk, through the curtains, and Lofty looked down. I pointed toward the nose, jabbing with my finger.

"The Kid says 'carry on,'" said Lofty.

I heard someone chuckle in the intercom. I thought it was Pop. It was certainly his voice that said quietly, "Good for you, Kid." Lofty didn't say anything. He just kept flying the kite, jinking through the moonlight on his course for the target. I rubbed and rubbed at my ray-gun ring as *Buster* bobbed and dipped. Will said he could see Krefeld up ahead, the flak bursting in the searchlight beams. He said it was particularly heavy. "Hang on," he said. "We're going to get shaken like dice."

Buster yawed to the left, banked sharply right. Lofty muttered something; then he swore. "To hell with it," he said. "Bomb doors open."

There was a lever at his right arm, and he must have pulled it before he finished speaking. Already I could hear the great doors swinging open.

But he didn't drop the bombs right away. We turned away from the target and fell from the stream.

Buster wallowed in a wail of wind, changed now with the doors open and an engine gone. I waited for the click of the latches that freed the bombs, for the jolt as the weight fell away.

We leveled off and dropped a flare. Ratty watched it sizzle down behind us, over empty fields turned bright in its whiteness. "Nothing there. Not even a cow to hit," he said.

Lofty jettisoned the bombs, their latches tapped like

metal fingers. My seat pressed against me as *Buster* lifted in the air. The doors pulled shut, and home we went with no one talking.

The wreck of *J for Jam* was still smoldering when we touched down in Yorkshire. It was a pile of red embers and a coil of smoke, and the smell hung around as the erks guided us to a stop at dispersal. Sergeant Piper wasn't pleased. He hardly looked at us, and he didn't believe there was very much wrong with our engine.

We took our parachutes and our gear and waited for the truck to pick us up. Lofty sucked so hard on his pipe that the air whistled through it.

In minutes the erks had the cowling off the engine. They shone torches over the metal, and rapped at things with their wrenches. Then they drew away, and the engine whined as it turned over. With a puff of smoke and a roar, it started right up. The airscrew buzzed and buzzed, and I saw Lofty's shoulders slump.

"We should have gone on," he said. "Damn. We should have gone on."

"Don't bind yourself," said Will. "It's too late now."

Lofty was angry. "The ruddy old ship. The ruddy old engines. It must have run out of fuel; the ruddy tank went dry."

Maybe he thought the old guy was half deaf, but Pop heard him all right, and spoke up from the grass. "There was plenty of petrol, Skipper," he said.

"Look, it was nobody's fault," shouted Simon. "It was just a bloody balls-up."

Then Ratty laughed. Poor little Ratty, he always found a laugh in everything. "It's like I'm back at home," he said, lounging on the grass. "You guys sound just like my dear old mom and dad."

He was trying to cheer up Lofty, but Lofty wouldn't be cheered. It was the skipper who made the decisions, who had to explain it all to the CO and the grim-faced officers who sat around the debriefing table. We thought they'd be angry that we had failed to reach the target, and they did sit with their arms crossed as Lofty talked. They sat as still as lumps of earth. Then they said they understood; they all said that. Uncle Joe just shrugged. "Your engine conked out; you came back. I might have done the same thing."

Or he might not; we knew what he meant. Uncle Joe had crossed all of Happy Valley on only two engines once, and had come home in a kite so riddled with holes that he'd taxied it straight to the boneyard. He'd got a gong for that, one of the long row that hung across his chest like Christmas bulbs.

I felt sorry for Lofty, who was kicking himself so hard inside that his eyelids were quivering. It was only our third op, and not a good sign to come back early. I imagined he was worried that Uncle Joe would think of him as a coward. He kicked himself out of debriefing and kicked himself into the mess. And then he saw the Morris list, and a little smile came to his face.

Ratty ran to the blackboard. It was too high on the

wall for him to reach the first name, the now-dead navigator from *J for Jam.* Even hopping up and down, he couldn't quite reach it. So he dragged the piano bench over, jumped onto that, and smeared away the navigator in a smudge of white chalk.

CHAPTER 13

SERGEANT PIPER SAID THERE was nothing wrong with *Buster*'s engine. The others seemed pleased, but I only found a new worry. When we flew to Wuppertal two nights later, I spent every moment listening to the pistons and the valves, my heart leaping with every ping and rattle. I kept seeing pictures in my mind of the kite slowly tipping, one dead airscrew dragging down the wing. I saw us spinning, heard the shouting and the crying, and *felt* the world going round and round.

Lofty took us to a staggering height, higher than we'd ever flown before. Even I felt the chill as I sat in the heater's blast of warm air, taking navigational bearings for Simon. I could only imagine what it was like for poor Ratty, way back in his whistling turret that was partly open to the sky, so cold that his breath sometimes froze in his mask. We flew so high that the engines had a different sound, and Pop fretted endlessly about his mixtures and his blowers. We flew so high that the color of the sky changed—or so Shakespeare said; I never looked out my window. Then I heard slithers and scratches on the metal outside and shouted at Lofty, "What's that?"

"Ice," he said. It was forming on the wings and the airscrews, breaking away with those terrifying sounds.

We crossed Wuppertal at twenty-six thousand feet, and Will described the bombers down below us, the stream of Halifaxes like toys, he said, like cardboard cutouts pasted on the flames and smoke. He described the puffs of flak and twisting tracers. Then he hunched over his bombsight and called out directions to Lofty. "Left, left. Steaaaady, Skipper."

A night fighter cruised below us, and Ratty begged to shoot it down. His teeth were chattering as he told us that he could see it "as clear as a pig on a lake." Whatever that was like. "I could get him, Skipper. He's right in the sights; no lie." But Lofty told him no. He shouted, "No! We're safe as long as he's down there."

The night fighter eased past. I didn't see it, but I felt it. I *sensed* it out there in the frozen night as it hunted for a bomber. I remembered being in the bush, in an open meadow, and watching the alders at the edge bend and shake as a bear lumbered by. Now I felt the same way as I had then, that if I was spotted, I would die. Lofty gave the throttles a boost, the column a tug, and lifted us up in a slow turn to the right.

Around we went, above the target. The air was hard and busted up, and we rattled through the turbulence. Even the white flares from the night fighters floated below us. Will watched the searchlights coning; he saw someone get the chop. Again he steered us over burning Wuppertal. "Right a bit. Steady now," he said.

I clung to the edge of my desk.

"Bombs gone!" said Will.

I started counting seconds as I shrugged my harness off. I felt us rising even higher without the weight of bombs to hold us down. The kite seemed to press at my feet as I went aft to the flare chute. We took a picture, I sent my signal, and we headed home with a tailwind, rushing to England at a ground speed of three hundred miles an hour.

I rubbed and rubbed at my ray-gun ring. It seemed we'd have an easy op for once, that we'd go out and back with no real trouble. We crossed above Holland and started over the sea. Then Pop said we were running low on fuel. We'd gone so high that the engines had used too much to get us there. "They sucked up the petrol like strawberry ices," he said.

Lofty throttled back and put us into a shallow dive. Simon gave him a new course to steer.

We thrummed along through the darkness. Gilbert stirred in his box, thrashing with his wings. I gave him water and a bit of crust from a sandwich. In the nose, Will called out, "I can see the coast, Skipper. Hello, England."

Suddenly Ratty shouted. "Corkscrew left! Go!"

Down we went toward the water, wheeling round in a sickening whirl. "A fighter!" shouted Ratty. His guns were firing. "Right on our tail."

We banked to the left and banked to the right. Buzz

cried out, "Where is he? Where is he?" But Ratty had lost him.

Then we leveled out, and everyone was looking for the night fighter. Even I was looking, my face pressed to my window, staring at nothing but blackness. We raced for the coast, for England, holding the course that Simon set.

"I don't see anything," said Buzz.

"He was there," said Ratty. "No lie. He was there."

It could have been a smudge on his Perspex, a spot on his goggles. To us a night fighter in a sky as black as that would be only a speck, a fleeting shape. But to him *we* would be huge and clear, as plain to see as the Bat Signal, as the Green Lantern flying with his cape spread across the stars. We would glow red bull's-eyes from the hoods of our exhaust.

We searched and searched, but saw nothing. We hugged the sea; then we crossed the coast at a hundred feet, and I looked out and saw flak above us, a black cloud that was tidy and round. Another passed, farther away. I couldn't figure it out, why there was flak over England. I said, "Skipper. Is that flak up there?"

"Huh?" asked Lofty. Then, in a breath, he said, "Jesus."

"Barrage balloons!" shouted Will.

They floated at five hundred feet, a host of them, like black daffodils swaying on their wire stalks. We flew below them, between their cables, then suddenly rose so quickly that Lofty must have nearly torn his column from the floor. He banked the wings and brought us up in a steep turn.

He said, "Simon, where are we?"

Across the ground dashed the shapes of houses, the spire of a church. Simon had steered us toward beaches and moors, but we had stumbled instead on a village. A searchlight came on, its bright eye seeking us out.

A cable creaked across the wing. It slowed us down and slewed us round, and I heard it grating on the leading edge.

Lofty swore; the old guy yelled at him to turn, to get higher. Then the cable was severed in the cutters, and we rose above the balloons, banking past the last one.

Our fuel was nearly gone, and we didn't know where we were. I twiddled the wireless knobs, cranking them too far and too fast with my trembling fingers. But I got a bearing from London, and then another from York, and Simon lined us up for home so perfectly that the beacon from our field came blasting through my wireless the moment I listened for it. Lofty sent me to the flare gun mounted in the roof, and we went in between the hills, firing flares like a stricken ship; we didn't have fuel to stooge about in a circuit.

Lofty was furious. He was hardly Lofty at all. The fellow who had always shrugged things off now tore strips from the rest of us as we taxied to dispersal. He swore at Simon for getting us lost, at Ratty for seeing phantoms, at me for not getting a bearing sooner. He was still frothing when the erks threw down the chocks, and the moment the airscrews whirled to a stop, he went stalking down the kite and nearly bashed his way out through the door.

He went for a walk across the field as we piled out. There was eight feet of cable dangling from the starboard wing, and one of the erks was swinging on it like a monkey. Simon stood looking around, and Pop sort of folded up on the grass. Ratty took off his gloves and thumped his hands to warm them. "What got the skipper's wind up?" he asked.

"Just let him think," said Pop.

Sure enough, when Lofty came back he was already his old self, whining his funny sayings through his nose. "I say, old chaps," he said. "Frightfully sorry I blew up. Who's for tea, then? What, what? A nice cuppa char."

Simon didn't answer. It would take more than a few mutters to soothe the big Australian. "You can stuff your cuppa char," he muttered.

It turned out that it wasn't his fault that he'd steered us to a village instead of empty coast. Sergeant Piper told us later that *Buster*'s compass was off by five degrees.

Lofty got mad at *him*. "How can the compass be off?" he shouted.

"Gremlins," said Sergeant Piper. "That's how I see it. No telling what a gremlin will do."

That was a lovely word. It made me think of a long-legged, sharp-toothed little monster that delighted in pulling out wires and unfastening bolts. It was a gremlin, I thought, who had shut down our engine over Krefeld, and a gremlin who had laid his scaly hands on the compass. But Lofty said gremlins wore coveralls and carried wrenches in their pockets. "A gremlin," he said, "is just a careless erk."

Whatever they were, the gremlins loved *Buster.* On our next op, the autopilot went U/S—unserviceable—and nearly tossed us from the sky. The week after, over Cologne, the wireless failed. The truth, though none of us said it, was that our old bus was slowly falling apart. Ratty said that if it kept on going, the fuselage would fall away, and we'd be left strapped in our seats, flapping our arms. But we hadn't proven ourselves enough to Uncle Joe that he would give us anything better.

We didn't fly every night, but every night I *dreamed* of flying. Sometimes I saw night fighters, sometimes flak and searchlights. Always it ended with me falling. And then it took a little more courage to step again through *Buster*'s door, up from the grass to eighteen thousand feet. Each time I did it, I thought it was with all the courage that I had, but the next op I had to find a little more.

Most of it came from Bert. Each morning I went to the loft on trembling legs, and came away happy again. Bert would point at a bird on a perch and tell me everything about it. "That's Blitzen," he would say. "Why, I remember Blitzen when 'e was just an egg. Oh, 'e was the roundest little egg, sir." When I sat with him, surrounded by pigeons, I never thought about engines failing and bombs blowing up. All his stories of pigeon heroes, all the tending to the babies, let me forget about flying for a while. A visit with Bert was a tonic for me. It was as though I borrowed from him the courage that he didn't need—or I *took* it, really, because I had none to give back.

And as strange as it seemed, the rest came from Percy, that bright little bird who would sit forever and listen to my troubles and my secrets. I confessed everything to Percy. I told him over and over that I didn't want to fly anymore.

But I did; I kept flying. We bombed Aachen in the middle of July, and we torched the city into such a blaze that the paint blistered on *Buster*'s belly. Then, a mile from home, at treetop height, we hit an owl. It shattered the bubble in the nose, ripping through the Perspex in a burst of blood and feathers. If Will hadn't been in the second dickey seat, he would have had his head torn off. But he somehow managed to joke about it. "What would they have told my wife?" he asked. "'We regret to inform you that your husband was owled to death.'"

That same night, Lofty moved up again on the Morris list when *M for Mother* smashed in the Channel. The bomb aimer had been on the list, but he never got his chance with the little black bus. He had been third, right below the guy who had it now, the pilot of *T for Tom.*

Then our leave came up, a few days of rest that we'd earned by weeks of flying. We went down to London. "The smoke," we called it. The whole crew went, even Pop, who would rather have gone home to his wife and his boys. It was the way Lofty wanted it. "Kid, you're coming, too," he told me. "No excuses this time."

We took the train and arrived in the morning, and it was strange to see bombed-out buildings, whole streets reduced to rubble, but the great city just humming along. At night, though, it lived in darkness; it closed up and hid itself from the German bombers. Will saw it and went Shakespeare on us. "Look around," he said, holding out his arms. He told us that nothing had changed in hundreds and hundreds and hundreds of years, that the same city that now huddled from bombers had huddled in the darkness from men armed with spears. We watched people carrying electric torches to guide their way down the ruined streets, as though they followed blots of light. I wanted to warn them that nothing could save them, that a city couldn't hide from bombers. But it was plain to see that they knew it already. There were buildings banked by sandbags, and buildings propped up with poles and posts. As darkness came, the underground stations choked with people who carried their belongings down in suitcases to build tiny rooms for themselves all across the platform.

We felt lost in London. It was too big, too loud, and too expensive. On our third day our money was gone.

Our crew came apart then, the fellows breaking off like the bits of *B for Buster.* Pop went north to his home; Will wandered away to see the museums. Simon met some Australians and went chumming with them. Only four of us were left to bum around for another day, gawking at old buildings and double-decker buses. We sat astride the lions in Trafalgar Square, in a cloud of pigeons thicker than the smoke in Happy Valley. Every inch of the place was covered with birds, every bench and every step of the Nelson column. Lofty smiled, but tried to seem disgusted. "Won't I ever get away from damn pigeons?" he asked. Buzz knocked one from his arm. "I bet the Kid thinks he's gone to heaven."

He was right. The sound of all those birds was as calming as wind in a forest. I even bought a postcard of the place, and sent it up to dirty Bert. I didn't know his proper name, so I addressed it to "The Pigeoneer."

We spent our last night, penniless and sad, in a service club, with a crowd of desperate-looking airmen who had just arrived from Sussex and had gone in a fever from one bit of fun to another. They sang and laughed through their first night of leave, and we moped through the last of ours. We sat staring at nothing, then suddenly raised our heads. We all heard the air-raid sirens.

It was a mournful sort of howl, something like wolves in a forest. It rose and fell in a warbling pitch.

A rush of people went down to the shelters, while the desperate and the drunk stayed where they were. Then the sirens stopped, and we heard the sound of bomber engines. They were different from ours, a harsher kind of clatter, a tremble that shook cold sweat from my hands and my armpits and forehead. It wasn't the thought of bombs that terrified me, or the thought of being caught on the ground; it was the idea of being *up there,* of flying through the night.

Lofty put on his cap. I thought he was going down to the shelters, and I stood up beside him. I wanted to get under the earth, deep enough that I wouldn't hear the engines. But he headed for the front door. He said, "I think I'll take in the show. You chaps coming along?"

We went with him; it might have looked cowardly not to. We took our caps and went out to a city that was nearly empty. A little knot of people hurried by, their shoes pattering. A fat man in a business suit scurried from doorway to doorway like a frightened mouse. When he disappeared around the corner, there was no one but us on the street.

Across the sky, searchlights were wheeling. In the distance, to the south, bursts of flak looked small and harmless. There didn't seem to be the slightest chance they could hurt an armored bomber. But with each flash, with each bang that followed, my skin twitched and jumped, and I sat on the curb so that I wouldn't fall over. The others sat beside me, then leaned slowly back until they lay across the sidewalk with their feet in the gutter.

The engines grew louder. We listened to the old, familiar *ooom-ba-ooom,* and watched for the bombers. "Only ten or so," said Lofty. "No more than a dozen."

"Just the first wave, I guess," said Buzz.

Guns started firing. Tracers rose up from the city, and it hardly seemed possible that they were the same sort of thing we'd seen coming *toward* us over Germany. They didn't start off slowly and suddenly rush along. And they didn't seem the least bit frightening. There were so many searchlights, so much tracer and flak, that we could see the roofs and the domes of the buildings drawn as clear as etchings. We saw glimpses of the bombers, gleams of light thrown back from the searchlights. They passed right above us, and then we heard the bombs coming down.

"Wheezy jeezy, I didn't know they whistled," said Ratty.

It was an unnerving sound in an unnerving place. The city seemed to have drawn up, struggling to defend itself. The machines above, the lights and guns below, it made me think of a war being fought without people, just thing against thing.

The whistle became a shriek. Then we saw the flashes and felt the bursts, heard the absolute roar of bombs exploding. Stick after stick rained down, each one a little closer. Flames and smoke soared up. The flashes tore across the sky, glowing on every roof, in every window. Fire engines and ambulances rushed along distant streets in a clamor of bells and sirens. The roar went on and on as walls crumbled and roofs collapsed. A gas main broke, spewing fire stories high. People screamed.

We lay on our backs and watched. We watched the ruin spread, the city burn, all because a dozen men were pushing their thumbs on a dozen little buttons. We saw a bomber explode, and nobody cheered.

The raid lasted only minutes. The *ooom-ba-ooom* of the bombers faded toward the east, followed by the wave of guns and searchlights. Then we got up and weren't sure what to do. We didn't *decide* to go and help, we just gravitated there, as though the flames had sucked us in. Firemen in weird, medieval helmets were spraying water into buildings full of fire. Soldiers and air-raid wardens dashed all over the place. There was smoke and heat and dust, and rubble everywhere. In the middle of it all, a group of Red Cross girls were setting up a tea stand in a little truck that folded open.

So we spent the last hours of our leave amid the ruins of a bombing raid. I saw corpses laid out on the street, a dead baby cradled in the hands of a weeping fireman. I was shocked by the destruction that a dozen bombers could bring, and I wondered what Krefeld must look like, or Wuppertal or Aachen, after ten times as many—or thirty times as many—of us had gone by. Then I was put to work pumping water, and I watched the mother of the dead baby take her child away. And I didn't think anymore, except about pumping.

CHAPTER 14

WE GOT BACK TO the airfield on Friday night, the twenty-third of July. In the nine days we'd been gone, the world had changed. The Russians were advancing in the east; the Germans were nearly beaten in Sicily; and the war was closing in on Germany. But the Four-Forty-Two was just as we'd left it.

We went straight on to ops on Saturday. The target was Hamburg, far to the east of Happy Valley, nearly a hundred miles inland from the sea. The skies would be clear, the moon in its last quarter, and it didn't seem like the sort of night for a jaunt across Germany. It was night fighter weather, perfect for them.

But Uncle Joe told us not to worry about fighters. He brought a cardboard box onto the stage, and set it down by the lectern. "This is top secret," he said. "Top, top secret." He nudged the box with his toe. "The boffins have come up with something that will make the German radar useless."

We all leaned forward as Uncle Joe knelt down and opened the box. It had been our wildest dream that the scientists would invent a gadget to stop the night fighters from homing in on the bomber stream.

"This is code-named Window," said Uncle Joe, reaching into the box.

I was certain, for a moment, that he would pull out a ray gun, and that it would look just like the tiny one that I wore on my finger. But all he lifted up was a wad of paper. Packing, I thought. It was just packing.

"Window," he said, holding the paper as high as he could. He let it fall, and the wad separated into shining strips that glistened as they drifted down. They were bright and shiny, covered in a metal foil. Suddenly, the hut was so silent that I actually heard those bits of paper settle on the stage. Then Ratty whispered to me, "They've gotta be joking."

"The German radar will see the Window," said Uncle Joe. "It will see so much Window that it will be blinded to anything else. Their fighters will end up chasing bits of paper."

I liked the thought of that; it seemed like a Buck Rogers sort of trick. Our giant Halifaxes, crammed with bombs, would be invisible.

Out at dispersal that evening, it took Buzz nearly five minutes to find his lucky clover. He crawled all over the grass, with his bottom high in the air. Ratty said he looked like a big old bloodhound sniffing around. But everyone was happy when he plucked that clover and held it up for all of us to see.

"What are you going to do in the winter?" asked Simon.

Buzz just frowned at him.

"When there aren't any clovers, you dill."

"Jeez," said Buzz. "Jeez, I hadn't thought of that."

We climbed into the kite well before sunset. It was so far to Hamburg that we had to leave in the daylight and let the darkness overtake us.

"Ignition, number one," said Lofty. "Booster on. Coils on."

The first engine started, and the rest followed. I had the strongest urge to get up and get out of the kite. I had felt the same thing on every op, but never so powerfully. I buckled my belt and cinched the strap, just to keep myself from running away.

"Doors locked," said Pop. "Ready to taxi."

And then it was too late. I *was* trapped. I was trapped for eight hours, and I shook like a leaf.

We taxied to the runway and took off, climbing straight toward the sun.

"Skipper, steer one-six-five," said Simon.

"One-six-five. Roger," answered Lofty, and we banked around in our circle. We gathered with the others in our squadron, then with more bombers from other squadrons, then into the stream that stretched a hundred miles. And we headed out across the sea. It was a Goodwood, a maximum effort.

I was in charge of the Window. It was my job to chuck it out of the kite a bundle at a time, down the flare chute where I dropped the photoflash. I sat in the fuselage, by the entry door, just behind Buzz. Every minute over the North Sea, I took a bundle from the box and sent it down the chute, imagining the paper being ripped by our slipstream into a glittering cloud.

I did it a hundred times, maybe, before my hands brushed together and I realized that my ray-gun ring was gone. I searched through the Window box, across my desk, along the floor. I went frantically through every corner, but the ring was really gone. I thought of it falling behind us, still spinning down. How long would it take for that bit of plastic to fall three miles? Then I thought of it landing in the Channel, the tiny splash it would make as it hit that cold, dark water.

"It's just a ring," I told myself. "Just a stupid plastic ring." But I felt such a dread at its loss that I curled up on the floor until Buzz, looking down, asked through the intercom if I was all right.

Lofty snapped at me. "Come on, Kak. Keep awake."

I dumped another lot of paper, and another as we flew along. We followed the Elbe into Germany, and bombed Hamburg when we got there. We gave it such a pasting that forever after we would say that each city we wiped away had been Hamburgerized.

There wasn't a single night fighter all the way to the target. The Window did fool the radar, but I wished it had fooled the flak instead. High over the Elbe, I hung on to the chute as *Buster* rocked and lurched through the blasts. Ratty started firing at searchlights, and his ammunition rattled out of the boxes above me, through the feed tracks that led to the tail.

In the darkness I wished for my little window. It was more frightening to see nothing at all, and it seemed that hours and hours went by before Will started guiding us on our bombing run. Then our belly opened and our bombs spilled out, and part of my fear fell away with them at the thought that we would soon turn for home. I counted the seconds, dropped the photo flare, then moved forward to send my signal. I didn't bother with an oxygen bottle; it was only a few steps to the wireless. But when I reached the cockpit I stopped.

All the glass and all the controls glowed with a dull red light. Even Lofty glowed, in his helmet and mask. His pipe jutted out from the rubber, and an ember seemed to burn in the empty bowl.

I just stood there, stunned by what I saw. The whole earth was burning, and great clouds of smoke—glowing red and yellow—billowed up ten thousand feet. Bombers crossed through it, little dark arrows darting across the clouds and the fire. Some headed east and others west, and the searchlights swung and crossed from every side. The tracers curved, the flak was bursting everywhere, and I felt giddy to see it, to be standing there above it all. It was terrifying, but it was wonderful, too. In the darkness of the night, below the speckled band of the Milky Way, the flames were truly beautiful. They raged so hot and fast that I could see streets and buildings. I watched the colors change from red to orange, and saw the white bursts of bombs flicker like lightning through the clouds of smoke. I felt as though I was hurtling through space above a planet made of fire.

Lofty pulled me down beside him. He plugged me

into the oxygen and the intercom. "Lend us a hand here," he said.

His glove was hot and slick as he took my wrist and guided my hand to the column. He was soaked with sweat, and right away I saw why. The column seemed to weigh a ton as I pulled against it. I could hardly believe the pressure there, or the strength that Lofty had needed to keep us flying. Together we pulled and pushed, wallowing through air that churned like the white river below Kakabeka Falls.

I had never really seen our battleground before, and I was amazed by the hugeness of it, and the smallness of us. I watched the blasts that made *Buster* roll and tip. I felt the cold and the rush of the flak, and I heard the wind shrieking through the canopy as we circled back for home. I saw the gigantic fire in a tidy grid of city blocks, and it made me think of London and how the ground had shaken. Then, for the first time, I thought about the people below us. I imagined them scurrying from the flames, crowding into the shelters. But I didn't feel sorry for them. I only wanted to get them before they got me.

Lofty caught his breath, then sent me down to the wireless. "Send your signal, Kid."

I let go of the column. I braced one hand on the canopy and reached out to unplug my oxygen. My hand was on the hose when something below me exploded.

There was an enormous bang, a glare of light. A shock ran through the airframe, and *Buster* tipped on her side. I nearly fell down the passage before the nose went down, throwing me against the glass.

I lay there, my arms stretched out, staring straight at the fires and searchlights. I heard the panes creak and snap. Down and down we went as Lofty tugged at the column. The intercom was full of shouts. "Shutting down number two," said Pop.

Buster fell three thousand feet before Lofty straightened her out. The pipe bounced in his mouth like a bug's antenna.

"What happened?" I asked.

"She went crazy," said Lofty.

Then Pop came on. "Skipper, we lost an airscrew."

"Nah, it isn't lost," Simon said in his Australian shout. "I can see it stuck right here in the side of the bloody kite."

It had sheared through the fuselage right where I should have been sitting. It had hacked through my seat and into my desk, and it should have shredded me into strips as thin as Window.

I went down and looked at it, the hub still stuck in *Buster*'s side, the twisted propeller blades still shaking as they stretched across my little space. *Buster*'s skin was bent inward. The pigeon box was dented, and Gilbert thrashed inside. His head poked out, then a wing, then a tail. He battered himself around as though a cat had been shut in there with him. My chair was hacked and twisted, the scraps of leather fluttering in the wind that screeched through the punctured hole. I looked at it all, and fainted, crumpling to the deck.

I wasn't out for long. We were still over Germany when I woke up. Will was sitting on the deck, cradling my head in his lap. He was holding an oxygen bottle over my nose and mouth, and I could feel his fingers stroking at my helmet, moving backward again and again.

That was the last straw for me. There was nothing in the world, I told myself, that would ever get me into a kite again.

All the way home I lay on the deck, thinking of what I could do. I remembered Donny Lee telling me that if I ever wanted out, I could talk to Uncle Joe. "Uncle Joe will understand," he'd said. So as soon as we landed—the moment we were out of the kite—I let Gilbert loose to fly home, and I dashed off to find the CO.

I fidgeted and bit my fingernails as I planned the things I'd say to Uncle Joe. I talked it out, half aloud, what I would tell him and what he would answer. I cocked my head to the left and muttered something, then cocked it to the right and answered for him. I imagined him calling me a coward. "You've got no moral fiber, boy," he said. And I didn't have the courage, in the end, to go into the office. I collected my dented pigeon box and went down to the loft instead.

Bert was there, feeding suet treats to the birds that had gone to Hamburg. Percy fluttered from his shoulder and landed on mine, and the moment I took him in my hands I felt almost peaceful.

It was the first time I had been to the loft since the day before my leave. I breathed the barnyard smell and looked around, and felt that I was home. I saw that Bert had put my postcard on the wall above the feed bags. I felt a bit embarrassed to think that he hadn't liked it enough to keep it in his room. But he saw me looking and said, "Thank you for the picture, sir. I put it up for the birds to see."

"You would like Trafalgar Square," I said.

"I know it well, sir," said Bert. "In the first bit of the war I lived near the Square for a while."

It was rare for him to tell me anything about himself. But he quickly turned away and went back to his pigeons and his suet. He said, "It must have been 'ard, sir. A difficult op. The way they're twitching, sir."

They didn't look any different to me. I couldn't tell which had been on ops, and I couldn't see the lonely one anywhere. The mass of birds swarmed at my feet. "Where's Ollie's wife?" I asked.

"Oh," said Bert, "I wish you 'adn't asked me that, sir. You never should 'ave asked me that."

"Why not?" I said.

"She died, sir. While you were down in London." He blinked at the suet he was holding. "She wasted away, sir. And the babies, too. They both passed on." He sniffed loudly, then used his fingers for a handkerchief. "I buried them all together, sir, the mother and her babies."

I was sorry they'd died, but more sorry for Bert. He kept his back toward me as he sniffed and nearly sobbed. "I think you'd better go now, sir," he said. "You might be flying tomorrow. There's bound to be ops."

He was only partly right. Three of our kites went off to bomb Essen, but *Buster* wasn't among them. She couldn't have gotten off the ground with a slingshot. The erks had wheeled her into a hangar and were working round the clock to patch her latest wounds. Like a gang of dirty, cursing surgeons, they slaved with an urgency that made us guess there was something big in the wind.

That feeling built up as the following day, the twenty-sixth of July, passed without ops. Ratty begged the old airscrew from the erks, and he hauled it into the mess, such a twisted bit of metal that every sergeant wanted to hear the story about it. Ratty was happy to keep telling the tale, as long as mugs of beer were planted near his elbows. He said he could probably stay drunk for a week. But the next morning we were on. Another Goodwood.

It was Hamburg again.

Even Lofty went pale at the news—Lofty, who wasn't really scared of anything. He drew in his breath when the curtain opened to show the red ribbons twisting down to Hamburg. Seven hundred kites were going, nearly every crate that Bomber Command could put in the air.

But I just couldn't do it. The moment I saw those ribbons, I knew I couldn't go back to Hamburg.

I turned to Lofty, in the middle of the briefing. "*Buster* isn't ready," I said. I whispered at him, harshly. "We can't go if *Buster*'s not ready."

"Shut up, Kak," he said.

I tugged his sleeve. "But, Lofty."

"Shut up, will you?"

He turned away, crossing his legs. So I looked to Pop, on my other side, and told him, "We can't go. We can't go to Hamburg."

The old guy patted my knee. "Shush, shush," he whispered. "I don't think we'll be going, Kid."

But the erks did. They promised us, as though they thought it such a favor, that they would do their best. "Touch and go," said Sergeant Piper. "That's how I see it. You'll have to taxi from the hangar. Yes, you'll have to taxi right from here. But *Buster* should be ready."

I had never spent an evening in such horror. Anyplace but Hamburg, I told myself. Anyplace but there. I couldn't go back to that burning city, to the solid flak and the searchlights. I couldn't go back without my ray-gun ring, that stupid, stupid ring. If I didn't have that, I was Captain Marvel without his powers, just a regular boy with nothing to save me.

For hours I hung around the hangar, listening to the hammering. I imagined they were building a scaffold, a gallows, in there. Whenever Sergeant Piper came out, I pestered him to tear the flare chute apart and see if there wasn't something in it.

"Like what?" he snapped when he was sick of the sight of me. "Something like what?"

"I don't know," I said.

"Then how can I look?" he asked. "How can I look for nothing?"

I grabbed him as he turned away. "My ray gun," I said desperately. "My ray-gun ring."

He laughed. "Do I look like a wet nurse, boy? Is that what I look like? Go on; leave us alone."

I went to Lofty, hoping he would help. I was sure he would take one look at me and say, "Oh, Kid, you're sick. You can't go flying." But he didn't notice how I sweated, how I trembled. He was sitting on his bed, writing a letter, and was neither startled nor worried to see me. He *smiled.* "Hi, Kid," he said.

His pipe was in his teeth, and he seemed as calm as the padre who spent his days sitting in the sun. It was the closest I'd ever seen him to the way he must have been before the war. Perched on the side of his bed, the paper on his lap, he might have been a shoe salesman again, getting ready to slip a pair of oxfords on my feet.

"I'm writing to my dad," he said. "Telling him that . . . Sorry, you wouldn't understand."

"Why not?" I said.

He was embarrassed. "Being an orphan and all."

"Oh, yeah," I said stupidly. I'd almost forgotten that he thought I was an orphan.

"Well, anyway." He folded his sheet of paper. "Listen, Kid. About the briefing. I'm sorry I binded you."

"It's okay," I said.

"You're a good guy, Kak. I guess I never told you that."

I knew then that he was getting ready to die. He was saying so long to his dad, and apologizing for things that bothered him. But he didn't look frightened, or even very sad. I didn't know how he could settle down so calmly to put everything in order.

"Lofty?" I said.

"Yes?"

I meant to tell him everything, all my lies and all my fears. I knew he might laugh, but I didn't care anymore.

I was sure that *I* would sob and weep, but even that didn't bother me. I just didn't know how to tell him, or where to start, so I blurted out, "I lost my lucky ring!"

It was worse than I'd feared. He *did* laugh, just a giggle at first, then more and more, until it exploded out of him. He had to take his pipe from his mouth and wipe at his eyes. "Your lucky ring," he said, and started off again.

"It's true," I told him. "I dropped it down the flare chute, I think. But Sergeant Piper won't go looking. Oh, I hate him, Lofty."

He couldn't have ever laughed harder at Buster Keaton or Laurel and Hardy. He laughed like a crazy man. And I sat there on the bed, my insides shaking themselves apart. It was true, I thought: my moral fiber *was* unraveling.

Lofty finally gathered himself together. Tears were smudged across his cheeks. "Your lucky ring," he said. "Look what it's got us. Shot up and shot *at* and damn nearly killed. Kakky, if that's what's been bringing us our luck, you should have thrown it away after the first op."

I heard engines outside: a kite coming in with a wounded rattle, one engine missing in its beat, another missing altogether.

"Who's that?" I asked.

"Who's what?"

Wheels touched the runway; engines growled, propellers changing pitch.

"*That,*" I said. "Who's that coming in?"

"Kid, are you okay?"

Lofty hadn't heard the sounds. I didn't know if I was imagining things or if he was deaf. So I went to the window, and looked out.

There was nothing on the runway.

CHAPTER 15

LOFTY SAID I HAD the twitch. The jitters. "A lot of guys get them." He put on his British mutter, as he always did when he was a bit uncomfortable. "I say, old boy. It's the waiting, you know."

He puffed through his empty pipe again. He kept folding the corner of his letter, bending it open and shut.

"You'll feel okay when you get in the kite," he said. "When you're on your way it's not so bad."

"Do *you* ever get scared?" I asked.

He looked at me for quite a long time. Then he smiled. "Don't worry, Kid," he said. "Last time was a dicey do. Tonight will be a piece of cake."

"But *do* you?"

"Naw," he said with a flip of his hand. "Now go for a walk. Get your mind on something else."

He didn't want me around, that was all. He didn't want to listen to my worries. So I left the hut and went walking. I passed a group of airmen sitting in the sun, in canvas chairs. Most of them wore their blue jackets and their blue trousers, but one was lounging in leather flying clothes, in big, unbuckled boots. He lifted his head as I passed.

It was Donny Lee.

I forgot in that instant that he was dead. I whirled around to smile at him. "Hey, Donny!" I was going to shout. But he wasn't there at all, and I remembered that he could *never* be there. A flying jacket was draped across the canvas, and a pair of boots stood empty on the grass. I stared at them with the oddest feeling; I was *sure* there'd been a person in the chair. Then I turned around again and stumbled off. I went faster and faster, and I went straight to Uncle Joe.

He was sitting at his desk when I got there. I saluted, but he only waved that off. "Sit down," he said, watching me. "I know you, don't I?"

"Sir, I . . ."

"Oh, yes," he said. "You're the bloke who laughed at all the flak."

That day, my first briefing, seemed so long ago that I could hardly remember.

Uncle Joe snapped his fingers twice. "Kakabeka," he said. "Have I got it?"

"Yes, sir." If he wanted to think that was my name, I wasn't going to correct him.

"What's on your mind, son?"

I told him straight out. My voice trembled and creaked. "I don't think I can fly anymore," I said.

He sat up in his chair behind the desk. There were pages of lists laid out, and he spread his hands across them. "Why not?" he said.

"I'm scared," I told him.

Right away I regretted coming.

"You're scared," he said flatly.

"Yes, sir."

He grunted, and it was as though he coughed out all his kindliness. He changed suddenly into someone fierce and angry-looking. Uncle Joe became my old man.

"Where are you from, Kakabeka?" he asked.

"Kakabeka," I told him.

Things like cables tightened in his neck. He must have been trying to figure out if I was a fool, or if I was trying to show that he was one.

"Well, *Mister,*" he said, "how do you want the folks in Kakabeka to remember you? As a coward?"

I really didn't care how they remembered me.

"And what about your crew?" asked Uncle Joe. "Do you care about *them*?"

"Someone else can take my place," I said. "There's lots of sprogs, sir."

"I see. So it's just your own sorry self you worry about, and the devil with anyone else?"

"It's only me who's scared," I said.

A look of utter disgust came over his face. He shoved back his chair and stood up. "If every frightened boy came to see me, there'd be a queue from here to York," he said. "They're *all* frightened, Mister. I'm scared to hell myself. But we do the job and we don't let anybody down."

I looked at the floor. I didn't want to cry, but I couldn't help it. Uncle Joe didn't understand at all.

"You volunteered for this," he said.

"Yes, sir," I sobbed.

"Do you think you can just change your mind? Do you think you can just tell me, 'Sorry, I don't belong here'?"

"But I *don't* belong here," I said.

"Who does?" he snapped. "Your pilot's a shoe salesman. Your navigator trimmed hedges and planted flowers. I was one year away from being a doctor, so what makes you think you're different from anyone else?"

His shadow lay on the planks, on my feet and my ankles. I wished I could disappear into its darkness.

"Why?" he demanded.

"Because I lied, sir," I said.

"What?"

"I'm only sixteen."

The shadow flowed up my legs, over my hands and my lap. I saw his hand reach out, and I cringed away. I thought he was going to slap me, but he only touched the top of my head, his fingers in my hair. "Really?" he said.

"Yes, sir."

Uncle Joe tipped back my head until I *had* to look at him. He stared right into my eyes.

"Well," he said. "This changes things."

My heart lifted. It soared to twenty thousand feet.

He was Uncle Joe again, smiling and friendly, the CO that all the sprogs met and loved right away. He took his own handkerchief from his back pocket and gave it to me. I dabbed my eyes, proud to be using it.

"There's only one problem." He stepped back. "How

do I know you didn't tell the truth then, and *now* you're telling me lies?"

"You can ask my old man," I said.

"You told me you were an orphan."

"I lied about that, too," I said. "I've got a dad. And a mom. I'm not really an orphan, sir. I lied about everything."

Uncle Joe sighed. "All right, son," he said. "If you're telling the truth, I'll see what I can do. I can get you off ops, but I won't get you out of the air force. I'll move you to other duties."

"I could look after the pigeons," I said.

"Well, yes, I suppose you could." He jammed his fingers together. "But I think we can find something more—more *meaningful*—than that." He went round his desk and picked up his papers. "I wish you'd come sooner, son."

So did I. "Yes, sir," I said. "I wanted to, but—"

"You'll have to fly tonight. If your kite's ready."

My heart plummeted again.

"There's no choice, son," he said. "It's a Goodwood."

"All right, sir," I said. I thought I could do it once more if I knew it was the last time.

"Fly tonight, and in the morning come and see me. We'll get this straightened out," he said.

"Thank you, sir."

He rolled his papers into a tube, then wedged them in his tunic. "We'll both have to hurry now," he said.

I stood up and saluted. His handkerchief, still in my hand, waved like a white flag. I put it on his desk and walked to the door.

"And, Mister."

"Yes, sir," I said.

"Not a word to your crew. Not yet."

"No, sir," I said.

"And if it turns out you're lying, I won't have any mercy. You know what happens when someone refuses to fly, don't you?"

"LMF, sir," I said.

He nodded. "But do you know what that means?"

"Not really, sir," I said.

"You'll be stripped of your rank, your stripes, and your badges. You'll be called a coward, and everyone will know it. You'll lose every friend you have, and I doubt you'll ever find another." He took his flying jacket from the rickety coat stand. "And if you think that's the end of it, you're wrong, Mister. It's just the start. If you're lucky, you'll be shifted into a drudge of a job. If not, you'll be put in the infantry and your cowardice will go with you. For the rest of your life it will follow you, wherever you go and whatever you do." He took his hat next, and jammed it on the back of his head. "You might find yourself in prison. Or maybe in a coal mine, and there isn't much difference. Whatever happens, you'll regret it every day you live."

"Yes, sir," I said.

"If you don't believe me, ask the pigeoneer."

"The *pigeoneer,* sir?" I said.

"Yes. He'll tell you a story about a fellow who was branded LMF."

I imagined that Bert had watched a lot of people come

and go. He must have known at least one who refused to fly. Maybe he'd known hundreds.

"But listen, son." Uncle Joe touched my arm. "If you're telling the truth, you're all right. You're not 'home' yet, as you might say. But you're, um, 'safe on third.'" He blushed wonderfully. "Understand?"

"Yes, sir," I said.

"Now you'd better hurry up."

Hamburg was still a terror for me, the flak and the night fighters as frightening as ever. But I kept pushing my thoughts ahead to the moment that we'd land. I imagined myself stepping from the kite for the last time, down to the grass and clovers. And I felt a calmness then. If *Buster* was ready, so was I.

I ate all my eggs and bacon. I swabbed up the grease with a slice of bread, and ate that, too. In the hope that someone would notice, I rattled my empty plate. I patted my stomach as though it was fit to burst. But the only thing the others were interested in was *Buster,* and the only thing they talked about was whether she'd be ready or not.

When we got to the hangar, the erks were still working. They had wheeled *Buster* onto the tarmac, and she looked bigger than ever now, all by herself on those acres of gray. There were new metal patches here and there, and especially around my little part of the kite, where the airscrew had torn through the fuselage. *Buster*'s kicking mule had lost a hoof, and the little Hitler had lost his arms now, as well as his legs.

Lofty went straight to the erks. "What's the gen?" he asked.

"No worries," said Sergeant Piper. "Yes, sir, no fear. You'll be going to be Germany, and that's for certain."

Buzz dropped his chute and his gear. He dashed away in his heavy boots, in a jangle from all his buckles and harness fittings. Ratty called after him, "Hey! Where are you going?"

I thought he had given up; I really did. I thought Buzz had packed it in, and just wouldn't fly to Hamburg. He was fleeing toward the hangar, as though he hoped to hide in there, and I envied him for it, and admired him. But mostly I just hated him for doing what I had thought so long of doing. "He's scared!" I shouted. "He's cracked."

"Oh, shut up, Kid," said Ratty.

Buzz kept running. Even the erks watched him go, a brown bulk like a charging bear. Ratty cupped his hands to his mouth. "What are you doing?" he bellowed.

Buzz held up his arms and waved them as he ran. "My clover, my clover!" he cried.

Pop rolled his eyes, and Simon chuckled. But everyone looked toward Buzz with the same fond smile, and I wondered, *Will they do that for me?* Will they be sad or angry when *I* run away? Will they be disappointed?

Buzz reached the hangar and threw himself down at the little strip of green along the base of the wall. He bent into his old bloodhound position, head down and bottom up, and a laugh rose from the erks. Sergeant Piper yelled at them. "Get to work, you miserable lot!"

We gathered in *Buster*'s shade, below the starboard wing. But even there, bubbles of pitch oozed on the tarmac, and we couldn't lie down, or even sit. On any other day I would have had a pigeon box to use for a seat, but Bert had finally got his motorized loft running, and I had to wait until he brought out the boxes himself.

My feet were baking in my boots when I saw that thing puttering toward us. Simon pointed and said, "Take a squint at that."

The motorized loft shimmered in the heat of the tarmac. Like a mirage on a desert, it was warped and stretched until it seemed as thin as a pencil floating on wheels that were six feet high.

"What the heck is that?" asked Ratty.

"It's the pigeoneer," I said. "It's old featherhead." Then I felt embarrassed for myself, and hot with shame, and I hoped my voice wasn't loud enough to carry to the loft.

"He's got kangaroos loose in his upper paddock," said Simon.

They kept joking about the pigeoneer as I went off toward him. I didn't run, but walked as quickly as I could. I didn't like the others to hear me talking to Bert, or Bert talking to me. Behind me Ratty was shouting in a funny high voice, "Pigeons, pigeons! Get your fresh, hot pigeons!"

Bert stopped the loft, but didn't shut off the motor. He didn't even get out of the cab. "Sorry, sir," he said. "But I'm late. No time to chat." He put his head out the window, and I saw Percy on his shoulder, standing at attention. "Could you 'elp yourself to Gilbert, sir?"

"Okay," I said.

"At the back, sir."

I found the proper little box; it was marked with Lofty's name and *Buster*'s numbers. I took it out and slapped the side of the loft. Bert drove away in a puff of smoke. "Thank you, sir," he cried. His arm jutted from the window, his hand waving. "Good luck, sir."

He went off toward the other kites, and I carried the box back to *Buster.* I sat on it, then lifted my feet from the hot tarmac. "See?" I said. "I told you the pigeons were useful."

"Yeah," said Ratty. "It's going to bake just right in that little tin oven."

I thought of the box heating on the ground. I stood and picked it up, and I waited as the others did, shuffling my feet as the box seemed to stretch my arm.

Lofty signed the 700 on Sergeant Piper's clipboard. He took out his pipe and wedged it in his mouth. "Right," he said. "Let's go."

We formed a queue at *Buster*'s door. I was at the end, shuffling forward as the others stepped up and disappeared into the fuselage. I saw Will take a peek inside his helmet. I saw Ratty touch his rabbit's foot, Pop his hidden crucifix, and I smelled perfume as Simon patted across his pockets. Suddenly I missed my lucky ray-gun ring so strongly that I didn't want to go.

I rubbed at my finger as I watched Simon vanish into the plane. The line moved a step forward. Then Pop was leaning up to *Buster*'s door, and it was my last chance not to go. A clear picture came to me, but not of the flak and the searchlights. I saw old *B for Buster* creaking in for a landing with a dead man flying her. I saw his eyes that couldn't see, his hands that couldn't feel, fixed to the throttles and controls.

I was alone outside the kite. Buzz was still way off at the hangar, and the others were settling in. I put my hands up to the door, and knew that another wop had done the same thing. Exactly the same thing. He had gripped the metal in the same place, then stepped up through the same door, only to disappear forever.

I shook that thought away. The erks were still busy with a job they might not even finish. And if *Buster* did get off the ground, we would be landing again in just eight or nine hours. When we did, at that moment, I would come *out* of this door free and alive. I saw myself doing it; I *knew* it would happen.

I put my knee on the sill. I boosted myself into *Buster.*

Buzz came a few minutes later. He went right through the kite, showing everyone the clover he had found. Then we sat and waited, sweating from the heat.

Across the field, the other crates started their engines. They began to taxi out from dispersal, the tangle of wings and tail fins sorting themselves into a tidy parade. Lofty had his window pushed open, and he kept shouting through it at Sergeant Piper to either get the job finished or say it wouldn't be done.

The first kite took off. It rose, wobbling, into a red sky. "There goes Uncle Joe," said Will. The next followed. The third.

I leaned back in my chair. There, above me, were the

penciled lines of the poem. "'I have slipped the surly bonds of earth,'" I said.

Outside, Sergeant Piper shouted, "Let's give it a try, Skipper!"

"Switch to ground," said Lofty, starting the checklist. A moment later the engine was running, the erks, below, were grinning, and we were off, on our way to Hamburg.

We were the last kite in the air. We flew along with the throttles set at maximum cruising power, hurrying to catch up. I counted the hours left to go. But as it turned out, we didn't get home that night.

CHAPTER 16

I LISTENED ESPECIALLY CLOSELY to the engines as we flew across the North Sea. I kept my head turned away, my hand against my cheek, as though that could save me if an airscrew came thrashing through the metal skin. I sweated the hours away, taking bearings on the wireless, dumping Window now and then.

Hamburg was still smoldering. Will saw the glow from miles and miles away. He watched the target markers tumble down, then the bursts from the first wave of bombers. By the time we got there, the city was a mass of raging flames—from end to end, it seemed. We flew in greasy clouds of smoke at eighteen thousand feet.

Again we rocked and twisted through the flak. Again the intercom erupted with shouts and cries. Our guns fired and *Buster* rattled, and I cowered in my chair with my hands clasped, praying us right across the city. Then we dropped our bombs and I sent the flare falling for our photo. I could feel hot air gushing up that tube, and I smelled the burning of the city.

We turned for home. I tapped out my signal as Ratty

watched the flames. I thought he would never stop talking about their colors and size, and the way they leapt through the whole sky. But he fell silent after only a minute or two.

It seemed our luck had changed. I started thinking that maybe I wouldn't have to quit flying after all, that I might go to Uncle Joe and tell him to wait a bit before he moved me off to something else.

Then, as though I'd jinxed us, *Buster* started leaking fuel. It dribbled from a valve, from a tank or broken hose. It streamed out behind us in a silvery mist that Ratty said was just like fizzy soda pop.

"Flight engineer, what's the story?" asked Lofty.

"I think we'll make the coast," said Pop. "I think we'll get to England, Skipper."

We had to feather number one, then feather number four. The airscrews stopped, their blades edged to the wind. For every mile we flew, we fell a thousand feet, and we flew so slowly home that daylight almost caught us up.

But Pop was right: we got as far as England, and a little more. Lofty said he'd put us down near Chelmsford, where the Yankees had a base.

Ratty cheered. "Wheezy jeezy," he said through the intercom. "I'll get to speak American!"

We landed on a runway that was long and fat and smooth, built for the great Flying Forts. We taxied in amongst them, a black sheep, dented and leaking, amid a flock of grand machines.

I carried the pigeon box out of the kite, then lifted

Gilbert from it. I opened the metal cylinder on his leg, pulled out the paper, and penciled out a note for Bert. Then I packed it up again as the others watched, cracking jokes about how the pigeon finally had to work for its living.

I tossed it up. "Fly home!" I said.

Gilbert spiraled above us. Round and round he went, wheeling in a widening circle.

"He's lost!" cried Buzz.

I said, "Shut up. He's not."

We all stood staring up, turning like beacons as the pigeon whirled above us. Then off it went across the runway.

"Straight to Trafalgar Square," said Simon.

Ratty laughed. "No lie. That's where I would go if *I* was him."

The Americans took over *Buster* as though they had captured the old crate. They pulled her into a hangar and stripped the cowlings from all four engines. It was their first look at a Halifax, and they called this one "a haywire job." They sent a fellow off in a little one-engined hack to fetch a part from the nearest Halifax squadron. "Take your time," shouted Ratty to the guy.

We spent all that day with the Americans, and the night as well. They filled *Buster* with fuel, and filled *us* with the best food we'd had in all our time in England. We sat in a gleaming mess and gorged ourselves—like storybook pigs at a fine restaurant—on meat and chips and apple pie and ice cream. "We've landed in Oz," said Lofty.

The Yankees lived in riches, and shared them all with us. They gave us sacks of chewing gum, a pile of boxes full of candy bars. Ratty really did speak American: it turned out to be a loud language in which everyone was Buddy and Pal. He slapped backs and shook hands and said, "Gee, this is swell."

Buzz hovered at his side, as though he was sure our little rear gunner would jump ship and stay forever below the big Stars and Stripes that fluttered from the flagpole. But if I had been Ratty, I wouldn't have joined the Americans for anything in the world. They had it worse than us, and I could see it in their faces, in the twitches in their cheeks. A gunner who came to sit with us said he'd racked up eleven ops. "Missions," he called them. "I'm not halfway," he said. "I got fourteen more to go."

"Jeez, we gotta fly thirty," said Ratty.

"Yeah, but at night, pal." The gunner pointed up. "Try hanging there in the sun. Biggest, brightest thing up there. You're floating bare-assed in a river full of gators."

"At least you see them coming," said Buzz.

"Wish I didn't, pal. You're flying along at twenty thousand feet, and you see 'em crawling up, you watch 'em spiral round and round like a bunch of buzzards coming for you. You see 'em gather, then in they come all at once, from here and there and up and down." His hands jerked out, as though he was flinging things all over the room. "You see the bits of metal jumping off the Fortresses, then the smoke and then the fire. You see the Forts drop away, and you see 'em break apart. You see your buddies tumble out."

The gunner closed his eyes. The corner of his mouth flickered back and forth. "My seventh mission, a guy fell past me. Boom!—right past. He didn't have a parachute. He was just falling. His legs, they were kicking, and his arms were going like this." The gunner's hands, in fists, moved liked a sprinter's, but only inches forward and back. "He was running in the air, buddy. He was trying to run away. Then I seen his face as he fell past. He looked me right in the eyes, right in the eyes as he went running past me in the air." The gunner shook; his breath nearly sobbed. "You see that, you don't forget it, pal. Live to be a hundred, you still end up looking eye to eye every night with a guy falling twenty thousand feet."

In the time that the gunner had flown his eleven ops, half his group had gotten the chop. He figured the other half would get it before the end of September. "Reckon I'll be one of them," he said.

Ratty didn't say very much after that. When we finished eating, he started asking around, trying to find someone from his hometown. Buzz went with him, right at his side, like a bodyguard who was more frightened than the guy he was guarding. I saw them standing in a big mob of Americans, little Ratty right at the center. Buzz was pointing around with his finger, asking, "So, did all of you guys live in cardboard boxes?"

There wasn't a chance that Ratty would stay. Even if he could have done that, I didn't think he would. The Flying Fortresses certainly looked huge and beautiful as we walked out to *Buster* in the early morning. Looking up at their bellies and the bottoms of their wings, the

Forts were the color of the summer sky, while our Halifax—just a few feet smaller—was like a chunk of the night. And that suited us, I thought, as I saw how everyone squinted at the sunlight. Ratty, like each of us, had become a minion of the moon.

We flew across England in the daylight. We flew north as the Fortresses went south, high above us, in their vast and tight formations. Each one had a long white contrail streaming out behind it, so many lines across the blue that it seemed the Forts were plowing the sky.

All of us must have seen them, but not even Ratty said so. It was too beautiful a morning to think of the Forts and what they were off to. England lay below like a painting of summer, and I could almost smell the flowers and the trees, and the yellowing grass of late July. Soaring above the fields and the rivers, over tiny forests and pretty villages, I was suddenly sad at the thought that this was probably my last flight. I didn't want to stop flying, only to stop being afraid. I hoped that Uncle Joe would find something that wouldn't keep me forever on the ground. I wondered if I could join the ferry service and fly the brand-new Lancasters from their Canadian factories, across the ocean to England.

The moment we landed, I went to see Uncle Joe with that idea in my mind.

I knocked on his door. A voice shouted, "In!" I stepped through, and didn't bother saluting. I said, "Sir, I'm—"

It wasn't Uncle Joe sitting at the desk. It was a fat little man with a red face and a mustache so thin that it might have been drawn with a pencil. He said, "You're a *disgrace,* is what you are. Stand at attention, man!"

I snapped my feet together. "Sir," I said. "I was supposed to see the CO."

"You're seeing him," he said. "*I'm* the CO."

"What happened to—"

"Shot down. He bought it last night."

I nearly fell over. My hands trembled so badly that I clasped them against my trousers.

"What did you want?" he said.

"I was supposed to see him, sir," I said. "I—"

"You *told* me that!" he shouted. "What about, man?"

"He was going to take me off ops," I said.

"Oh, was he? Well, I *shan't.* So you've no fear of that."

"But I wanted him to," I said.

"The devil you did!"

It went downhill from there. I tried to tell the new CO that Uncle Joe had promised to move me into other duties. But the little red man, with stripes and brass all over him, wouldn't even let me speak.

"There will be no malingerers in *my* squadron," he said. "No cowards here."

He went on and on about it, and all I could do was stand there as he ranted. He got up from his chair, taking a swagger stick from his desk, swishing it back and forth until I was certain that he would lay into me with it. He demanded my pilot's name. He said, "Go and find him. Send him to me." Then he threw me from his office, and I stumbled out in tears.

I found Lofty in the sergeants' mess. He was staring at

the blackboard, and I saw that other names had been erased from the Morris list. *T for Tom* had bought it on the way in, and *S for Sugar* had caught a packet coming home. There wasn't a name now below Lofty's, and there were only two above him. I had no doubt anymore that I was looking at a chop list.

"You know, Kid," said Lofty, "I'm not sure I want that bus anymore."

I didn't want to tell him I felt the same way. "Skipper," I said, "the CO wants to see you."

He smiled. "Jolly good show. What does Uncle Joe want with me?"

I said, "It isn't Uncle Joe."

He understood exactly what I meant. That smile fell away, and those funny eyes of his looked especially hollow and sad. Then he patted my shoulder. He took out his pipe. "Well, not to worry," he said.

Lofty went off to see the red man. I never learned what happened in the office, but when Lofty came back with the gen, his calmness was gone. "We're on tonight," he told us. "If *Buster* isn't ready, we have to take another kite."

Even Ratty didn't want to go flying. "This isn't fair," he said. "No lie. It isn't fair."

"Nothing's ever fair," said Lofty. "You haven't heard the worst of it." He took a very deep breath. "We're on for *every* op. Every night we're on."

Simon groaned, "I should have stayed a gadna."

"Cheer up, mate; you'll get your chance," said Will. "You'll be planting daisies pretty soon, I think."

Lofty got a huddle going. He formed a circle, arms on

shoulders, but I didn't make myself a part of it. I only watched as the six of them swayed together and swayed apart, the circle never breaking. I didn't hear anything that Lofty said until the end, when his voice rose into his British whine. "Now, who's for a nice cuppa tea?"

I decided not to go with them. It would give Lofty a chance to tell the others what had happened, how I'd schemed to get out of flying, and how they were all being punished for my cowardice. I cleared out as far as I could, hurrying down to the pigeon loft.

As soon as I saw old Bert coming out through the door, I broke into a run. He thundered toward me in his huge, stamping boots, and we collided on the grass, banging together. He held me by my shoulders. "What a turn you gave me, sir," he said. "When Gilbert came 'ome on his own. What a fright I got. My 'ands were shaking so, I could 'ardly open 'is little canister to read 'is message."

"I'm sorry," I said.

"No, no, sir," he said. "I'm just so glad to see you alive."

At that moment he must have been the only one in the world who felt like that, I thought. He opened his arms and wrapped them around me, the first time that *anyone* had hugged me in ten years or more. I fell against him, collapsing into his arms. I couldn't stop crying. I just shook and sobbed at all my fears and shame.

"What's the matter, sir?" Bert's hands rubbed across my shoulders. "I'm sorry if I shouted, sir. I'm not really angry at you, sir."

"It wasn't you." I told him how I'd lost my ray-gun ring, how I'd heard a kite that wasn't there, and how I'd seen the ghost of Donny Lee. I told him what Uncle Joe had promised, then all about the fat red man.

"Yes, that's Fletcher-Dodge," he said. "Wing Commander Fletcher-Dodge. 'E came in the morning, sir. In a big black car as long as an 'earse."

Bert took me into the loft. My hand was still on the door when Percy landed on my shoulder.

"My, you're 'onored, sir," said Bert. He got me sitting down on the feed sacks, and Percy nestled in my hands. He gave me a drink from the pigeons' water as a clutch of birds clung to his arms. They fluttered their wings when he gestured across the loft. "Fletcher-Dodge was 'ere, sir."

"Here?" I nodded at the floor. "Right here?"

"Yes, sir. First thing 'e did, sir, was drive down 'ere in that big 'earse. With 'is little stick, all 'is buttons polished. You should 'ave seen Percy, sir." Bert shook off the birds. He stood with his neck thrust out, bent forward with his arms tight at his sides and his elbows pulled back like wings. I smiled at his picture of Percy striking a puffed-out pose at the sight of all the red man's brass and stripes and bars. "Fletcher-Dodge came right through that door, sir. Said 'e wanted to see the pigeons, sir, and didn't I think, 'Now 'ere's a pleasant change'?" Bert sighed sadly. "Uncle Joe—bless him—never came to see the pigeons, sir."

"I know."

"Fletcher-Dodge, 'e looked in the nesting boxes. 'E

looked in every one." Bert pecked his head around to show me how the CO had looked. "Then 'e asked 'ow the breeding was going, and 'e told me to step it up, sir."

"That's good," I said.

"I don't know. I don't see it, sir," said Bert, his head shaking. "This war will finish pigeons, like the last war finished 'orses. They're on their way out already, sir. Won't be long until there's no use for pigeons, then they'll be gone; their sun will set. The big Lancs, sir, they don't carry pigeons."

"I didn't know that," I said.

"It's true, sir."

"Why not?"

"Don't need them, sir. It's . . ." He paused, looking anguished.

"It's what?" I asked.

He sighed. "Your wireless, sir. It's your wireless that's replacing the pigeons."

"How?"

"The boffins keep making them better, sir. The Lancs have a portable that goes in the life raft. If you can transmit from the life raft you don't need a pigeon, sir."

"Are we going to convert to Lancs?" I asked.

"Sooner or later," said Bert.

"What will happen to the pigeons?"

"I don't know, sir," he said. "Not exactly. I suppose they'll go 'ome, sir—the ones that 'ave a 'ome. Back to their lofts 'ere and there. And the others, sir? The poor things?" He looked down at the birds that milled on the floor. Then he shook a fist at the roof and shouted, "Damn you!" loudly enough to set the pigeons rustling.

"Why are you shouting at God?" I asked.

"At God?" He laughed, then clamped his hand over his mouth. "I'm sorry, sir. But I'd never raise my voice to God, sir. I get angry at *'im*!"

"Who?"

"Bomber 'Arris," he snarled.

The chief of air command. Dirty Bert's "man upstairs" really was a man.

"'E doesn't care," said Bert. "Sitting down there in High Wycombe; 'e doesn't even *think* about the pigeons, sir." Bert reached up to a shelf above me. He took down his little tin of suet, and I realized how close I was already to flying again. "The brave little birds. I just wish I knew what will 'appen to them, sir. It doesn't matter what becomes of me, but I can't sleep when I think about the pigeons."

I felt ashamed that I hadn't even wondered what would happen to old Bert. "Where will *you* go?" I asked.

"Wherever they send me, sir," said Bert. "Somewhere terrible, I'm sure."

He pried the lid from the tin, then pulled out a twisted old spoon that he clanked on the rim.

The birds swarmed up to his shoulders and his arms again, and to the roosts above him. They flapped and whirred through the loft, and Bert laughed like a boy. But Percy didn't move from my hands. He only watched the other birds as the little halo gleamed in his eye.

"What's wrong with Percy?" I asked, shouting over the clamor of the pigeons.

"Nothing, sir," said Bert. "'E knows 'e won't be getting suet, so 'e doesn't bother asking."

The others weren't as smart. They whirled around the tin like a cloud of giant bees, until Bert had to guard it in the crook of his arm and fend off the birds with his huge right hand. But he never stopped laughing as he doled out the suet to the pigeons that were on for the night. There were only four of them, and I watched him feed big dollops to the first three, then look around for fat little Gilbert. "Where are you, my pet?" he said. "Gibby!" He clanked the suet tin again.

Then his laugh died away. "Oh, crikey," he said.

"What's the matter?" I asked.

He was looking down at the nesting boxes. "Gibby doesn't want 'is suet, sir." The swarm of birds moved with him, across the loft toward the nesting boxes. His coveralls were clotted with white splotches.

I could see Gilbert cowering in the box as the mass of pigeons flew back and forth. His feathers were ruffled, his eyes rolling. His beak was open, and he pecked at Bert's hand when the pigeoneer reached toward him.

"Oh, crikey," said Bert again. "'E doesn't want to go. 'E's frightened, sir."

The pigeon was crying in a strange, croaky voice. I saw absolute terror in his eyes, and that fear seemed to leap from him to me. *"They always know when their number's up,"* the pigeoneer had told me.

I tossed Percy away and ran from the loft. I saw him

tumbling down in a feathery heap on the floor, but I just plowed past him and fled to the sunshine.

Bert came after me. He seemed surprised that I hadn't kept running, that I was just standing a couple of yards from the door. He said, "Gilbert's only a bird. They don't *always* know, sir."

"Well, I'm not flying," I said. "I'm never going again."

"You've got no say in it, sir."

"Oh, yes, I do," I said. "I'll just refuse to go. What's the worst that can happen?"

Bert looked down at me. "You don't want to know, sir," he said very solemnly. "You don't want to even think about that."

"You know someone who refused to fly," I said.

"Who told you so?"

"What happened to him? Just tell me what happened," I said.

The pigeoneer turned his back. I shouted at him, "You tell me that!"

"Well, sir," he said, looking up at the sky. "'E wouldn't get in the kite one day. This fellow, 'e just stood at the door and said 'e wouldn't get in. The pilot told him, 'Get in.' 'E said, 'No.' The pilot fetched the CO. The CO said, 'Get in.' 'E said, 'No, sir. Sorry, sir.' The CO—"

"But what *happened*?" I shouted. "What do they do to someone like that?"

Bert turned to face me again. His hands went up to his throat, and his thick fingers fumbled with his buttons. He opened one, then the next and the next, all without a word. Then he pulled his filthy coveralls apart, and I saw his tunic underneath. He tugged the coveralls from his arms, and let them flop from his waist.

I stared at him, amazed. There were patches on the blue where badges and ribbons had been. I could see the holes where thread had held them on. There had been a chevron on his arm, a wing at his breast, thick stripes around his cuffs. Bert had been an officer once. He had been an airman.

"They 'umiliate you, sir," he said.

His eyes were blinking quickly. He was red with shame, as though he stood absolutely naked.

"What happened?" I said.

"I was a navigator, sir," said Bert. "On the *White Knight.*"

The *White Knight.* I remembered the wreck on the Yorkshire hill, the painted knight with his visor open. "You crashed," I said.

"No, sir." He started pulling on his coveralls again. "I saw the target pictures, sir. At the briefing. They were 'ouses, sir. Not factories. Just rows and rows of 'ouses. I saw that picture, sir, and decided right then that I wouldn't take us there to drop our bombs on 'ouses, sir."

He had his coveralls half on, and was shrugging them up to his shoulders. "The CO was furious, sir. If 'e'd had a gun, I think 'e would 'ave shot me on the spot."

"How many ops had you flown?" I asked.

"Twenty-nine, sir," he said.

"You had only one more to make thirty."

He nodded. "After thirty I was going to become an instructor."

"Why didn't you do it?" I asked. "Just one more op."

"Why, sir? To teach other boys 'ow to drop their bombs on 'ouses? Not me, sir." He started on his buttons, his head turned down. "No, sir, I wouldn't do that. So I didn't go flying."

"But the *White Knight,*" I said. "It *did* crash."

"But I wasn't on it," said Bert. "They sent a sprog in my place, sir. I imagine 'e lost 'is way coming 'ome, and 'e was killed for that. They all were, sir. Even Captain Flint, and I didn't know then what a good bird 'e was. I didn't appreciate pigeons then, sir."

I should have thought about what was going through his mind, all the terrible memories I must have raised. If our positions had been reversed, that's what *he* would have done. But I only cared about myself, just as Fletcher-Dodge had told me. I only worried about "my own sorry self."

I said, "What happened next?"

"They made my life a misery, sir. They made it a living 'ell."

"But they made you a pigeoneer," I said.

"Only in the end, sir. And only Uncle Joe. 'E took pity on me, sir, because we'd flown together once."

I didn't care how it had happened, or how long it had

taken. I only saw that Bert was safe and happy. “I’ll do the same thing,” I told him. “I’ll refuse to fly. And then I can be like you, Bert.”

He smiled, but little tears came into his eyes. He smiled and cried together. “Oh, no, sir,” he said. “You don’t want to be like me, sir. I won’t *let* you be like me.”

“But I *can’t* go flying,” I told him. “I just can’t go tonight.”

His lip was quivering, his eyes blinking. “I know what you need,” he said. “I’ve got just the ticket, sir.”

CHAPTER 17

HE GAVE ME PERCY, that bright little bird. He gave me his closest friend, and grinned as he did it.

"But Percy's a breeder," I said. "You told me you can't risk losing him."

"We won't lose 'im," said Bert. "Not if you're with 'im, sir. You look after Percy, and 'e'll look after you."

Bert knelt on the floor as I held the pigeon. "Remember, sir, 'e's got the eye-sign. No matter what 'appens, 'e'll always get back. Just put your trust in Percy, sir."

It amazed me that he would give me the best bird in the loft, his favorite of the bunch, and that he would do it with a smile. But maybe the most amazing thing of all was that I *believed* that Percy would save me.

I looked into the bird's dark eyes, at the halo of sparkling stars, and I *did* believe it. There was a strength inside him that seemed to pulse through my hands. I felt his heart beating, his little breast heaving, and something passed from him to me. I knew what the Green Lantern had felt the first time he had touched his ring to the magical lantern. I just *knew* that I was safe, that I was suddenly strong and unbeatable.

Bert closed his hands around mine. His fingers encased them, and wrapped Percy double. "Now you'll 'ave to remember," he said, "that it will all be new to 'im, sir. Percy's never 'eard the flak, 'e's never even flown in a bomber. So you'll 'ave to watch out for 'im, sir, and 'elp 'im through it, the first time or two."

"All right," I said. "I'll try."

"If you get frightened, don't let 'im see it, or 'e'll get frightened, too."

"Okay," I said.

"And never fear, sir, never fear; Percy will keep you safe."

I closed my eyes and tightened my hands. The heat from Percy's belly warmed my fingers. His pulse sent fire through me.

Bert put a message cylinder onto Percy's leg, fastening it to the metal ring. He got one of the metal boxes ready, and padded it with straw. And last, he took the pigeon, to put him in the box. He held Percy up to his face for a moment, the pigeon's head against his lips. He whispered something as he stroked the stripes across a wing.

Maybe I was only desperate, clinging to the very end of my tether. But I believed what Bert told me, and I put all my trust in Percy. He didn't let me down.

Across the North Sea and all the way to Germany, I tossed Window through the chute. I kept the pigeon box beside me, and after every toss I put my hand inside to make sure that Percy's little heart was beating. I counted the faint flutters that trembled through his feathers.

When we reached the coast I went back to my wireless, carting the box along as though I was some sort of refugee wandering through the kite with all my belongings. I strapped it down and looked inside.

For once I worried more about another than I did about myself. When I found Percy twitching in his box I worried that he was dreaming terrible things, whatever nightmares a bird might have. When I found him asleep I worried that the thin air had knocked him out, and that he would never wake up again. Whenever I started to quiver or sweat I thought of Percy and forced a calmness into myself. I shoved my fears away, and whispered to him, "Don't be scared. We're going to be all right."

We crossed the target at eighteen thousand feet, with the night fighters above us and the flak all around. We rolled and pitched, and the air filled with the smells of gunpowder and smoke. And I did get frightened; I couldn't help it.

Percy stirred in the box. Maybe it was the sound of the battle, or maybe my fear, but something upset him. He bashed himself against the corners. His beak opened, and fluttered, and I was glad that the thunder of our engines hid the sounds he made.

I opened the door and took him out. I *snatched* him out, and held him as we pitched along through the flak and the boiling air. He nestled into my hands, soothed as I squeezed him. I wedged myself into my place as the bomber banked and turned. I held the little bird as tightly as I dared, knowing that if I could keep him safe, he would save *me.*

Will took over in the nose. Beside the twinkling lights of his Mickey Mouse display, he guided us along as searchlights splashed across us. The flak and flaming onions came up in a storm. A night fighter shrieked past our tail, and our guns opened up with their startling chatter.

But Percy stayed quiet. His little heart thudding, his feet gripping my fingers, he lay in the darkness.

"Left, left," said Will. "Steaaady." Then he cried, "Bombs gone!" and old *Buster* leapt in the sky.

I kept Percy in my jacket as I dropped the photoflash, as I came back to send my signal off, as we wheeled around and turned for home. When Hamburg was far behind us, I lifted him to my shoulder. I let him ride there as we droned north across Germany, across the sea, and over England. I leaned against the fuselage to let him look out the window. It was pitch-black out there, but I imagined that he could see everything in a strange world of black and white, and that he was thinking how great it was to fly at a hundred and fifty miles an hour without even flapping his wings.

We flew one circuit round the airfield, then went in for our landing. Will, in the second dickey seat, pulled the throttles back.

"Flaps down thirty," said Lofty.

"Flaps thirty, okay," answered Will.

Buster trembled as the hydraulics hummed.

"Hello, Skipper," said Pop. "Port tank two—sixty gallons; starboard tank two—sixty-three."

"Roger," said Lofty. "Landing gear down."

"Landing gear down, okay," said Will.

They talked in low, comforting voices, as though they hadn't been shrieking and shouting at each other only an hour or two before. I imagined doctors talked like that around an operating table.

Percy watched the fields go by. His feet shifted on my shoulder, the tiny claws plucking at my jacket.

"Seven hundred feet. Speed one-three-five," said Will.

"Propeller speed twenty-four hundred."

"Okay." The engines slowed. "Two hundred feet, Skipper. Speed one-two-five."

"Full flaps."

"Flaps down, okay."

We touched the ground and hurtled down the runway with the brakes squealing underneath me. Percy stiffened to attention as we passed the tower and the huts. Then we wheeled off to the right, taxiing along, and I told him, "You did it! Your first op."

I carried him from my kite on my shoulder. I didn't care how the others joked, each calling me Captain Kid or Captain Kak, thinking he was so clever. Even Sergeant Piper got in on the act. "*Arrr,* must have been a rough crossing, Cap'n!" he cried as I stepped down. "Your parrot's gone gray as a ghost."

I didn't let Percy fly back to the loft. It wasn't yet daylight, but I worried about hawks. So he rode in the truck, like part of the crew, and I carried him down to see Bert. He got the sort of welcome from the pigeoneer that I imagined most boys got from their fathers after a long adventure. I didn't really know, as the best *I'd* ever gotten was a cold stare and a drunken mumble, but it seemed right when Bert nearly cried to see Percy come home.

He kissed the bird. "Oh, 'e's fit as a fiddle," he said. "You've done well for 'im, sir."

"Thank you," I said.

We returned to Happy Valley the next night, and it seemed almost easy after Hamburg. Only *A for Apple* didn't come home. They copped it over Remscheid, and the mid-upper gunner was erased from the Morris list. Only two names remained on the blackboard. If the pilot of *G for George* bought the farm, Lofty would get the bus. But the thought that we were so close to having the Morris didn't terrify me anymore. I believed that Percy would protect us even from a chop list.

CHAPTER 18

ON THE SECOND OF August, when the moon was new, the bowser king went out at first light and fueled the bombers. The smell of petrol wafted across the field, and the gurgle of the pump set my nerves on edge.

The target that night was Hamburg. But the worst news, for me, came when Drippy stood up.

His weather map was covered with circles and lines. He smiled at us and said, "Thunder, boys. Expect thunder and lightning all the way."

Bert shouted at his man upstairs when I told him that. "Poor birds," he said. "It's going to be 'ard on them, sir. 'Ard as nails." He worried about Percy, who had never seen a thunderstorm from the air. "You'll 'ave to 'elp 'im through it, sir."

I did the best I could. The moment we took off, I lifted Percy from his box. I opened my jacket and slipped him down into a sheepskin nest, where he settled against my heart. We climbed through churning clouds and heavy rain that dashed against *Buster* like shotgun pellets. At five thousand feet the lightning started, and the rolls of thunder that followed them were louder than the engines.

Percy lifted his head, and I could feel him quivering. In each bolt of lightning I saw his eye-sign glow, the little stars twinkling round his pupil. I pressed my hand against my jacket, pressed the bird against my breast. But he didn't try to struggle free; he lay in there and twitched with each lightning bolt and every peal of thunder.

Ratty told feeble jokes from the rear turret. He called the lightning by its German name. *"Blitzen,"* he said in a terrible German accent. "It's'n blitzen everywhere." It dawned on me that he didn't care for the lightning, and that he was genuinely frightened in his lonely dustbin far behind us all. None of us really knew what would happen if the lightning hit old *Buster.*

The flashes lit up clouds that looked like fists and gremlin heads that were torn and twisted by strong, high winds. Simon shouted like an old sea captain, "It's howling a fury up here." In stranger Australian than ever, he added, "It's London to a brick that we'll be blown to the never-never." He couldn't account for the winds that shifted with our altitude, blowing first against us and then behind us.

Will's maps were useless; he couldn't see the ground. I started taking navigational bearings, tuning the loop antenna onto Berlin, onto London, onto anything I could find. I wrote the bearings on bits of paper and passed them to Simon as the rain blasted against us. It dribbled through the bubbles and the canopies, until Lofty sat in a little waterfall, soaked from his shoulders down. Then the rain turned to ice as we climbed. It froze along the wings and on the edges of the tail fins. It froze to the whirling blades of the airscrews, then flew off in chunks that banged against the fuselage. The kite got heavy and clumsy; the engines ran faster.

I rocked Percy in my jacket. "It's okay. Don't worry," I told him.

Then a weird blue glow filled the Halifax. It shimmered on my wireless, on the struts beside me, on the frame around my window. It was a pulsing jelly, like strands of bluish fire. I switched over from the wireless to the intercom just as Lofty shouted, "Pop! What is it?" Buzz said, "My goddamn guns are blue." And Ratty yelled over top of them both. "It's lightning! We're gonna get hit."

"Shut up!" cried Will, in the nose. "Saint Elmo's fire. It's just Saint Elmo's fire."

I looked up, round the curtain and past the bulkhead. Lofty sat in a flaming seat, his hands on a fiery column. The glow shimmered all around him, on the framework of the canopy, on all his levers and controls. It even pulsed on the end of his pipe.

It was an eerie thing to see at eleven thousand feet—a cold blue fire consuming the kite. It terrified me at first, until I thought of the Green Lantern and the glowing metal that gave him his power. I reached toward the window frame, hoping to touch the flames, to capture their power. "Shazam," I said to myself as my fingers trembled. But the glow suddenly vanished, fading away like a ghostly fire, to leave us in darkness again. *Buster* went roaring up through the clouds, tossed by the wind as she climbed.

Will spoke in his deep Shakespeare voice. "There appeared a chariot of fire. And Elijah went up by a whirlwind."

I had never learned the Bible stories. I didn't know what he was blathering about.

We flew on through rain and ice, through lightning, clouds, and stars. The wireless filled with static, and Simon tried all his little tricks. Twice we dropped flares and let Ratty measure the angle of our drift by lining them up on his guns. But we never found the target. We blundered over Germany, in and out of flak and searchlights. We didn't even know where we dropped our bombs; we just let them fall, and turned for home.

The lightning chased us, and little Percy shivered in my jacket. He fell asleep over the North Sea and dreamed some sort of dream that had him twitching all over. I tried to calm him, but he twisted round and nipped me through my pullover.

I felt awful for him, to see him dream. It was as though my own nightmares had been passed to him, for I hadn't had my spinning dream for days, not since I'd taken Percy flying. For three mornings in a row I had woken full of peace, feeling rested and content.

That night was the same. I ate my fresh egg and sat through debriefing, then fell asleep as soon as I crawled into bed. Thunder rumbled in the distance, and I thought of Percy dreaming, but no fiery world went twirling around me.

I woke to the patter of rain on the hut's tin roof, a sound I'd come to love. If it drummed like that, there would be no flying, and it drummed like that all week. Yet I found my stomach churning as much as ever as I sat at the breakfast table waiting for the WAAF. Through all the week of rotten weather it churned away each morning. But on the third day I noticed that Buzz and Pop and Ratty were worse—much worse—than me. Their breakfasts sat unfinished as their fingers shook and fluttered. Buzz had a twitch in his left eye, so that he looked a bit like the American gunner we'd met. Pop kept tapping his foot on the floor, his whole leg moving, his knee going up and down like a grasshopper's. Only Lofty didn't seem to mind the waiting; he took turns chewing his sprouts and chewing his pipe. Sometimes he chewed the two together.

I spent the days in the pigeon loft as the rain went on and on. I wondered sometimes if it would ever stop, if we hadn't dropped so many bombs that we'd wrecked the whole sad planet. That was what had happened in Buck Rogers; it made sense it could happen again.

Around the huts, the bit of grass became such a muddy wallow that the erks packed away their cricket bats and wicket things. But the Canadians didn't give up their baseball. They played the same wild game they always had, a sort of tackle baseball that was even wilder in the mud. They turned themselves into clots of earth, into black snowmen that were often heaped in piles among the bases.

At night the sergeants' mess filled to bursting, a dangerous place to be. The twisted airscrew that might have slashed me to ribbons became a giant spinner that was hurled around the room in a lunatic's version of pitch-and-toss. Then the big leather sofa got so badly wounded in a crashing round of Tank that Ratty fetched a pistol and put it out of its misery. Six sergeants bore it up on their shoulders and carried it outside. They dug a massive grave behind the hut, and Buzz played taps on a pocket-comb kazoo as they lowered it down in the rain.

The war went on—it always did—from the South Pacific to the Russian steppes. But it didn't affect our little bit of Yorkshire. At the Four-Forty-Two, the only battles were waged within ourselves. Lofty and the rest went from one feverish game to another. If they weren't getting drunk, they were getting sober; but I wasn't a part of any of it.

I was becoming more and more like Bert, always alone except at the pigeon loft. I spent more time talking to pigeons than I did to people. I collected little treats for Percy, and made a game of letting him choose which pocket they were in. He looked at me, his head tilting, then pecked at one of my pockets. Four or five times a day we played the game, and he never failed to get it right.

I was at the loft, near the end of the week, when Fletcher-Dodge came to see the pigeons. The sun was setting when Percy suddenly snapped to attention, and in through the door came the CO, with a black umbrella that frightened the birds silly. They flapped away as he squeezed it through the door; they squawked while he shook off the rain and closed it.

His buttons were polished, his badges shining. He squinted and frowned at me, as though trying to figure out where we'd met. "What do you do here?" he asked.

Bert answered for me. "Sir, 'e 'elps with the pigeons."

"Good show," said Fletcher-Dodge. Below his mustache, his teeth grinned crookedly. "I say, that's jolly dee."

His red face and perfect clothes made him seem foolish, like a character from a music hall. He tapped his umbrella on the floor and shouted at Bert. "Pigeoneer! Any eggs today?"

"No, sir," said Bert.

"Blast! That's a bother." The CO made a puttering sound with his lips. "I was counting on you, Pigeoneer."

"Yes. I'm sorry, sir," said Bert.

Fletcher-Dodge set off on a circuit round the loft, tapping his umbrella at the nesting boxes, prodding at the straw. I watched him poke and trundle round, not knowing why he was there. Bert watched him, too, avoiding my eye.

"This is a shower," said the CO. "An absolute shower. I was expecting better, Pigeoneer."

Bert nodded. "Sir, I'm trying."

"Beastly things. They're a miserable lot." Fletcher-Dodge swept the pigeons away with his umbrella. When he looked up, I was right in front of him with Percy on my shoulder. "Now that's a wizzo bird," he said. "I should like to see more like that, Pigeoneer."

"Yes, sir," said Bert.

"He's jolly dee."

I was quite pleased, but Bert was miserable. His head drooped lower and lower until the CO—with a "Cheerio, then!"—opened his umbrella and went out through the door. Then Bert shook his head at me. "Do you see what he's up to, sir?"

"No," I said.

"Why, 'e wants to eat them, sir."

"The pigeons?"

"Yes," cried Bert. "Eggs 'e wants. Or squabs or birds. It doesn't matter to him."

"But they're not his pigeons," I said. "He can't eat them, can he?"

"Who am I to say what the CO can do?" asked Bert. "But 'e *won't.* No, sir, not on *my* watch 'e won't."

Bert turned away and pulled the birds from their nesting boxes. "'E's a 'orrible little man," he said. "I know 'is type, sir. You won't ever see 'im fly nothing but a desk. If that swaggering pigeon-eater ever goes on an op, you'll 'ave nothing to worry about, sir. 'E won't ever risk 'is own skin, that one."

Bert worked himself into such a fit that he went off for a walk. He left me alone with the pigeons, and the rain came down and the darkness settled. Hours passed, but he didn't return.

I guessed it was nearly midnight when I heard the Morris outside. Through a window I saw its hooded headlights veering down the runway, glowing in the rain. They reminded me of searchlights swinging up from the ground, and I felt a twitch of fear as they turned right at me. I heard voices shouting as the car rushed along. The muffler popped; the tires squealed.

I took a lantern from its hook and went outside.

"Left, left!" someone cried. "Corkscrew left!" and the car spun sideways. There must have been a whole crew aboard, with all the bellowing and laughter. The headlights disappeared, then reappeared, as the car slewed in a circle. Gears clashed and the motor spluttered and someone shouted, "Bomb doors open!"

Something dark and gangly separated from the Morris and tumbled across the ground. "Bombs gone!" cried a voice, and others laughed as the car accelerated. It went racing back toward the huts.

The dark mass on the ground picked itself up and came toward me. It was Lofty, smearing mud from his jacket. "Thank God they slowed down, the silly buggers," he said. "They pitched me off the running board."

He was staggering a bit, but not from his landing. Somehow he was still holding a bottle of beer. He tipped it up, but found it empty. Then he belched and said, "You're missing the party, Kid."

"There'll be another one tomorrow," I said.

"Maybe not. We might be on."

Up went the bottle; he'd forgotten already that it was empty. Then he peered through the neck. "U/S," he said, tossing it away. He staggered up to the pigeon loft, leaned against it, fitting his fingers through the wire mesh. I held up my lantern, and the pigeons twitched and blinked.

"What do you see in these birds?" asked Lofty.

"I'm not sure," I said.

Lofty was so much taller than me that I could lean in toward the wire below his outstretched arm. I looked at the birds inside, their eyes glowing.

"God, they reek." He sniffed. "Or is that you? Kid, you stink of birds."

Lofty banged on the bars; he thumped and rattled at the mesh. Half the pigeons rose in a startled mass, bubbling up in gray and brown, little downy feathers flying.

"Don't do that!" I shouted.

He only laughed, loudly enough to keep the pigeons in a whirring cloud. His hand fell from the wire and landed on my shoulder with a mighty slap. "Kid," he said, "I think you should spend more time with the *other* birds."

"What birds?" I asked.

"The two-legged ones."

I frowned. "They're all two-legged, Lofty."

"Huh? Oh, yeah, I guess they are." He snickered to himself. "The two-*breasted* ones, I mean. There's a couple of WAAFs at the party who'd like to get their feathers stroked."

I was glad for the darkness as I felt myself blush. The WAAFs, in their pretty blue suits, scared me nearly as much as the ops had ever done.

"Come on," he said. "You can navigate for me."

"I want to stay here for a while," I said.

"Very well." He took a breath that nearly toppled him sideways. "I'll go on instruments, then."

He headed off, stumbling on the wet ground. I

couldn't let him go alone, not after he'd come all that way to see me. He was my pilot, after all; I owed him a bit of care. "Hang on," I said.

I put the lantern back inside, blew it out, and said so long to Percy. Then I walked away with Lofty through the rain, letting him bump against me to keep him on the beam. He didn't talk at first; he was far too busy just staying upright.

When we were nearly at the huts, he stopped. His feet stopped first, and then the rest of him, reeling in a circle like a Happy Valley searchlight. "Kak," he said. "Hey, Kakky?"

"Yes?" I said.

"What's the matter with us, huh? Don't you like us, Kakky?"

"What do you mean?" I said.

"You're always by yourself. Here or there with your ruddy birds. Why don't you hang around us anymore?"

He was drunk. And what drunks said didn't matter for anything.

"We need you, Kak." He turned toward me, wobbling, and put his hands on my shoulders. "We're a crew," he said. "Me and you and Ratty and the rest. We've got to stick together, Kid. We *have* to stick together, or all of us are lost."

I didn't like him being so close that he could hit me before I could move.

"Oh, cripes! I forgot," he said. His right hand lifted from my shoulder, and I cringed. But he only thumped himself on the head, knocking himself into a funny little dance that ended when he tripped and fell. He lay in the mud, giggling. "I pranged," he said. "My undercarriage collapsed."

I hated drunks.

"I forgot to tell you," he said. "What I came to see you for."

"What?" I said.

"I got some gen. It's hot."

Lofty held up his hand. He was like a long beetle lying on the ground. "Help me up!" he said. "Pull my chocks away."

I took his hand, and pulled, but he didn't come very easily. He rose only halfway before his fingers—wet and slick—popped from mine, and he dropped back on the grass.

"Once more," he said, and I tried again. He kicked and struggled. "Boosters on!"

I got him up, and we nearly fell together. His arms and legs were muddy, his cap still somehow on his head. All I wanted was to get rid of him, to get back to the loft and the birds.

"So what's the news?" I said. "What did you want to tell me?"

"Oh, yeah." He laughed again. "We're getting rid of *Buster,* Kid."

"Really?"

Lofty nodded. "That's the pukka gen."

It had to be true if it was pukka gen. That was the most reliable news there was. "But why?" I asked.

"We're getting Lancs," he said.

I almost let him fall. He grabbed for my arms to steady himself. "We're converting soon," he said. "A week or two at the most. The first one will be here any day."

"But I don't *want* to change," I said. "I don't want to fly a Lancaster."

"Are you nuts?" he asked. "Why not?"

"They don't carry pigeons," I said.

Lofty groaned. He shook his head and pulled his hands away. "You're hopeless, Kak," he said. "You really are a twit. You've got those birds on the brain."

"But we need Percy," I said.

"Aw, go on." He gave me a push that didn't shift me at all but sent *him* reeling sideways. He staggered to a stop and slowly straightened. "Go back to your pigeons," he said. "That's where you belong, I guess."

CHAPTER 19

IT WAS THE NINTH of August when we flew again. The skies cleared and the moon was in its last quarter, and three kites were sent off. Of course *Buster* was one of them. We wouldn't be "driving the train" exactly, but we'd be close to the head of the stream. There would be a bunch of kites, then old *Buster* and *G for George* and *V for Victor;* then the rest of the stream would be spread behind us for mile after mile after mile.

No one was keen on the target. We were going to Mannheim, way down by the bulge of France, in the valley of the winding Rhine. "Wheezy jeezy," Ratty said. "Can't we ever bomb something close to home?" Old Pop said, "We only pay the piper; we never call the tune."

For most of the sergeants it was just another night on the ground, and the party kept rolling on. In the mess, they stood amid the wreckage and sang about Happy Valley, about the flak and the blinding searchlights. For me it was hard enough to sit outside and listen. It seemed so strange that we were flying off across half of black Europe while the others were carousing. I didn't understand how Ratty and Lofty and Buzz could join the party. But there they were, in the last hour before the op, surely the only ones not drinking. I could tell it was Ratty banging away on the piano; I heard his funny squeak that filled in for each missing note when he hit the empty key.

It was especially hard to be alone that evening. I kept thinking of the Lancasters, and what changes they would bring for me and the pigeons and Bert. A movie played endlessly in my mind: the birds screaming as they were slaughtered; Fletcher-Dodge grinning over his roasted pigeon; the loft sitting empty and forgotten. I knew I couldn't cope without my little friend.

The singing from the mess grew louder. The voices howled like mournful dogs.

> *"There was flak, flak*
> *Bags of bloody flak*
> *In the valley of the Ruhr."*

And then others chimed in for the chorus:

> *"My eyes are dim, I cannot see,*
> *The searchlights they are blinding me."*

A sergeant came out of the mess and walked right past me, as though I wasn't there. It made me remember how

I had seen Donny Lee in almost the same place, and I turned cold at the thought that I was joining that lonely world of the dead men. I got up and went through the door.

Buzz was sitting on the piano bench beside Ratty. Lofty was in his favorite corner, reading a paper that was crinkled by his fists. Pop wasn't there, but it didn't surprise me. He always spent the moments before an op lying on his bed, holding the crucifix, talking to a photograph.

I found a chair that still had four legs, turned it upright, and sat by myself near the door. The cigarette smoke was as thick as the clouds over Hamburg, and I squinted through it, with my eyes burning. I watched Ratty's hands slide along the keyboard. I tried not to think about pigeons.

From outside came the clatter of the Morris. The car came closer, then stopped by the hut with the bang of a backfire. Shoes pounded up the steps, and through the door came the pilot of *G for George,* the fellow who owned the Morris then. He went straight across the mess, straight to the piano, and stepped in front of Ratty. The music stopped; the singing stopped.

In the silence someone coughed. The pilot looked around the mess and asked, "Who wants the bus?"

He didn't say it the way that Donny Lee had done. He sounded desperate and frightened. He shook the keys; he held them up. "Who wants the damned bus?" he shouted. "Anyone can have it."

There was no rush for the keys. No one even answered.

"Doesn't anybody want the thing?" said the pilot. "Doesn't *anybody* want it?"

The mess was absolutely silent except for his voice. There was no rattle of bottles, no scuffing of feet. There was only a faint jingle as the keys trembled in his fingers.

The pilot looked again around the room, all around at every face, then sort of sighed and sagged. His hand came down. His eyes darkened and his brows lowered, and he marched across the room to the blackboard on the wall. He stared at the names on the Morris list, all the smudged-away names, and then his and then Lofty's. He turned toward the corner. "Lofty," he said.

He had to say it again before Lofty seemed to hear him. Then the newspaper tilted down, folding backward over itself.

Lofty looked as calm as ever, and I felt a happy twinge to think that he was my skipper, the best of the bunch. "Hmm?" he said. "What's that, old boy?"

The pilot swallowed. "You want the bus?" he said. "You can have it now."

"Thanks, old boy," said Lofty, more British now than Fletcher-Dodge.

Buzz stood up from the piano bench. He looked frightened, ready to shout at Lofty. But Lofty didn't even look toward him as he folded the paper on his lap. "Thanks awfully," he said. "But no, I'll wait my turn."

The pilot stared at him.

"Cheers, though. Ta very much, old boy." Lofty slowly picked up his paper. He shook it open in front of his face with a snap that made the poor pilot blink.

The fellow looked miserable. He turned around, scanning the faces, and an expression of rage came over him. "Well, it's not mine. Not anymore," he said, his teeth gritted. "I'm rid of the damned thing."

He put the keys on the nail; he snatched up the chalk brush. He touched it to the board, beside his name. His hand quivered as he held it there.

But in the end, he didn't rub out his name. I supposed he just couldn't do it; I didn't think that *I* could have done it either, if I had been him. I couldn't have added my own smudge to the other smudged-out names of dead men.

He put down the brush, and chalk flurried around him in a white cloud. Then he turned and left the mess, weaving round two broken chairs, his feet drumming on the floor.

"I shouldn't worry, old boy," said Lofty from behind his paper. "It's only a lot of names, you know. Everyone's on a list, after all. I say, we'll all get our tickets; it's just a matter of time."

That was an odd thing to come from him, and it put a damper on the party. The singers moved apart, and the room emptied by half. Buzz and Ratty left, then Lofty himself, and he smiled at me as he passed. "Come on, Kid," he said. "It's a long way to Germany. We'd better get moving."

We changed into flying clothes, got our chutes and gear. I went behind the others, from one hut to the next, hardly a part of the crew. Again we were all being punished for what I had done, and I kept myself away to save them the bother of driving me off.

I got my pigeon box from Bert, and made sure that Percy was inside it. For the first time, the pigeoneer shook my hand. "Good luck to you, sir," he said. "'Appy 'unting, as we used to say." His fingers wrapped right around my hand, so that he held me just as my mom had held me when I was a tiny boy. "No worries, sir," he said. "Just think of Percy and 'is eye-sign."

I nodded.

"I'll see you when you're 'ome."

I sat right at the tailgate of the truck as we rumbled across the runway. I lingered at the edge of the dispersal, nearly a wing-length away from the others. Lofty stood staring up at the engine that had failed over Germany, his pipe going in and out of his mouth. Both Sergeant Piper and Pop joined him for a while, pointing at the thing from the front and the back. Then Sergeant Piper held out the 700, but it seemed that Lofty didn't want to sign it. They talked again and pointed some more before Lofty signed his name. He shoved the clipboard back at the erk, stalked to the door, then told us, "Come on, boys. Let's go."

Buzz was still crawling around, looking for his clover. He had grazed over the same bit of grass again and again, like a sheep in a pen, and now he was worried. "Help me, Ratty," he said.

"Never mind that," I told them. "It's not the clover that helps us."

It was a dumb thing to say. No one had ever spoken aloud about Buzz's clover or Ratty's rabbit's foot, or the others' lucky charms—the photograph, the crucifix, the handkerchief. My ray gun was the only thing anyone had mocked, and that was no wonder, the thing had been so stupid.

But I blundered on. "You don't need it. You don't need *any* of that junk," I said. "Percy keeps us safe."

"Oh, shut up, Kak," said Simon. His hand was in his back pocket, but he snatched it out.

"It's true," I said. "He's got the eye-sign."

"Shove off, Kid," said Ratty.

"Never mind him," cried Buzz. "Just help me look."

Simon helped, and Will. Even the old guy got on his hands and knees. I pretended to look in the grass right beside me, but I really only searched for the little yellow shoots that Percy loved to gobble down. At *Buster*'s door, Lofty called, "Hey, let's go!"

"No!" said Buzz. "Wait a minute."

He moved faster and faster, scuttling over the grass. Even Lofty poked his toe around, but it was Simon who found the lucky leaf. He held it out in his palm like a little green jewel. "There you go, Cobber," he said.

"Gee, thanks," said Buzz. But he got Simon to put the clover down so that he could pick it up himself. "It's best that way," he said. "I think that's the way I have to do it."

The tiny leaf fluttered down, and Buzz snatched it up again. "Okay," he said. "Okay. *Now* we can go."

I laughed at him. I thought everyone would, but the only laugh was mine, and it seemed so loud that it echoed in my ears for ages. I could hear it as I stowed Percy's basket, and even the engines didn't drown it out when they started.

We followed *G for George* along the perimeter and onto the runway. Engines boomed and droned. I felt us rock as *George* took off; I heard the spray of grit thrown back by its airscrews. "We're next," I told Percy. "Don't be frightened."

"Testing magnetos," said Lofty.

It was a change in his routine. He had tested them already, as he always did. But now he wound the engines up and tested them again. Pop told him he wasn't doing it properly, but Lofty said that *he* was the skipper, that he would do what he wanted. "These damn engines," he said. "You can't trust them."

I couldn't really follow what was happening. Switches were being thrown back and forth, engine revolutions read out from the gauges. All I knew was that each engine had two magnetos, that *Buster* had eight altogether, and that Lofty seemed very worried. I sat in my compartment, in the darkness of the kite, and listened to the voices on the intercom, each sentence beginning and ending with the click of a mike.

"I'm getting excessive mag drop," said Lofty.

"It's not a problem," said Pop.

"Something's wrong. Maybe the engine's U/S."

"It's not. Everything's tiggety-boo."

Will, in the second dickey seat, said, "Seems all right to me, Skipper."

"What do *you* know?" snapped Lofty. "Look at the bloody gauges!"

"But, Skipper," said Pop.

"It's U/S, and that's it. We're not going anywhere tonight."

"But, Skipper."

"This old crate should be out in the boneyard. It's a wreck; it's a bloody disaster."

Pop sighed through his intercom. "You're the boss," he said.

"That's right," said Lofty. "And we're going back."

The engines quickened. We taxied down the runway, lumbering along with our great fat bottom dragging behind us. The intercom clicked. "There go the rockets," said Will.

I was on the wrong side of the kite to see those signals shooting up from the tower. But Will kept talking, and I imagined the fiery trails burning into the sky. Fletcher-Dodge must have been raging in the tower to order so many signals so quickly. They soared up one after another, until Will told us, "It looks like the *Titanic* going down."

Lofty pulled off onto the perimeter. The runway flares lined up in a row in my window, then fell away behind as we taxied our way back to dispersal. The engines seemed strong and loud to me, wheeling us along with our thousands of pounds of bombs in our belly. But I was glad that Lofty had tested them. "That was a lucky break," I said.

Buzz, in his turret, started asking his crossword questions; he knew them all by heart. But no one was interested, and his voice only bleated in the darkness.

Sergeant Piper was astonished to see us back, and Fletcher-Dodge was furious. He came roaring out in a truck, demanding to know what was wrong. Lofty stormed through the door and stood in front of him, right below my window. I looked down at the top of Lofty's cap, at the CO's red face tilted up, shouting at Lofty. The swagger stick whistled through the air.

Fletcher-Dodge didn't give us a ride to the huts. Percy flew back, weightless and free, while the rest of us had to hoof it with all our clobber, lugging our chutes like schoolboys with satchels.

There was a *feeling* that hung around us, a sense of being beaten, as though we had lost a battle we didn't know we were fighting. I felt sorry for Lofty, who tried to struggle ahead with his buckles jangling. It was *almost* as though he had refused to fly, or that was how it felt in a way. No one *said* that he should have flown, but no one backed him up. I was only glad that I had a pilot brave enough to refuse to fly if he thought he had to. What would have happened, I wondered, if we had been halfway across Germany when the magnetos gave out? Could we ever have gotten home again? I wondered about it, then had to know.

"Hey, Lofty," I said, calling ahead to him. "If we had kept going, what would have happened?"

"Oh, shut up, Kak," he said. "No one wants to hear from you."

I had heard the same sort of thing a thousand times from my old man, but it really hurt, coming from Lofty. "Gee," I said. "I only asked."

"Well, don't," he snapped, without even slowing.

I felt terribly sad. I let the others move past me, and followed along behind them all, the tail-end Charlie now for sure. But Pop glanced back, then fell in beside me, puffing from the weight of his chute and his black bag of gear. "He's not angry at you, Kid," he said, quietly enough that no one else would hear. "Not really. He's more angry at himself."

"Why?" I said.

"Well, Kid, you should know."

"What's that supposed to mean?" I asked. "*I* don't understand magnetos."

"I thought you were smarter than that."

The old guy surprised me sometimes. He knew things that other people didn't. But now I thought the duffer just didn't make sense.

"Lofty's playing it safe," I said.

"Sure he is," said Pop.

CHAPTER 20

I WENT DOWN TO the pigeon loft. Bert was sitting with the birds all around him, as though he'd been telling them stories. Percy stood on top of his head, and Bert was smiling.

"Well, 'allo, 'allo, sir," he cried as I came through the door. "You scrubbed it, did you?"

"One of our magnetos was busted, or something," I said.

Bert laughed. "That old dodge? That won't work twice with the new CO."

"What do you mean?" I said.

Bert stretched out his legs. The pigeons moved off in ripples around him, and Percy rose from his head to flutter over to me. "Let's say you don't want to fly. Well, you foul the plugs, and Bob's your uncle, sir. You get too much magneto drop."

"On purpose?" I asked.

"It's easy to do, sir," he told me. "Magnetos seem to 'ave a 'abit, sir, of causing problems before a difficult op."

"But Lofty wouldn't do that," I said. "He's not afraid to fly."

"No, sir. You're quite right, sir."

I hated that maddening way of his. Every time the pigeoneer agreed with me, I felt that I was wrong. But I would never lose faith in Lofty. "He might get the jitters," I said. "I guess he might, but that's all. He doesn't really get scared."

Bert wouldn't talk about it anymore. He got up and went to work with a bucket and a rag, washing down the walls of the nesting boxes. The birds hopped up to the rim of his bucket, two or three at once, and he splashed them with water. They shook the drops away and giggled little pigeon laughs. Others squeezed between them to get a turn at the bath.

Bert patted their heads and talked to them. He told them he had to work, that he couldn't sit and play all through the night. But each time he tried to move away, the pigeons squawked and shouted, and back he went to the bucket. "Oh, all right," he told them. "Just for another minute."

I watched him play and laugh with the birds, his coveralls filthy, wrinkled and torn. I asked him, "What will you do when the Lancasters come?" Right away I wished I hadn't.

He stood up, his little game at an end. He looked down at the pigeons and all around the loft. "I don't know, sir," he said. "I don't know what will become of us."

"Fletcher-Dodge," I said. "Will he really . . ." I couldn't finish the sentence.

"I don't know that either, sir," said Bert. "But I 'ope not." He stood in a slouch, his shoulders bent, the rag dripping water round his boots. "But what can I do, sir? If 'e wants to slaughter them, 'ow can I stop it?"

I didn't have an answer. I shook my head, and Bert's shoulders slumped even more.

"I'm scared of that Fletcher-Dodge," he said. "If I take one step out of line, 'e'll pull out 'is files and whatnot. Soon as 'e does, 'e'll see who I am and what I've done, and *then* there'll be 'ell to pay." He looked down at the rag, as though surprised to see it in his fist. "When Uncle Joe made me a pigeoneer, I thought I'd gone as low as I could go. I didn't know what a kindness 'e was doing for me. I love the birds, sir; I love the loft. I love them with all my 'eart. But if I don't do what I'm told, sir, I don't like to think what might 'appen to me."

"But you're not breeding them," I said. "You were told to do that, and you didn't."

"It's different, sir," said Bert. "I thought I could get away with that." He started washing the boxes down. "I 'ave these mad ideas, sir."

"Like what?" I asked.

"I thought I could put them all in the motorized loft. Every blessed bird." His hand rubbed up and down over the same bit of wood. "I thought I could make a run for it, sir. Up to Scotland maybe. Up to the 'ighlands, sir. I could maybe 'ide myself among the 'ills."

"Hide yourself?" I laughed. "That loft and fifty birds?"

"That's the catch, sir, isn't it?" said Bert.

"What will happen when they find you?"

"The birds will be safe enough. They'll be 'alf wild by then. For me it'll be prison, I suppose, sir. Years of 'ard labor." He breathed three quick breaths. "But what else can I do, sir? When the pigeons are gone, and the loft's destroyed, there'll be no use for me 'ere anymore. Fletcher-Dodge will get out those files, and it will all be there in black and white. A coward; a malingerer."

"He won't even look," I said. "He'll send you somewhere else. To another loft at another squadron."

"The files will go with me, sir. I could sooner 'ide the loft than 'ide those blasted files." He mopped his face with the rag. Then he looked up and shouted at his man upstairs. "Damn you! Damn you! 'Ow can you let this 'appen?"

His anger filled him, then drained away, as it always did. He sighed and went back to his wiping. "Some of these birds, sir, they belong to people," he said. "People in the fancy, sir, who lent them out for the war. When a pigeon gets the chop, I write to the breeder, sir. I tell 'im the bird went out in the line of duty, that it went out a 'ero, sir. 'Ow can I tell a man 'is bird went out as a *pie?*"

I felt like laughing, but there was nothing funny underneath it all.

"I'll make sure those birds get 'ome," he said. "No matter what 'appens, I'll see to that, sir. But what about the others, the ones like Percy that I bred myself? Who will speak for them, sir, if I don't do it myself?"

I didn't answer. But in a flash of guilt I knew it wouldn't be *me.* I couldn't face an angry Fletcher-Dodge for a second time.

Bert dropped to his knees and called the pigeons around him. He whistled and clucked, and they flew up to his arms and shoulders, to his hands and his head. Even Percy went over, and I felt a jealousy that I shouldn't have felt. The birds were so happy with Bert, and he was so happy with them, that I couldn't imagine them ever being apart.

"Oh, it's awful, sir," he said. "It's 'orrible to think about." He was covered with birds, and the sound of them made his voice faint. "I would rather a fox got them, sir. Or a cat, God forgive me for saying it. I would rather burn them."

"No!" I said.

"It's 'appened before."

He waited until the birds were calm, until they nuzzled at his clothes and his neck. Then he told me a story from the last war, about a pigeoneer who had set fire to a loft full of birds as the German army advanced toward him. They were beautiful birds, said Bert, such good fliers that the Germans couldn't be allowed to have them. He told me how the pigeoneer had wept as he'd held a torch to the wooden loft, how the birds had panicked as the fire caught.

"It must have been frightful, sir. It must have been . . ."

Bert shook his head. He got to his feet, knocking the birds away. "I 'ave to be alone, sir," he said.

Bert went off to his room, and I washed the boxes for him. I washed the floor and the roosts, looking at Percy every few minutes. Inside, I felt cold. Through all the thoughts about birds and pies, and the fate of the pigeoneer, my own selfish dread kept oozing to the top. I knew I'd be lost if I couldn't take Percy flying.

On his roost by the roof, he blinked at me, with his eye-sign shining in the lantern's yellow glow. Then he stood at attention, and I was sure that Fletcher-Dodge would come in through the door. I turned to look, to wait, and there was Lofty standing at the window, his face a frightening skull in the moving shadows of the light.

"You scared me!" I said.

"Sorry, old boy." He slipped sideways from the window; then the door opened beside it and he walked in.

"Who came with you?" I asked.

"Simon. But he's gone right by." Lofty looked surprised. "How did you know that?"

"You're a sergeant."

He frowned, not understanding that Percy only stood at attention for officers. "Well, never mind." He shook his head. "Listen, Kid; about tonight."

"It's okay," I said.

"The bloody old bus. Those damn magnetos."

"I understand," I told him.

He'd been drinking. I could smell it on his breath.

His face was pale and blotched; his hands shook as he jammed them into his pockets, nearly shoving his trousers right off his hips.

"You know, Kak, you've changed," he said. "You were such a kid when I met you. So young and wide-eyed. You couldn't wait to fly, to be a hero. Then you got scared, eh? You got the jitters, didn't you?"

"A bit." I backed away as he came closer. "You know I did."

"Yeah, but now you've changed again." He brought out his pipe. He poked it against his cheek before he found his mouth. "You're not frightened anymore, and I want to know how come. How'd you do it, Kid?"

I had told him already, and I didn't want to do it again when he smelled of beer. He would only laugh at my faith in Percy. "I just don't worry anymore," I said. "I know we'll always get home."

"How?"

"I just know it, Lofty. Okay?"

He nodded in that clumsy way of a drunk. "But what about the list? Aren't you scared of the Morris list?"

I looked up at Percy. He seemed to be watching me, his head turned sideways. His eye was enormous and bright, the tiny stars sparkling round his iris.

"Eh?" said Lofty. "It scares everyone else. What about you?"

Percy winked at me. His eye closed and opened again, and I could hardly believe he didn't understand everything we were saying.

"I think it's maybe just a list," I said. "I'm not sure it really matters."

"Yeah, why should it?" Lofty puffed his empty pipe. "Just a bunch of names, eh?"

He squatted down in a boneless, drunken way and tried to call one of the birds toward him. It only scuttled out of his reach, but Lofty stayed there with his arm stretched out. "I like you, Kak," he said. "Have I told you that?"

"Yes," I said. "The last time you were drunk."

I didn't want him in the loft. It was *my* place, where I came to be away from him and everyone. But when I tried to help him up, Percy made a funny noise and hopped a circle on his roost. And then, beyond the wire roof, into the lantern light, came a pigeon. It dropped down with its wing feathers splayed, with that soft whistling sound growing louder. It landed above me, pushed through the trap, went straight to the bell, and tapped it with its beak.

"Where's he been?" asked Lofty.

The bird hopped down to the roosts, down to the floor. It took a drink of water from one of Bert's fountains, and other birds hurried to nuzzle against it. They crooned in that peculiar voice that Bert said was singing.

Lofty belched. Moving his hand like a bandleader, he started to sing. "Been to London to visit the Queen."

I could have hit him. "That bird went flying tonight," I said. "He was out on *George* or *Victor*."

"No kidding?" said Lofty. "Then why's he back? What's he—"

I could see the truth sink in for Lofty. A soberness came over him, in a way I'd seen a hundred times with my old man, as if beer could be shocked from his blood. He took his pipe from his mouth; he pushed it back in. "They've bought it, haven't they?" he said. "That bird's come from *George,* and they've bought it."

I picked up the pigeon. Its heart was pounding, its breath coming in gasps. I turned it over, but there was no message, no cylinder. There wasn't even a *leg* on that side. It had been shot off or torn away, and streaks of dried blood covered the feathers on the pigeon's belly.

"It's *George,* isn't it?" said Lofty. "It's that damned list."

Bert came in, zipping his coveralls as he rushed through the door. "I 'eard the bell," he said. "Who's 'omed, sir?"

I held out the bird. "He's hurt," I said.

"Oh, mercy," cried Bert. "That's Geordie! Wee Geordie!"

"I knew it," groaned Lofty. "It's *George.*"

"No, no," said Bert. "This is Geordie from *Victor.*"

He took the bird in one hand and felt through its feathers. He pulled at the stump of the pigeon's leg, and the poor bird thrashed wildly.

"What's happened to *Victor?*" said Lofty.

We never found out. Only the pigeon came home. The kite and the crew vanished completely, as though *V for Victor* had flown off to that other place of Donny Lee's.

But right then in the loft, it was the pigeon that Bert

cared about. He got out his salve and his bandages and went to work. "Oh, 'e'll be all right. Don't you fret now, sir."

Lofty still hadn't sorted it out. "Are you sure that one's not from *G for George*?" he asked. "How can you tell?"

"I think I know my birds," said Bert.

Lofty hung around, though neither of us wanted him there. He lurked by the nesting boxes, whistling through his pipe with a sound that grated at me. I helped Bert wash Wee Geordie, changing the water as the redness brightened in the bowl. We had just finished and were settling the pigeon into a nest when we heard the sound of engines, a single kite coming in.

"You'd best go, sir," said Bert. "You and your chum 'ere, sir." He was signaling to me with his eyes; Bert had never cared for visitors.

I took Lofty outside. "We'll watch him come in," I said. But we were nearly blind in the darkness, and we had to half grope our way around the corner of the loft. Then we struck off toward the huts and nearly stumbled over Simon, who lay on his back in the grass, looking up at the sky. He was even drunker than Lofty, cradling a brace of bottles that clattered as he got up.

The bomber passed above us, flashing its recognition signal. Everyone knew the code for V, the three dots and a dash that had come to stand for victory. And that wasn't the signal that came from the aircraft. It was *G for*

George coming home, all right. It went round in its circuit.

The runway lights were on, shining across the ground in watery pools of crimson. Lofty stood with his pipe jutting straight from his mouth, looking up as the Halifax came sliding from the sky. All we could see were its landing lights, glowing brighter and larger. The engines raced for a moment, then slowed to a putter.

"You see, Simon?" said Lofty. "There's no such thing as luck. You don't get the chop because you write your name on a blackboard. Even the Kid says it's true."

G for George leveled off above the runway to let its airspeed fall away. It flickered in the runway lights, its black bulk seeming only partly whole. Wheels down, it hurtled along the flare path, flashing redness from the struts and the bubbles of glass, but aloft—still flying.

"Put her down," muttered Lofty. "Put her down."

George touched the ground with a squeal, then another. The engines hurried in a mad, deep roar, and the kite struggled up again.

"Oh, God, he's botched it," said Lofty.

I saw him clearly in the blast that followed. The ball of fire lit him up, and I saw his eyes staring, his lips apart. I heard his breath in the moment before the explosion reached us, before the hot wind tore across the field and plucked the caps from our heads. I saw the look on his face, and wished I hadn't seen it.

In that instant Lofty moved to the top of the Morris list. The little car that Donny Lee had driven, that had passed four times from owner to owner, now belonged to him.

Simon stared toward the fire in the north, in the field beyond the runway. A fire truck and an ambulance were racing toward it.

"Well, Cobber," he said. "Fancy a ride in your Morris?"

CHAPTER 21

I HAD NEVER SEEN ribbons as long as the ones that stretched across the map the next day at briefing. They dodged across France and over Belgium, then wound their way to the east, so deep into Germany that they almost reached Poland.

The target was Nuremberg, an ancient city full of castles and cathedrals. I asked Ratty, beside me, "Why are we going *there*?"

He whispered back, "I guess that's where they ran out of ribbons."

The intelligence officer showed us the things to watch for. He pointed at a photograph taken from twelve thousand feet and showed us the monastery and the royal castle and the bronze dome on the tomb of a saint. He said the starlight would shine on that bronze; we were lucky it was there.

"And now," he said, "here are the defenses."

We all leaned forward as his pointer scratched along the picture. I thought he would show us a hundred searchlight batteries and a thousand flak towers. But he smiled and ran his pointer along a ditch a hundred feet wide, and back up an ancient wall that nearly circled the city. "That's about it," he said. "They shouldn't give you much trouble."

He got a chuckle out of just about everybody. But those defenses seemed very sad to me. I thought they must have been built centuries before, to keep out men and horses, but it seemed that the people inside them hoped they would keep out bombers, too. I remembered someone saying almost the same thing about London, and I thought of the dead baby that I had seen there in the Big Smoke. I supposed there would be a lot of dead babies in Nuremberg, and that struck me as sort of a shame.

The intelligence officer let the laughter fade away. Then he got down to serious business, showing us the things that could *really* hurt us. All along the route there were guns and searchlights and night fighters. But our worst enemy, he said, would be time. To Nuremberg and back, it was eight or nine hours in the air. The darkness wouldn't last that long. "Don't relax when you've dropped your bombs," said the officer. "You'll battle the fighters all the way home."

"What about Window?" somebody asked.

"It will help, but I'm afraid they've largely found their way around that."

There were mutters among the airmen, little coughs and nervous breaths. If it hadn't been for Percy, I would have been terrified. I couldn't have hauled myself into the crate that night if it hadn't been for him.

We drove to dispersal in the Morris. Or most of us did, at least; Pop refused to get into the thing. He wouldn't even throw his chute aboard. So he legged it across the runway as the rest of us drove, with Ratty balanced on the bumper. Lofty parked behind *Buster,* jamming the binders too suddenly. Buzz slid right off the fender and sprawled on the grass. He shouted, but not from anger. He'd landed right on top of a four-leaf clover.

For the first time ever before an op, the keys were left in the Morris. Any change in routine was normally met with fears of a jinx, but no one said anything this time. They must have thought it really didn't matter what we did if we were already on a chop list.

Pop arrived five minutes later, out of breath, frowning at the Morris. "I hate that thing," he said. "It gives me gooseflesh just to look at it."

"Then don't look, old boy," said Lofty.

"I'll never get in it."

"That's fine, Pop. You don't have to."

Lofty sounded kind and caring, but the old guy looked nervous. He took out his crucifix, and it was still in his hand when we climbed through *Buster*'s door.

In bright daylight we started the engines. We wouldn't see the sun go down until we were halfway to France, and *Buster* was hot and muggy, thick with kerosene fumes. Along the wings, the airscrews thrummed as Lofty and Pop tested the temperatures, the pressures, the flaps and magnetos. They did it carefully, and they did it twice. Each engine was run up and throttled back, each magneto switched to left and right and back again.

"It looks good," said Pop.

"I don't know," said Lofty. "Gee, I don't know."

The bombers started passing, nose to tail along the perimeter. I watched them through my window as they lumbered by, huge and black, shimmering heat from their wings.

The erks pulled our chocks away. Sergeant Piper held up his thumbs. Will, in his place beside Lofty, nudged the throttles. By the sound of the engines I knew he was pushing the levers farther than ever to get *Buster* moving with all the weight of bombs and fuel. We turned onto the runway, then braked to a stop.

"Magnetos," said Lofty.

"We checked them already," said Pop.

"I want to check them again."

Pop sighed. His breath whistled in the intercom. But he did as he was told, and Lofty worried that something was wrong with the magnetos. "Damn," he said. "There's too much drop."

That old dodge? I heard Bert's voice in my mind. But suddenly Lofty said, "To hell with it. Full throttles! Lock 'em, Will."

If anything really was wrong with *Buster,* she managed to hold herself together. She took us through the evening to the night, all the way to Nuremberg without a murmur from the engines. She took us across the city, lurching through the flak and the billowing smoke from the fires. Percy lay inside my jacket, and I held him tightly as we rolled to the left. Through my window, eighteen thousand feet below, I saw the dome where a saint was buried, and I saw the castles burning.

Buster brought us home again. She brought us to a land of clouds, and went shivering through them as I tuned the loop and listened on the wireless. I picked up the streams of dots and dashes. "Skipper, we're on the beam," I said.

Two nights later the old crate took us to Italy, and it was such an easy show that even Fletcher-Dodge came along in his perfect *R for Rags.* It was our best machine, bright and new like a showroom car. He had renamed it for his favorite old dog. More than five hundred bombers went, and all but three came home to England. But Fletcher-Dodge stepped out of *Rags* as though he was Jimmy Doolittle returning from Tokyo. He was still swaggering the next day, when the first of the Lancasters came.

The entire squadron watched it circle round the field. We watched it tilt and sideslip down, then level off above the field, beyond the hedge. We heard the engines fade away, then rise again.

Fliers and erks and WAAFs, they all cheered as the Lancaster touched the ground. No one could have cheered more loudly if the king had arrived inside it. Then they surged forward, and I saw Ratty practically skipping along at the front of them all, Lofty—somewhere in the middle—grinning round his pipe. But I stayed where I was, feeling empty and sad. I saw the ending when that Lanc arrived.

Over the next few days I watched others arrive, one at a time, and a line of Lancs began to grow at the farthest end of the field. I never went near them until I had to, when our turn came around to go up for a spin on the fifteenth of the month. It was a night flight, under a big full moon.

I felt strange getting into a kite without a pigeon box to carry. I kept thinking that I'd forgotten it, that I heard—from a distance—the flutter of Percy's wings, the bubbly coo of his voice. For the others our first pigeonless flight was something to joke about. Simon said he was glad he wouldn't have to smell the bird anymore. "No lie," said Ratty. "We'll never smell pigeons again, soon as the Kid takes a bath."

I settled at the wireless, not wedged down in the nose, but high in the fuselage, right below the astrodome and just behind the engines. A trainer took the pilot's seat as Lofty hovered near him. He fired up the engines, taxied to the runway, then steered west to the coast in the moonlight. Down into valleys, up over hills, we took the same sort of winding route we'd taken in *Buster* our first time up, and I loved it all over again.

The Lanc made our old crate look like a dodo bird. Despite what I *wanted* to think, I loved flying in a thing so fast and big. I leaned sideways and looked forward through the front office, out through the windshield at the moon straight ahead. We were climbing toward it, with the engines in their perfect, powerful drone. Lofty was driving now, and it seemed that he could take us there if he wanted to, that he could put us down among the craters, or just loop the loop around that moon. But he throttled back and rolled us over, and I saw the ocean—all bright and sparkling—slant across the glass.

A shiver of delight ran through me. For a moment there was nothing in my thoughts but the joy of flying. I reveled in the weightlessness of dipping into the dive, then felt myself grow huge and heavy as we leveled out above the sea. I grinned as we turned and gamboled through the sky.

"Roaring rockets!" I said, and this time nobody laughed at me. Then I reached inside my jacket to stroke at Percy's feathers, and when I found only sheepskin, all my joy dissolved.

I suddenly missed my little friend so strongly that my heart ached. I felt a terrible guilt that I'd forgotten that he wasn't there. And I thought of what it really meant to be flying in a Lanc—that he would never be with me again.

CHAPTER 22

WE DROVE IN THE Morris to the Merry Men the first night beyond the full moon. It was the sixteenth of August, and we'd been with the Four-Forty-Two almost exactly three months. "Time to celebrate," said Lofty. I had no choice but to go along. The moon was so bright that there couldn't be an op for days to come. But more importantly, I was the only one who had saved any money, so I was shanghaied to pay for the rounds.

Lofty drove the bus flat out. Will and I clung to the bonnet, Buzz to the boot. Little Ratty rode on the bumper with his goggles on as our slipstream of road dust swirled around him. Simon was in the passenger's seat; Pop had refused to come along.

We flitted through the valley; we raced up the hill. For a moment, at the crest, we were airborne. Then we landed in a thudding four-pointer, jinking across the road. Lofty drove so fast and recklessly that I couldn't decide if he wanted to smash the little bus or if he believed that it *couldn't* be smashed. Maybe he thought that the Morris was somehow blessed on the ground, that it made sure we were safe until it got a chance to smash us in the air.

I leaned back against the windshield, holding on more tightly than I'd ever held to *Buster.* I watched the moonlit road twist toward us through the headlights' gleam and flash underneath; I saw white ghosts of milestones hurl themselves past. We went laughing into the bar, and for once I enjoyed myself. I played darts and sang songs, not even bothering to pretend that I was getting drunk. But early that morning, back in my bed, I had my dream again.

It was more frightening than ever, coming out of the blue like that. I woke up shouting, dizzy from a spinning world of sky and flames. Then I lay in a sweat, with a racing heart, staring up into utter blackness.

I was glad the moon was full, that its brightness would keep us on the ground. But I couldn't shake away my dream as I sat at breakfast. Lofty was planning a trip to Leeds for the evening when the speaker hummed and the WAAF told us, "You are on for tonight."

I could see from Lofty's face that he didn't believe it. "It's a full moon," he said. "This is a joke. Some silly clot is playing a prank."

But it was no joke. The erks right then were filling *Buster*'s tanks. They were getting ready to stuff her belly full of bombs.

The briefing scared me. It scared us all. The red ribbons went straight across the North Sea, over Denmark's narrow throat, then down along the islands of the Baltic.

They ended at a village called Peenemünde, a little seaside place that none of us had heard of.

But six hundred kites were about to attack it. Six hundred kites from all over England, they would meet above this little village and bomb it to hell, and none of us could even guess why. It was just another Goodwood, Fletcher-Dodge told us proudly. "It'll be a wizard show," he said. "Every squadron in England is putting every crate in the air."

Someone asked him, "Are you coming, sir?"

The swagger stick swished against his leg. "I only wish I was," he said.

Short little Drippy told us the skies would be clear. "Spectacularly so," he said. "You might get a glimpse of aurora borealis." But once the intelligence officer got up, I doubted that anyone would be looking for northern lights. He said there would be flak and searchlights on the ground, a smoke screen laid out as a welcome. Flak ships would be anchored in the Baltic. "Now mind you, watch for those," he said, as though it might not have occurred to us to do that. We would drop our bombs from just eight thousand feet, below the spotlight of a moon.

I told myself not to worry. I tried to think of Percy and his eye-sign, of his magic as a homer. But I only saw my hands trembling, and I held them together as the briefing went on, each bit of news worse than the last. Ratty and Buzz kept sighing and shaking. Simon doodled slashes on his notepad. Lofty, stoic as ever, stared straight ahead with his empty eyes.

They all had heavy lines scarred in their faces and their foreheads, as though they had been sitting for twenty years inside the hut. I touched my own cheeks, the corners of my mouth, certain that I would feel those same creases and wrinkles. It seemed that my world had gone into a tailspin, and I was more afraid than ever.

The CO ended the briefing with a little talk. "This is the last op for our Hallibags," he said, his crooked teeth showing in a grin. "The next time we fly, we'll be doing it in Lancs."

So that was it. His bit of news fell like a wet blanket on the benches full of fliers. He didn't get a smile, let alone the cheers he was probably expecting. He tapped his stick on his toe.

For me it was worse than the flak ships and the full moon, even worse than the low-level bombing. Though I'd known it was coming, and every day I'd expected it, his news made me gasp.

Tap-tap went the stick. Tap-tap. "Any questions, gentlemen?"

I put up my hand. I was the only one who did.

The swagger stick pointed at me. "Yes?" said Fletcher-Dodge. He didn't seem to remember me either from *Buster* or from the loft.

"What will happen to the pigeons, sir?" I asked.

Everybody laughed. It was as though I had touched a pressure valve, releasing it all in a rush and a roar. With the flak and the full moon, and the miles of sea to cross, the birds seemed a silly thing to worry about.

The briefing ended then. Fletcher-Dodge wished us

luck, and the airmen rose from the benches. We all stood at attention as the officers filed from the stage. Then I ran for the door.

Lofty shouted after me, "Kid! Hey, Kak." But I kept going, through the crowd and outside, beyond the huts, along the grass, down to the pigeon loft.

From a hundred yards away I heard the birds squawking. I heard their wings beating at the bars, and I thought of the pigeoneer who had slaughtered his flock to keep them from the enemy. I sprinted the rest of the way. I bashed through the door and into the loft.

Bert was there, in the midst of a swarm of pigeons. He was just beginning to sort out the ones that were "on" for the night. He had his bucket of suet waiting, and the birds circled round him.

"'Allo, sir," he said, shouting over the noise.

I couldn't see Percy anywhere in the mass of flapping wings. But Bert saw me looking and raised an arm that was covered with pigeons; six of them clung to his sleeve. He pointed to the top of the roosts, and I saw Percy up there, sitting patiently on the highest perch.

"Percy's too smart to mix 'imself up in the melee, sir," shouted Bert. "Oh, 'e always gets 'is turn."

I held up my finger and whistled, and Percy came whirring over to perch on my knuckle, his feathers all happily ruffled. He tipped his head to peer at my tunic, trying to figure out what I had brought him and where I had put it. His head moved forward and back, left and then right. He blinked and cooed, then gazed at me with his starry halo.

"I'm sorry," I said. "Gee, I didn't have time."

He took another look, peering at each of my pockets. Then he blinked at me, his little brow all puzzled.

"Oh, Percy, I'm sorry," I said.

He flew away and left me. He joined the crowd of pigeons fighting for the suet. I sat down on the feed bags, moaning to myself. "It's the end for them," I said.

"What do you mean, sir?" asked Bert.

"This is the last op for the Halifaxes."

"Oh, Crikey." Bert raised his head and swore. The birds whirled away from him, rising from his arms and shoulders. He came toward me through a storm of feathers, sad and slumped, a bowed-down giant. "Are you sure, sir? Did they tell you that?"

"Yes."

"Did they tell you what will 'appen?"

I shook my head.

He sat down beside me, the little suet tin looking sad and tiny in his hands. "So that's it, is it?" he said. "It's all over after tonight."

"I don't know what to do," I said.

I started to shake, more from fear than anything. I rocked forward until my head was nearly on my knees. Bert's arm pressed across my shoulder, his hand tightening on my arm.

"I thought you knew," I said. "I came down here, and I heard the pigeons flying, and I thought you were getting ready to destroy them."

"Never," he said. "I'd never allow it, sir."

"But . . ."

"It will all work out in the end. I don't know 'ow, sir, but it will."

I leaned against him, and he pressed me even closer. The birds came hopping on the floor, turning back and stopping, advancing warily toward the suet tin.

"Going to 'Appy Valley tonight, sir?" asked Bert.

"No," I said. "Peenemünde."

"I don't know it, sir."

"On the Baltic. On the way to Berlin."

"Oh. Double rations, then." He collected the tin and stood up. "It's a long 'aul, sir, for the poor little bleeders."

I started to speak, but he stopped me with a look. "Tonight's just another op, sir," he said. "No point in upsetting the birds, is there? We'll worry tomorrow about tomorrow."

He doled the suet out. Though he was doing it for the last time, he did it no differently, making sure that every pigeon got a proper share. I fed the others, the ones that weren't flying that night. They came pecking round my feet as I tossed down handfuls of seed.

We fixed message cylinders to the birds that were on. I clipped them in place as Bert held the pigeons, and it surprised me to see how the birds struggled. "They're uneasy," said Bert. "Not to worry, sir, but it might be a difficult op."

I didn't believe that birds could see the future. I thought they were scared because *I* was scared, that they sensed the fear that was growing inside me. When I saw how they fought at the doors of their boxes, I decided not to put Percy inside one.

I carried him from the loft on my shoulder, with his empty box in my hand. Through the rest of the afternoon I kept him right with me. I even ate my eggs and bacon with Percy tucked inside my jacket.

It was still daylight when Lofty drove us out in the Morris. We sprawled on the grass below *B for Buster,* and Buzz went looking for his clover.

Ratty tugged on the string at his neck and pulled out his rabbit's foot. Whole patches of its fur had been worn away by rubbing on his chest. He tapped it on his lips, then slipped it back into his flying suit. The others all saw him and, like people yawning after one person yawns, touched at their clothes for their own little charms. I put the empty box on the ground and let Percy hop around beside it.

We lay there too long. We should have climbed into the kite right away, before our thoughts could work around to the target and all the terrible things that the sun held at bay. Ratty was smoking cigarettes as though he would have no tomorrow to do it. There was one in his mouth, and a butt smoldering in the grass, and already he was fishing another from his packet. Buzz was still searching for his clover, and Will kept asking, almost to himself, "What the hell's at Peenemünde?"

An hour passed. Then we saw a little figure wandering toward us, a man in air force blue, dwarfed below the bombers. He came around the tail of *D for Dog,* through

A for Angel's shadow. His hands in his pockets, his head down, he crossed the grass toward us. The sun shone on his white hair.

"Wheezy jeezy, it's the padre," Ratty said.

"Come to do the last rites, I guess," said Will.

"No lie."

It was unnerving to see him coming. He had never walked out around the bombers before. Even Buzz stopped his search and watched that figure growing larger.

The padre stopped and stood above us, his back to the sun, his face a shadow below his cap. "Evening, boys," he said. "I wanted to wish you Godspeed and good luck."

He got mutters of thanks, a grunt from Ratty.

"I wish I was going with you, boys," the padre said, just like Fletcher-Dodge. "I really do. But there's no room for passengers on a Hallibag."

It bothered me that he said that, taking a word meant only for fliers. Ratty must have felt the same. He cocked himself up on an elbow and told the padre, "You can take my place if you like, sir. Lots of room for gunners."

The padre forced a thin little smile. "Anything I can do for you, boys?"

"You could help me look for a clover," said Buzz. "Bet you could find one easily."

The padre must have wondered if his leg was being pulled. Then Ratty said, "It's true; he needs it, sir. He never flies without one."

"No, he doesn't need a clover," said the padre, smiling. "God will be with you all."

Will looked up. "Do you really think so, sir?"

"I beg your pardon?" said the padre.

"Do you really think God goes flying in bombers?" asked Will.

The padre was standing directly in the sun; I couldn't look at him without squinting, and I couldn't see the expression on his face. He reminded me somehow of the pigeons that got millet while the others ate suet, and I felt the same pity for him, and the same envy, too. Jolly or not, his well-meaning visit had turned to a trial. He said in his calm way, "Wherever you go, He is with you."

"Then why do so many of us die?" asked Will. He sounded sincere, almost sad, as though the question had tortured him through many nights and days. "If God is with us, why do we die?"

"Knock it off!" shouted Buzz. He threw a little pebble at the bomb aimer. "I don't want to talk about this. It's wrong; it's bad luck."

Then Ratty surprised me by siding with Buzz. "No lie," he told Will. "Shut up, okay?" And he turned toward the padre and said, "Oh, Father. Bless us."

"No!" Will was pushing himself up. "*Tell me!*" he shouted. "Why do we die?"

Beams of sunlight seemed to burst from the padre's hair, from his collars and his boots. He put a hand up, as though to bless us, and the shadow of it fell across Will. "You go in the name of God. You go with His blessing," he said.

But the bomb aimer got up on his knees. I didn't

know if he meant to stand up or only to kneel there. But the padre stepped forward and put his hand on Will's shoulder. And Will didn't push it away; he held on to it, and asked again, "Why?" Then his back bent in an arch, his shoulders sagging. His head bowed toward the earth. "You don't know," he said quietly. "*Do* you? You just don't know."

His hand stayed clutched to the padre's wrist, on the stretch of white skin below a gold-braided cuff. In that moment it looked as though they were locked in a struggle. The padre, stiff-armed, might have been pressing Will into the ground. "Are you frightened?" he asked.

Will shook his head. "That isn't it."

"God bless you, son," said the padre. He pulled his hand up, and Will's arm rose with it—as high as he could reach—before it dropped to the grass. The padre backed away a step or two, then turned around and walked off toward the next kite.

"Father!" shouted Buzz. "Help me look."

"I can't," the padre said. "I don't have time." Already the first bombers were starting their engines. Puffs of white smoke were swirling up from the tangle of wings and tail fins. The air was shaking with the rumble of airscrews.

Ratty started searching for a clover, then Simon, then I. Will didn't move from his bit of grass; he didn't even rise from his knees. He held his helmet upside down, and stared at the picture inside.

Then Lofty and the old guy came around *Buster*'s tail.

Pop stood by the door. Lofty called to us: "Right, chaps. Let's go."

"My clover!" said Buzz.

Lofty got down and looked—the old guy, too—and Sergeant Piper watched us crawl across the grass as though we'd lost our minds. Far to the west, toward the sun, the first kite taxied to the runway. Another came into line behind it.

"I've *got* to find one," said Buzz. "Aw, Geez, I can't go without a clover."

"All aboard!" shouted Sergeant Piper.

Lofty walked over to Buzz and tried to haul him to his feet. Pop had already given up, and then Simon did, too. "Don't worry," he told Buzz. "She'll be apples tonight." He shrugged at Lofty, and the two of them wandered over to the kite. They stood at the door, and Lofty said, "Buzz, we have to go." Will shuffled over to stand with them there. I carried the pigeon box, and Percy on my shoulder, past Buzz and Ratty as they still ferreted back and forth.

The bombers passed in their thundering parade. "Buzz," said Lofty again. "We can't wait anymore."

"Another minute," said Buzz. "I gotta find one."

Ratty put his hand on Buzz's back. "Come on," he said. "You can take my rabbit's foot. Okay?"

Buzz shook his head. "It won't help me." He kept searching, frantic now.

Will climbed up through the door. Simon went behind him, then Lofty—ducking his head as he clambered through. Ratty was pulling at Buzz's collar, trying to get him up from the grass. Our engines started, one by one.

Buzz was nearly in tears when he gave up his search. He came running to the door, clumsy in his big boots. "Oh, Geez," he said. "I'm scared."

CHAPTER 23

WE THUNDERED OVER WHITBY and on across the sea, and the water was all aflame. High above it, with the sun behind us, we flew in a great battle fleet of Lancs and Hallibags. We could see them strewn for miles around us, on a sky of lurid colors.

I wished that Will had described it all with his poetry. He would have found just the right words to tell us how the sky looked as it changed from twilight to darkness, how the huge full moon came sailing up. But he was silent all the way; he never said a word.

I let Percy sit on my shoulder as we climbed toward the darkness. Our route took us over an airy mountain with a summit of eighteen thousand feet, so I thought he would feel a bit groggy as we crossed over Denmark. But for now he was happy to look out the window, and I felt his head turning from side to side as I listened on the wireless for a recall, for changes to the route and weather.

Silver moonlight flashed across the water. The engines throbbed as we climbed steadily to the east. Far in the distance I saw flickers of gunfire, little bursts of red tracer. I held on to Percy until we topped ten thousand feet, then tucked him inside my jacket.

A few minutes from the coast, Lofty told me to start throwing out the Window. I took Percy aft and plugged myself in by the flare chute. Someone sighted searchlights on our left; then Will broke his silence to say there were others to the south.

"Yes, I see them," answered Lofty.

I couldn't see anything where I was. But Will painted it all with his words, the way the beams of light were swinging and crossing. I was glad to hear him, until I realized that what he was really describing was a Halifax being coned in the lights. He talked on in a flat and dreadful voice, as another beam—and another—fixed themselves on the straggling bomber. Then he told us how the flak was bursting close around it, how the Halifax seemed pinned in place against the sky. Suddenly he stopped, and it was just his breathing that I heard.

"Poor buggers," said Lofty. His pipe started ticking.

We crossed narrow Denmark, and Will looked down at prickles of light. "They're sort of twinkling," said Will. "Sort of bursting. Here and there. All over." The whole country was ruled by the Nazis, but on the farms and in the villages blacked-out windows were being uncurtained, doors and shutters opened as the bombers flew overhead. From the middle of an empty field came flashes of a torch aimed toward us—three dots and a dash, three dots and a dash—V in Morse code, the symbol for victory. All across the dark land lights flickered on as we droned across it, our friends on the ground cheering us in secret. It was a brave thing, and a sad thing, and I wished that I could see it.

"Skipper. Turn coming up," said Simon. "Steer one-five-four. Now."

"Roger," said Lofty, the kite already rolling to the right.

We started down toward Peenemünde.

There was no use for Window anymore; the Germans knew we were coming. I moved up toward the wireless, passing through the front office. With our turrets whining, our engines in a pleasant roar, we flew along below the moon and above the sea, in a brightness that was neither night nor day.

"A hunter's moon," said Will.

I held on to Percy as I stepped down and buckled in at my place. "Don't worry," I told him. "There's six hundred kites. They won't get *us.*"

The night fighters came into the stream before we reached the target. Sparks of gunfire shot from kite to kite. Then the searchlights wheeled toward us, and the flak opened up from the ships down below. It grew heavier and heavier, and we had never seen flak as bad as that.

"We're going to get the chop," said Buzz.

"Shut up," said Lofty.

"It's true," he said. "I know it."

I closed up my window. I didn't want Percy to see the beams of light, the tracers and the gunfire, the flames and the bomb bursts. I squeezed him against me as the crate was hurled up and then down. I put my hand into my jacket and rubbed his feathers. I felt his heart shuddering inside his little breast.

Our number three packed it in just as we dropped our bombs. The one that had quit before, the one that Lofty had fretted about, sputtered and stopped. Lofty shouted at Pop to close off the fuel. Then the flak hit us. It ripped through our metal skin in a hundred places. It knocked out the number one engine, puncturing the fuel tanks. It jammed the rear turret and set the wing on fire, and down we went in a howling dive. I lurched against my harnesses, then smashed against the fuselage. Everyone was screaming. Buzz, in a high voice, was shouting for his mother.

The airframe shook all over. *Buster* went into a spin that hurled me sideways and pinned me back in my seat.

"Pull up!" yelled Lofty. "Come on!"

We tumbled down in a circle of fire, corkscrewing down to the ground. I could see my parachute but couldn't reach it. I felt Percy struggling in my jacket.

"Come on. Come on!" cried Lofty.

In my window the earth went round and round. My ears ached and my arms were chunks of lead. But my head felt light and woozy, and I passed out for a moment. I dreamed that we were flying flat and level, cruising above puffy clouds lit by sparkling stars. Then I woke again to the spinning horror of the kite and shouting of the crew.

We came out of the dive at a thousand feet, roaring through the smoke of Peenemünde. Our own fire had blown itself out, but someone was crying in the intercom; someone else was babbling. It was Buzz, going on and on, "I told you so! I told you so!"

We headed home with two engines, with so many holes in the fuselage that I could see the stars right through *Buster*'s skin. Air blasted through the kite and froze me in my seat. It stank of petrol and cordite and scorched metal.

"What's the course?" someone asked. "What's the course for home?"

I shivered in my seat, suddenly colder than the air. It was the ghostly voice I'd heard so long ago. "What's the course for home?" it asked again.

I knew what the answer would be even before Simon spoke. Then he said, as I knew he would, "Steer two-one-niner."

The kite shook as it turned. *Buster* rattled and shook as it came around to a course that it had always been meant to fly. It seemed as though my ghosts had taken control, and I was so cold and frightened and lonely that I wondered if I was even alive anymore. I might have got the chop in that blast of flak, or we might have spiraled into the ground, and now we were on our way to that terrible place where all the airmen went. Two-one-niner. Was that the course that Donny had steered? Was it the one that everyone had to fly?

But Lofty's voice came over the intercom then. Calm

and strong, a little bit slurred by the pipe in his teeth, it calmed me in an instant.

"Sing out," he said. "Will, are you there?"

"Yes, Skipper."

"Simon?"

"Okay."

He got an answer from everyone. We couldn't *all* be dead, I thought, not dead and talking, dead and flying. I tightened my hand around Percy.

"How much fuel have we got?" asked Lofty. Pop gave him a number, and I heard the pipe clicking in the skipper's teeth.

"It should be enough," said the old guy.

We straggled home by ourselves, out of the stream and the sense of protection it gave us. The sky was clear and bright all the way to England. The sea was silver, the land a grayish mass of shapes and shadows. Then we crossed the hills with our fuel getting low. And we dropped into fog that *Buster* never came out of again.

I listened for bearings on the wireless, but couldn't even hear static in my headphones. I slammed at the box, then tore the covers off, and I saw the shattered tubes and knew the thing was useless.

We groped through the clouds, holding to our course, judging by our airspeed when we should find the runway. But it wasn't where it should have been. We flew five minutes farther, then circled around and circled again, like a pigeon trying to find its way. The fog turned yellow as dawn approached, a greasy, sickly color.

Pop said, "You've got fuel for twenty more minutes, Skipper."

We widened the circle and went around again.

"Kak," said Lofty. "Can you call the Darkies up?"

"No, Skipper." There wasn't a chance of getting help. "The wireless is U/S."

Pop said, "Fifteen minutes, Skipper."

"Okay," said Lofty. "Okay."

His intercom clicked off, then on again. "Boys, get your chutes on," he said.

I didn't see that we had any choice except to bail out. I took my chute from the rack, and waited.

"What about Ratty?" asked Buzz. "His turret's stuck."

"Yeah, what about me?" said Ratty.

"Don't sweat," said Lofty. "I'm staying. You guys get out, and I'll put the kite down somewhere. Me and Ratty."

"And me," said Buzz.

"Yeah, me too," said Simon.

Pop and Will, they both said they'd stay with *Buster*. No one was bailing out. "I don't want to get my boots dirty," said Will.

I didn't know what to do. It was a scary idea to step through the hatch and into the air. But I thought of the *White Knight* wrecked on the hillside, and I sure didn't want to stay.

Percy wasn't a problem. I had a paper bag to put him in; I had it for just that reason. Tucked inside, with its top crumpled down, he would fall away from the kite and out of the slipstream, then work his way free to fly on his own. I didn't have to worry about Percy.

"Pop, how's the fuel?" asked Lofty. "Kid, if you're going, you'd better go."

It didn't matter to him what I did; it didn't matter to anyone. There was nothing shameful about bailing out of a doomed bomber. It was the proper thing to do, and everyone knew it.

"Skipper, ten more minutes," said Pop.

"Okay. Kid, get outta here," said Lofty.

My old man had used those same words. He had shouted them at me in one long slur, too many times for me to count. But Lofty said them in a different tone, wanting me to go only because it was safer. I hadn't thought of my dad in ages, but suddenly I saw him clear as anything, as though his armchair was right in front of me and he was in it, trying to focus his drunken eyes. I wondered what he would say if he *had been* sitting there, what he would think to see me scared and uncertain. I knew right away; he'd be pleased. His red face would laugh, his blurry eyes glowing with the pleasure of finding he'd always been right. That I was good for nothing. That I cared for no one but myself. That even shadows scared me.

I lifted my parachute. The buckles tapped against the ones on my harness. I hoisted it up and put it on the rack. "I'm staying," I said. "We'll stick together."

"Jolly dee," said Lofty.

I opened my jacket and let Percy come out. He

hopped to my shoulder, up to the window. The fog seemed liquid-thick, flowing round the wingtip, churning through the airscrews.

"Flaps down ten," said Lofty. "Landing gear down. Field or forest, here we come."

I unfastened one side of my mask. "Where are we?" I whispered to Percy. "Where's the airfield? Where's home?"

He snapped to attention.

He stiffened; his head came up. His pink feet tightened on my jacket, and the chevrons rippled across his wings as he drew his feathers tight. His eyes staring around with their halos of stars.

He knew where we were. He knew how to get home. I peered into the splash of his eye-sign and tried to learn what he knew. But he only blinked at me, then pecked my lips.

"We're almost on the deck," said Lofty. "You see anything, Will?"

"No, Skipper."

"Full flaps. Everybody buckle up."

I wanted Percy to be inside my jacket. The lining, I thought, would keep him padded if we pranged. But when I reached for him, he hopped away. And again he stood at attention. "What's the matter?" I asked. And then I knew. I fumbled for my intercom button. I shouted, "Wait! We can still get back."

"How?" asked Lofty.

"Percy can save us."

I thought someone would laugh, but the intercom was silent. "If we let him go, he'll fly straight to the loft," I said.

"Yeah, and then what?" asked Lofty. "How's that going to help?"

"We'll get there with him," I said. "You'll follow him home."

The fog flowed past; the engines droned. I hoped everyone was thinking of the day over Scotland, our first flight in *Buster,* when Lofty had flown the old crate more slowly than any of us had believed was possible.

"Can you do it?" asked Will. "Can you follow a bird?"

Lofty's pipe clicked on his teeth. "How fast does he go, Kid?"

"Seventy miles an hour," I said. "Maybe more."

"You're nuts," said Lofty after a moment. "Kak, you've lost your mind." And then the old guy said, "I think it's worth a try."

"You too?" asked Lofty. Then, "Oh, hell. Why not?"

He opened the doors to the bomb bays, to slow us down as much as he could. Simon set to work opening the hatch in the floor. I took my paper bag and snapped it open. I put Percy inside, folded the top, and unbuckled myself from my harness.

"Kid," said Lofty. "When you let him out, come and help me. Everyone else, watch for the bird."

I crouched over the hatch with Simon, and he hauled it up and let it clatter onto the deck. I looked through the hole, down at a solid mass of clouds rushing past.

The wind whistled up through the floor, tugging at my clothes. With her nose up, shaking as though from fright, old *Buster* flew on. Her two engines raced to keep us in the air.

"Eighty-five knots," said Lofty.

"Don't stall her!" cried Pop.

"Eighty knots. Okay, Kid. Let him go."

I dropped the bag. I thought I'd be able to watch it fall straight into the clouds and see Percy flutter loose. But the instant it left my hand, the bag vanished below the kite, snatched away by the slipstream. I got up so suddenly that I put my leg through the hatch, and fell into the hole. My elbow hit the fuselage, and I jammed up against the metal with the clouds racing past my feet. Simon caught me. He pulled me up, and I staggered to the cockpit. I plugged in beside Lofty.

Ratty was shouting, "There he goes! Left, Skipper. Left!"

We wheeled in a turn so sharp that the clouds blurred across the windshield.

"Where is he?" said Lofty.

There was no answer. Round we went through a solid sky. I looked to the left and the right, but I couldn't find Percy.

"There!" shouted Will. "Twelve o'clock high. Look at him go!"

I saw him then, through the windshield. Percy was straight ahead and a bit above us, his wings flapping. He was a little black dot in the fog, and in a moment we overtook him. I watched him through the panes of the canopy, until our propwash hit him and rolled him on his side.

Lofty stomped on the rudder. Pulled at the column. "Throttle back," he told me. "That one. The middle one."

I pulled on the lever, and the kite slewed sideways.

"On the right," shouted Buzz. "There he is!"

Buster rolled the other way.

"Behind us now," said Ratty.

Round we went again, tilted far over. Through the glass, beyond the wingtip, I saw the little bird thrashing through the clouds. He seemed to skid forward across the canopy, right around it and over the windshield. A gray-and-green speck, he was flying like a rocket.

"Full throttle!" cried Lofty.

I shoved the levers forward. The wing lifted as we leveled off. Little Percy seemed to sink below it.

Will shouted, "I see him. To the right! To the right!" he cried as Buster swung around. "Now straight! Now steady, Skipper."

Lofty leveled the wings. He put the nose down a bit and cranked up the flaps. He aimed *Buster*'s nose right where Percy had been. But the pigeon was gone.

Lofty flew straight and level as we scanned the whole sky, all around and above and below, but no one could see Percy. We droned along, looking up and down, left and right. I stared down the steps to the nose, out through the open hatch, and saw a shadow rush by with the clouds, and then another.

"Five minutes left on the fuel," said Pop.

The clouds were scattering, burning off with the sun. I saw a fence go by, then a tree. And then we crossed the airfield.

We flew right over the pigeon loft, right across the runway. We roared over Hangar D, so close above it that our wheels nearly touched the curve of the roof. Lofty's leg straightened on the rudder pedal. "Throttle back," he told me as we skidded round toward the tower.

"Home! We're home," shouted Will.

We missed the runway. We missed it by a hundred yards or more, and landed on the taxi strip. Our port wing nearly brushed the noses of the Lancs that were ranged across the grass. Erks and airmen watched us hurtle past, our wing in shreds, our fuselage like the top of a pepper shaker.

Lofty braked, then turned the kite. I stood beside him in the cockpit as he taxied back, and I saw Sergeant Piper running out to meet us, with his gang of erks behind him.

We didn't have to shut the engines down. The first one quit as we rolled into our dispersal, the second a moment later. We rolled to a stop, and the erks came yelling round the tail fins, like a pack of dogs chasing a car. They banged their fists on the fuselage, and pounded on the door until Buzz went down to let them in. Then they swarmed up to the cockpit.

Sergeant Piper pointed at the wing. "You great clot!" he said to Lofty. "What have you done to my bus?"

CHAPTER 24

IT TOOK THE ERKS half an hour to free Ratty from his turret. Buzz looked at him squeezed into the glass ball, laughed, and said, "Just leave him there." But as soon as the erks were finished, Buzz was the first to help the gunner out. He held little Ratty upright and walked him round through *Buster*'s shadow to get the kinks from his knees and ankles.

We all stood together around the old crate, and I was right in the middle of the group. Will held up my arm as though I was a champion fighter. "The Kakabeka Kid!" he said. "The Birdman of Yorkshire!"

I felt happy and proud, and a bit embarrassed, too.

Percy hadn't really saved the kite. But he had tried his best, and maybe that was good enough for the others. They laughed their heads off about the little bird, telling each other how he had looked as he'd flown through the clag with his wings in a blur, how each of them had spotted him. They said it had been a crazy idea to follow a pigeon, that only someone like me could have thought of that. Only the Kakabeka Kid could have done it.

I wished that Bert was there to see the fuss over his best bird. It made me sad that he hadn't come out to see us.

"Okay, chaps," said Lofty. "Let's go."

We piled aboard the Morris. Even Pop climbed in, taking the passenger seat for himself. Lofty shifted gears and off we went, jiggling on top of the car as it rumbled on the grass. I thought we would go straight to the huts, but Lofty took us across the dispersal and over the runway, straight to the pigeon loft.

Bert came out to greet us as we skidded to a stop. Percy flew from his shoulder to mine, nuzzling against my cheek. Bert hugged me again, holding me in his bird-smelling grasp, then shook hands with all the others. He said he had lost a year of his life in the time between Percy's arrival and ours.

For the first time, the crew showed a real interest in the pigeon. Lofty held out his arm and whistled for the bird to come, but Percy just stayed on my shoulder. Will fetched him a bit of grass, then smiled as Percy's beak touched his fingers. "He looks like a corporal, eh. Those two stripes on his wings."

Bert stood at my left side. He leaned down and whispered—a Bert whisper that everyone heard—"The order's come, sir."

I knew what he meant, and it took my pleasure away. It made me more sorry for Bert than anything.

"I say, what order's that?" asked Lofty.

"I'm to slaughter the birds, Sarge," said Bert.

Lofty looked shocked. "All of them?"

"I'll send 'ome the ones that I can. But all the others, yes."

"When?" I asked.

"Tonight, sir," said Bert. "Old Fletcher-Dodge 'as got the cook making crusts right now."

I was sure that Ratty, at least, would laugh at that news. But the little gunner, barely half the height of Bert, seemed more surprised than anyone. "He's going to eat our birds?"

Bert looked down—way, way down. "Not if *I* can 'elp it, Sarge." Then he turned to me. "I'm going to make a run for it, sir."

He took us to the back of the building, where the ancient motorized loft had its bonnet open again. Oily rags were draped on the fenders, Bert's broken tools scattered around. The loft's great bins had their doors dropped down, ready for the birds.

Pop took off his flying jacket. He bunched up the sleeves of his sweater, stepped onto the front bumper, and leaned over the engine.

"I think I can 'old her together," said Bert. "Long enough to get me to Scotland, at least."

"You're taking the pigeons?" asked Will.

"Yes, sir. That's my scheme, sir." Bert tugged at his filthy clothes. "I'm giving it a try, sir," he said to me. "I'm going to take them north, sir, and try to 'ide them in the 'ills."

Pop was making the sort of sounds that every mechanic seemed to make, a lot of grunts and groans.

Just looking at the motorized loft, we could tell the plan didn't have much hope. It was almost funny to imagine the pigeoneer trying to sneak across England in that thing. It was a huge, rattly house on wheels, a lunatic's caravan that would be crazier still when it was stuffed with fifty squawking, stinking birds. And there in the cab would be Bert, spotted with droppings, with pigeons perched on his head and his arms.

"Just let them go," said Buzz. "Why not, eh?" He looked around, like a schoolteacher in a class full of idiots. "They're birds, aren't they? Turn them loose and let 'em fly away."

"Wheezy jeezy." Ratty punched him on the arm. "You let a homing pigeon go, where do you think he heads for?"

Buzz frowned. He couldn't figure it out.

"He thinks they'll go to Trafalgar Square," said Ratty with a laugh. "No lie. That's what he really thinks."

A dim understanding showed in Buzz's eyes.

I said, "Well, what if they *do* go there?"

Bert frowned at me. "Sir, I'm surprised at you."

"No. Listen," I said. "What if we *take* them there? You and I? We can go tonight."

"To London?" said Bert. "To *London,* sir?"

"Why not?"

"Well, sir . . . Well . . ." He blinked and muttered, and then he grinned. "Well, why *not,* sir? I've got mates down there. They could get the birds stuck, and—"

"Stuck?" asked Buzz.

"Oh, the birds 'ave to be stuck," said Bert. "They 'ave to learn that the place is their 'ome. My mates will do that." He rubbed his forehead, looking doubtful. "But you'll be AWOL, sir, if we don't get back before morning."

Pop raised his head from the motor. "Not a chance of that," he said. "Not a chance you'll even get as far as Sheffield. It's just rust and hope that's holding this together."

"Are you sure?" asked Bert.

"You might not get through the gate."

Bert sighed. "That's torn it, then."

"I say." Lofty took the pipe from his mouth. "We could make it there in the Morris, you know."

And so our plan was made, and everyone fell in with it. Bert told the crew what he had already told me, that he used to live near Trafalgar Square. Pop interrupted him. "You'd have to be mighty posh to live near the Square," he said.

"No, not really, Sarge," said Bert. "Not anymore." He said his friends would be there, and that they would be willing to help.

Pop sat down to calculate in his head the fuel we would need. Simon measured a pigeon box and went off to figure out the best way to stack fifty of them on a Morris.

Then Ratty spotted the flaw in our plan. "What about the cook?" he said. "What about all those crusts he's making?"

Buzz shook his head. "Are you really that dumb? We take them with us, eh? We dump them somewhere on the road, and we stop at a bakery coming back and pick up chicken pies."

Maybe Buzz wasn't so stupid after all. His was a better idea than anyone else could come up with. So we raced to the huts and sat through debriefing. Then we raced back to the loft and got everything ready. Simon went round and talked to the cook, who was only too glad to get out of the chore of baking his pies. He even came with us that night, in his white apron and his tall cook's hat. His pie crusts were stuffed in the car's little boot.

Bert took off his coveralls. He combed his hair and shined his boots, until he looked so spick-and-span that Lofty didn't recognize him at first. No one said a word about the blank spaces on his sleeves, and Bert didn't explain. He just kept his hands there at first, blushing and shy, until it was obvious that everyone had seen what he was trying to hide, and that no one would bind him for it.

As soon as it was dark, we roared out through the gate in the Morris. Will perched on the very front of the bonnet, with a road map in his hands. Simon navigated from the starboard fender. Buzz and Ratty, on the boot, watched for policemen coming behind us. Bert and the cook and I balanced the stacks of pigeon boxes that rose from the passenger seat and the running boards, that covered every inch of the windshield. Lofty couldn't see a thing except boxes, so the old guy got up behind him—just where he'd be in old *Buster*—with his helmet and goggles on, his head in the slipstream. He sat on the boxes and passed steering directions to Lofty, with taps of his feet on the pilot's shoulders.

We raced south toward London, flying through the blackness behind the dim glow of our hooded lights. We hurtled through Sherwood Forest, through little villages closed up in the blackout. Simon took us down the narrowest, emptiest roads, winding through curves with the boxes teetering and the pigeons shouting inside them. From county to county, we roared through the night—seven airmen, a cook, and a pigeoneer balanced on the little black roadster.

It was two hundred miles to London, and we made it in less than three hours. We came into the city through Chipping Barnet, then steered through the grounds of Hampstead Heath.

"Left!" shouted Simon.

Pop gave Lofty a kick. The little bus squealed round a corner. Gears shifted as we gathered speed again.

"Right!" called Simon.

A kick from the old guy, a turn of the wheel, and the pigeons settled into their squawks and songs. They were singing their old one as we hurtled south down Edgeware Road and onto Park Lane. The blacked-out city rushed by as Pop steered us past Hyde Park and Buckingham Palace, onto the Mall and through Admiralty Arch.

And then we were there. Stone buildings were all around us, a swarm of cars and buses. In the middle, like the still beam of the night fighters' guide, rose the towering column topped by Nelson's statue.

Lofty drove us over the curb with a great lurch and a clatter from the boxes. A thousand birds rose from the Square, scattering in front of us like a burst of flak. Then Lofty put the binders on, and we stopped below the column, below the huge lions with their bronze heads watching.

Lofty stepped from the car and stretched his arms. He looked at the big buildings and the faintness of the skyline. "You know," he said, "when the war's over, I think I'll set up a shoe store around here."

"I thought you were going to be a bush pilot," I said.

He shrugged. "I think I'll have had my fill of flying, Kid. I'll be happy to keep my ten-and-a-halfs on the ground."

We stacked the pigeon boxes in a perfect pile at the base of the nearest lion. They rose around it and made a wall that didn't look out of place. It looked as though it had been there since the war began, just like any of the funny little walls that had been built to protect strange things from the bursts of bombs. Before we were finished, the boxes were coated with pigeons.

Bert listened to his own birds singing inside them, and he looked like a happy, monstrous little boy. "This is wizard, sir," he said. "This is a proper snorter."

Lofty put the last box in place. The cook opened the

boot of the Morris and took out all the pie crusts. He flung one of them out over the Square, and it ricocheted off the paving stones. It went rumbling away like a wheel, and a flock of pigeons chased it. He threw another one, and it landed with a cracking thud.

"Wheezy jeezy, you'll bust the stones," said Ratty.

The cook stacked the rest of the pies between the lion's paws and told Bert to feed them to the pigeons.

"All right," said Bert. "They need the roughage."

Down toward the river, Big Ben started tolling the hour. We counted the strokes of the bell, two and then three of them. "We'd better scramble," said Lofty.

Bert nodded. "Yes, you'd better go."

I looked up at him; I thought he'd be coming with us.

"I'll be up in a day or two, sir," he told me. "I 'ave to find my mates and see the pigeons safe, then I'll make my way back on the train."

"But Fletcher-Dodge—"

"Oh, 'e won't know I'm missing, sir," said Bert.

Old Pop was gazing around at the buildings that encircled us, a ring of spires and domes and walls of carved stone. "Bert, where do you live?" he asked.

"Just over there, Sarge." Bert pointed in the vaguest direction, just a twitch of his arm as his hand went up to scratch his hair. He shuffled his feet.

They were such grand and beautiful buildings that I couldn't imagine Bert living in any of them, and didn't believe he ever had. But he smiled at me and said, "Come and I'll show you my digs, sir."

He took me across the Square, past the empty fountains and down to the underground. I imagined we would have to take the tube to the next station, or the next, but I saw right away that the last train had left long before. The platform was crowded with people. Even the tracks were covered with sleeping bodies.

Then one of them stirred and shouted, "Why, it's Bert." Another said, "Bert, is that you?"

It seemed that half the people there knew him, and greeted him warmly. An old lady called him Bertie, and stood up so that he could bend way down and kiss her cheek.

He told me, "This was my 'ome, sir, for many a month. I was bombed out in the blitz, sir," he said.

It made me happy to see all his friends crowd around him. They asked where he had been and why he was back, but he told them all that it would have to wait. "I've got to see my young one off," he said. And didn't that make me proud.

We went back to the Square, to the pigeon boxes, so that I could say goodbye to Percy. I asked which box he was in.

"Just whistle, sir."

I did. I whistled once more for Percy, as I had so many times. And he answered with a familiar little song. He chirped and cooed as I searched along the pile of boxes, and I found him standing at attention at the door of one near the bottom. I bent down and put my finger through the flap. "Hey, Percy," I said.

Lofty came up behind me. He told me in a quiet voice

that it was time to go, and I looked up to nod at him, and saw Pop and Ratty and all the others standing there behind him.

"One more minute?" I asked. "Is that okay?"

"Sure, Kid," said Lofty.

CHAPTER 25

I PATTED PERCY'S HEAD. I rubbed his cheeks, his throat, the little holes for his ears. He leaned against my hand with all his tiny weight.

"Goodbye," I told him. "So long, Percy."

"Take 'im out, sir," said Bert. "Give 'im a proper goodbye."

I unfastened the door, and Percy hopped out. He rose straight to my shoulder; he nudged at my ear.

Across the Square and down the street, Big Ben tolled another hour. I knew I had to go, but I wished I could have a few minutes more with Percy. I wanted to tell him how much he had helped me, and how scared I was to go on without him. But I was too embarrassed to tell him that with everyone standing around.

I gave him one more tickle, one more squeeze. Then I slid my hand across my shoulder, and he jumped up to my knuckles. "You'd better hold on to him," I told Bert.

"Yes, sir," he said.

We put our hands together, and I felt the little

prickles of Percy's claws as he walked across my fingers onto Bert's huge fist. I wanted to remember the feeling of that.

"I'll put 'im back in 'is box, sir. Soon as you leave," said Bert. " 'E'll 'ave to live in there for a while, of course. Until 'e forgets that 'e can fly 'ome and see you, sir."

"How long?" I asked.

"Oh, not too long, sir. A fortnight maybe."

I nearly sobbed. Percy had always been the bird with the greatest freedom, and it wasn't right that he would have to live two weeks inside a box. Two weeks without flying, without walking around in the sun. Hundreds and hundreds of birds around him; it would be almost torture for my little friend.

We all said so long to Percy. Simon told him, "Take care, Cobber." Buzz petted the bird, and it was the first time he had ever touched a pigeon. He ran his fingers down the double stripes on Percy's wing. "Look after yourself, little corporal," he said.

I couldn't move away. I wanted to stroke Percy for the last time, and then again once more. I felt a thickness in my throat, and tears coming to my eyes.

"Oh, this isn't right, sir," said Bert. "I think you'd better keep 'im."

"He's your pet," I said.

"Yes, but 'e's a flyer, sir. Percy doesn't belong 'ere, begging bits of bread from people."

"What about Fletcher-Dodge?"

"Blast him," said Bert. "You're right. Any stray pigeons will find themselves eaten." He sighed again.

"Oh, sir, 'e shouldn't stay 'ere and 'e can't go 'ome. I don't know what to do."

I could see that on his face. It sort of pulsed and twitched as all his undecided thoughts went running through his mind. Little Percy peered up at him, head tilted, eye-sign gleaming.

"We really have to go," said Lofty.

Buzz put his hand on my arm. "Come on, Kak. He'll be all right, the little corporal."

"Too bad he's not a sergeant, eh?" said Ratty. "'Cause then he could live in the sergeants' mess."

A warmness came over me. I looked up to see that Bert was smiling. His eyes were almost as bright as Percy's. He nodded his head, and I nodded mine. "We'll promote him," I said. "Hello, Sergeant Percy."

There was a bit of silence before everyone talked at once. They said it was a good idea, or at least one worth trying. Simon said it was "cunning as a dunny rat." The sergeants' mess was just about the only place where Fletcher-Dodge wasn't *allowed* to go.

Bert held out his hand, and Percy hopped from him to me. "Go now, sir. Please go, and 'urry 'ome."

I put Percy in my jacket, and we climbed aboard the Morris. Lofty ran his hands across the instrument panel. "Switch to ground," he said. "Landing gear locked." The motor coughed and started; it whined as Lofty ran it up.

"See you soon, sir," shouted Bert.

I touched my cap. I saluted the pigeoneer. Then I pulled my goggles down, and Lofty went off with a squeal of tires.

We drove across the Square, scattering pigeons left and right. We bounced down the curb and shot across the street. We looped the loop through Piccadilly Circus.

It was light enough to see the buildings, the towers and domes, the bronze lions in the Square. Old Bert was standing up on one, waving both his arms. I waved back, and then he disappeared behind me.

We took the same route home, out through Hampstead Heath and along the country roads. Then the city was behind us, and the sun was coming up.

From Leicester up to Leeds, we stopped at every bakery we passed. The cook dashed in and bought a chicken pie—or two if he could get them—from the money that we pooled, and the boot filled up as we rattled north. Then we sped through Yorkshire, and it was like flying through clouds, and we arrived back at the airfield before anyone was stirring.

Fletcher-Dodge held a big party for the officers, to celebrate the Lancs. He served his pigeon pies, and I would have given my lost ray gun to see how he gloated over the table that was covered with them all. But sergeants weren't invited. We heard from Simon and Will how he had called it a "wizard show," a "splendid scoff." Will laughed as he told us what an adjutant had said.

"He took a bite," said Will, "this fellow did. He chewed it carefully. Then the CO asked him what he thought, and the adjutant said, 'It tastes rather like chicken, sir.'"

Buzz giggled. "What happened then?"

"The CO was furious," said Will. "He turned red as beets, and sent the fellow packing. He said pigeon pie was wasted on a guy like that."

Percy took up lodgings in the mess. He got his own little paybook and a place at the bar, a wooden swing that he loved to stand on as people pushed. The harder they pushed, the more he liked it, and he would soar in great arcs, singing his little song.

CHAPTER 26

BERT CAME SLOUCHING INTO the loft the next day as I was feeding the few remaining birds. His hangdog look barely brightened when he saw how few there were. "Nobody even missed me, sir," he said.

"I did," I told him, and he smiled then. He put on his coveralls and went to work.

Over the next few days the pigeons slowly disappeared. Bert went down to the train station every morning and every evening with another basket tagged for a breeder somewhere. He expected to be sent away at any moment, and each time I went up for a training trip in the Lancaster, I was afraid that he would be gone when I landed.

By the time we made our first op in the Lancs, on the thirtieth of August, there was only one left. Or there was only one in the loft, while little Sergeant Percy was swinging in the mess.

I carried him in my jacket, out to the Morris, into the kite. Simon had fixed him up with a tiny oxygen mask made from the rubber tip of a medicine dropper. Percy didn't really need it, but I fastened it on at nine thousand feet, and Simon came back to have a look. He grinned at me, and I grinned at him, and Percy just looked foolish. The oxygen made him lively, and he hopped around as far as his little hose would reach.

We flew to Happy Valley, to a city with a name as long as the Ruhr—München-Gladbach. Will said it sounded like a pretty place, full of castles and bridges and churches. "Yeah, well, not after tonight," said Ratty. "It'll just be full of rubble then."

He was angry that we had missed out on Berlin. More than seven hundred bombers had raided the Holy City on the twenty-third of August as we were stooging around Yorkshire in an empty Lanc. It didn't matter to him that it had been the worst night of the war for Bomber Command. Fifty-six of our kites had got the chop. But Ratty had seethed in the mess the next morning when we heard on the wireless how badly the place had been plastered. "I missed it," he'd said. "I wanted to see Berlin."

Even now, as we flew on toward Germany, he asked if we could make a detour to look at the ruins.

"I don't feel much like sightseeing," said Lofty.

It was the night of the new moon, and the sky was clear. Stars shone down through the astrodome. I looked up at the Milky Way, imagining myself in outer space, glorying in the strength and speed of the Lancaster. All the way across the sea and on to Happy Valley, Percy explored the space around me. He stood staring through the astrodome, with his eye-sign gleaming in the starlight. Then he rose to my shoulder and pecked at my lips, and I knew that I had nothing to fear. I didn't think that any of us worried with Percy to keep us safe. "He'll always get us home," we'd said.

Fletcher-Dodge came along, so it was bound to be an easy show. We followed the markers that the Pathfinders dropped, along a ribbon of green on the ground, and the city was orange and red from the flames. Not one of our kites was lost; not one was even scratched. We came home laughing, and in the mess, someone marked Percy's paybook so he would get his two dollars and twenty-five cents for the op.

Ratty said it was silly for a pigeon to be saving money. "No lie," he said. "We should take him down to the Merry Men and let him blow it on a binge."

"He doesn't drink," I said.

"He can have a sandwich, can't he?"

"I say, that's topping," said Lofty in his whine. "We'll take the Morris out tomorrow night. Kak, are you in for that?"

I could hardly believe I was the first one he asked. I grinned and said, "Sure, I'll go." I was going to say "That's wizard!"—but I was afraid of sounding silly.

I went to bed as dawn was breaking, and I felt happy—safe and happy. The last thing I expected was to have my spinning dream again, but I saw the burning land below and felt the coldness of the sky, and I woke kicking at my blankets.

I lay there, staring up, waiting for the dream to fade. Then I rolled on my side and looked at all the sleeping sergeants in their mounds of sheets, and suddenly saw the beds again as rows of graves, the wrapped bodies only waiting for their burials. Nearly every bed already slept a dead man as well as the still-living fellow. I shared mine with one, and the thought of that chilled me more than the air in my spinning dream. What if he came back, I wondered, on one chill, gray dawn, and reclaimed his bed, crawling in beside me?

Once the idea was in my mind, I couldn't get it out. I lay with my eyes wide open, certain that a ghostly hand would fling back my sheets, that an icy body would slide in next to mine. I thought I saw a shadow passing through the door, an airman still in boots and leather jacket; I thought I heard his buckles jangle.

You'll see a lot of them, sir. Bert had told me that, one of the first times I had talked to him. *There, but not really there.*

I knew I couldn't sleep anymore. I got up and got dressed, and went down to the pigeon loft. I still wasn't used to going near it without setting off a rush of birds, and the silence that night seemed particularly lonely. The door creaked when I pushed it. In the darkness I found the lantern, and I hurried to fill the loft with its light.

I looked in every nesting box, along every roost, in every corner. But the last pigeon was gone.

"Bert!" I shouted.

I ran around the back, into the pigeoneer's little room. It was as empty as the loft. Bert's cot was set up on the floor, his blankets folded at its foot. In the middle of the canvas was a penciled note. "I couldn't bear to say goodbye."

I slumped to the floor, my elbows on the cot, my head in my hands. For a long time I sat there, thinking and remembering. Then I went back to the mess—I was the only one there—and stood at the bar, pushing Percy on his swing. I looked in his eyes, at the little twinkling stars round the black of his pupils. As always, it comforted me to be with him. The fear that my dream had brought back, the jitters that were gathering in my stomach, left me then as I talked to Percy.

I stayed with him until breakfast. I even slept for a couple of hours in a chair beside the bar. When I joined Lofty and the others they were already at the table, already planning Percy's night on the town. But the trip to the Merry Men had been scrubbed, and a different op was in the works. Lofty wanted to take the whole day and drive north into Scotland. "I hear they wear great clunking shoes up there," he said. "Sounds interesting."

It was the sort of plan that everyone fell in with right away. But the speaker clicked, and the WAAF said, "Good morning, gentlemen." She said, "You are on for tonight."

"Well, that's that," said Lofty. His smile disappeared; his wrinkles deepened. He took out his pipe and started whistling through it.

"Hey, we might not be on," said Ratty.

"We're always on," said Lofty.

I looked at my breakfast and didn't feel like eating. I said, "I'm sorry, I—"

"Forget it, Kid," said Lofty.

"But it's my fault," I said. "And I—"

"Forget it!" he snapped.

Ratty was looking at me. "What do you mean, it's your fault?"

"You know," I said.

He frowned. Then he shook his head, and I was amazed that Lofty hadn't told them everything. I wondered what he *had* told them to explain why we were always on. If I had been him, I would have made sure they all knew. I would have told them, "It's because of Kakabeka. It's because the Kid was afraid to fly."

Pop understood; I could tell from the way he looked at me that the old guy figured everything out right then. But poor stupid Buzz would never catch on. "I thought it was because we were so good at it," he said. "I thought we were one of the crackerjack crews."

"Wheezy jeezy," said Ratty.

I looked around at them all. I said, "I was afraid to fly."

"Who isn't?" asked Buzz.

"But I tried to get out," I said. "I went to the CO. I begged him, nearly. That's why we're always on."

"No lie?" asked Ratty.

"No," I said.

They didn't laugh at me. Nobody mocked my fears. Maybe they thought it had all worked out for the best, that we got Percy because I was afraid, and now—because we had Percy—we were safe. But nobody talked about it. We just stared at our plates for a while, then got up to leave.

I followed the others around the tables, out toward the door. I heard the sprogs talking loudly, and I saw the worried looks on the faces of the others. And then I heard a familiar voice, and turned my head toward the last table.

There, at his old place, with his old crew, sat Donny Lee.

"Hey, Kid!" he said. His face was as white as the china plates. His hand, too, was white—and thin—and he held it up and rolled it slowly through the air, waving me toward him. "Come join us," he said.

I didn't look twice, afraid that he was really there, that I wasn't only seeing things. I hurried from the hut, but I could still hear the laughter of his dead friends, and his voice shouting after me, "Come join us, Kak."

CHAPTER 27

I WATCHED THE FUEL bowsers nestle up against the Lancs. I watched the erks bombing up the kites, and anyone could guess that we were going a long way. They stuffed the bellies of the Lancs with enough incendiary bombs to start a fire that might burn forever. The bowser king moved from one aircraft to the next, missing only one. Fletcher-Dodge wouldn't be flying that night.

I went through the day in a trembling worry, not sure why my dream had started again or why the ghosts had come. I sat with Percy for a while, trying not to let him see my fear. Just holding him made me feel better, and I thought of smuggling him into the briefing. But it was a good thing I didn't. It might have scared him silly.

The target was Berlin. The Big City, the Holy City. There would be a belt of searchlights and flak nearly forty miles wide. There would be more night fighters than we had ever imagined. No city in Germany was defended as heavily as Berlin. But Ratty was pleased that we were going. "I'm getting my wish," he said.

That evening, for the first time since I'd left home, I wrote a letter to my mom and dad. I lay on my bed, with Percy standing on my pillow, and I wrote, "Dear Mom and Dad."

I didn't tell them that I loved them; I didn't tell any lies at all. I only said that I missed them very much right then. I said that I wasn't sorry that I had come to England, but that I wished I was home in Canada. I told them not to feel bad about anything they had done, and that was all I could think of. I wondered how to finish it, what to say instead of "Love." I was still lying there, looking at the letter, when the old guy came in and found me.

"Time to go, Kid," he said.

I signed my name and stuffed the letter in the envelope. I didn't know what to do with it; I held it up toward him.

"You can leave it on your bed," said Pop. "I think that's good enough."

He stood in the corridor two beds down. I took Percy in my hand, then put him on my shoulder, and walked past the old guy. His hand came onto my back. "First time for everything," he said. "An orphan writing to his folks."

I didn't ask him how he knew; he probably only guessed. "How old are you, Kid?" he said. "Seventeen?"

"Sixteen," I told him. "But my birthday's pretty soon."

His hand pressed harder for a moment. "My oldest boy's fifteen," he said. "I wish he was more like you."

It made me happy to hear him say that. I knew he was trying to tell me that he wished his own boy was as strong as me. Maybe he, too, thought he was going to get the chop above Berlin, and he worried about whether his son could carry on without him.

We collected our chutes and our escape kits. We changed into flying clothes. Percy stayed with me, always watching wherever I went. I noticed that he wasn't worried, that he didn't twitch at all or sing the mournful pigeon song. When I tucked him inside my jacket, into the sheepskin lining, I really wasn't frightened.

Then I stood at the edge of the tarmac with Lofty and Pop and others. Trucks full of crews were going by, puttering out to the kites. I saw Donny Lee waving at me from one of them, his white fingers spread. He didn't seem quite whole, more like a swirl of dust.

Even as I watched he disappeared, and I didn't find it so frightening as the first time I'd seen him. It seemed to me that he was on his way back to wherever it was he had come from. Or maybe he wasn't even there, and it was just the jitters that had made me think he was.

We sat below the Lanc exactly as we'd used to sit around *Buster*. Will looked at the photograph in his helmet, and Simon took a sniff of his handkerchief. Ratty smoked his cigarettes. Buzz found his clover right away, took out his crossword, and tackled some of the clues. We were sick to death of hearing them.

The Lanc was still new enough to us that Lofty and Pop ran carefully through their checklists when the time came. Blowers, boosters, ignition on. The engines started up, and the erks pulled away the chocks. We took off into daylight and gathered with a great flock of kites. Others joined us as we headed for the sea.

Then darkness came, and we sort of hid inside it. The engines roared and thrummed, and we flew along on autopilot. Lofty just sat behind controls that worked themselves and looked around, and up, watching the sky.

Others were doing the same thing: Will in the nose; Buzz and Ratty behind me. The Lanc was faster than old *Buster,* and it flew higher. But no one liked it better than Ratty. His tail turret gave him a better view than he'd ever had in a Halifax, and he told us—delighted—that he could see the Big Dipper and the sword of Orion and all of Cassiopeia.

"Just make sure you see the fighters," Lofty said.

We crossed the enemy coast in the middle of the stream, with seven hundred bombers ranged across the sky. We were like a great stampede of cattle rumbling along behind the leader, through bursts of flak from ships and shore, then on across black Europe.

Percy, in his oxygen mask, stood looking out the astrodome. I wondered if he felt the same as I did, that it was good to leave the sea behind us. He turned his head and blinked, then hopped across my back from one shoulder to the other.

Buzz saw squirts of gunfire off to the west, and we knew the night fighters were prowling through the herd of bombers. Then a Lanc exploded in a ball of yellow, and on the other side, a kite was streaming fire from an engine. It was turning a long, slow circle, said Will. It was going down. "They've bought it," he said.

The stream flew on and on. It stretched and grew, and it twisted through the sky like a huge, crawling snake. Its head was thrusting toward Berlin, its tail still over the sea. We worked our way along in the middle of the thing, rocked by the propwash and slipstreams.

We passed through searchlights and a belt of flak. Another crate went down. Ratty counted parachutes: "Two, three, four," he said quickly. That was all that came out. Lofty switched the autopilot off and nudged us higher in the sky. His pipe clicking inside his mask, he and Pop fiddled with the engines to get the settings and the mixtures right. And on we flew—on and on through the blackness.

I scanned through the frequencies on the wireless. I adjusted the antenna and twiddled with the knobs, and for a moment I heard music. It came from England, lovely Vera Lynn singing about the bluebirds and Dover. I fed it through the intercom, just a few notes, a few words about love and laughter that sounded sad as heck up there in the dark above Germany.

Then Will said, "I see it. There's Berlin."

The engines hummed their steady sound. We bounced through a pocket of air.

"God, it's burning," said Will. "It must be burning from end to end. It looks like the earth's on fire."

Ratty cried, "I want to see! Just jink us round for a minute, Lofty."

"Just *wait,*" snapped Lofty.

"Wheezy jeezy. I'm getting my wish. I'm going to see Berlin."

What a funny thing to have wished for, I thought, to see a city burning. But I couldn't help feeling happy for Ratty, maybe because I had never wished for anything as strongly as he had wished for this.

"I don't believe it," he said. "How many kids grow up in cardboard boxes and get to see Berlin?" His turret whined back and forth. "What's it like, Shakespeare? What's it look like?"

"Just like Hamburg," said Will. "Just like Nuremberg and Mannheim." He whispered through the intercom. "It's a mass of flames, a whirlwind burning. It looks like hell has cracked open, and it's bubbling up to the surface; it's spilling into the sky. I can see the devil down there, and all his demons, and that's what it's like. Boys, we're flying into hell."

Lofty clicked his intercom. "Just shut the hell up," he said.

He sounded exactly like my old man. I remembered hearing that so many times. Shut the hell up. Get the hell out. Go to hell, go to hell, go to hell. I wondered what he would say to me now if he could see me flying toward the fire, doing exactly what he had told me to do a thousand times. What he had always told me to do.

"The flak's heavy," said Will. "You ever seen so many searchlights, Skipper?"

No answer from Lofty.

"They're turning the whole sky white. They're weaving and crossing. There goes a Lanc. Christ, there goes another."

And then we flew into the flak. I smelled the bursts of it and felt the air blast against us. With shaking hands I grabbed little Percy and tucked him into my jacket. I pulled away his oxygen and hoped that he could sleep before he sensed my fear.

Lofty started weaving back and forth. He put us in a dive and pulled us out again. Ratty's guns were firing.

Then the searchlights coned us. They glared in through the bubbles and the canopy and lit up the kite with a white glow. We dropped at least a thousand feet; I was suddenly weightless in my chair. Then Lofty pulled us up with the nose high, with the whole crate slanted. Flak burst below the nose and tossed us higher. Something black and small broke off and came skittering down the fuselage. It bounced on the deck, leapt to my desk and again to the floor, and lay spinning at my feet.

It was Lofty's pipe, and I picked it up.

The stem was nearly chewed off. He had bitten right through it in places, leaving deep and jagged marks. He had worn the end away and shortened it to a stump. He must have bitten on that pipe harder than a wounded man would bite on a bullet to keep from screaming in pain.

I held it as the Lanc shook from end to end. I looked at that pipe and realized that Lofty was terrified all the time. *All the time,* whenever that pipe was in his mouth.

I felt ashamed that I had found him out. I remembered him scoffing at clovers and rabbits' feet, at my plastic ray-gun ring. There was no such thing as luck, he had said. But all along he had kept his own talisman with him. In the air, in the mess, through all the hours of waiting, he had whistled and puffed on that pipe. He needed it more than the rest of us together needed all our lucky charms.

It shocked me to see him coming toward me now, staggering down the fuselage. He was so desperate to get his pipe back that he had put on the autopilot and ripped off his mask, tearing away his oxygen and his wires. His arms held out, his mouth screaming, he lunged at me and grabbed at that thing.

Then the flak hit us. It tore the starboard wing in two.

A gusher of flames billowed out. We fell on our side and went into a spin, and the flames wrapped around the fuselage. The smell of petrol was thick enough that I could hardly breathe.

Everyone was yelling. The searchlights still held us, and the flak puckered all around. Simon was clawing toward the escape hatch in the top of the fuselage. But the spin of the kite pushed him away, and he went sliding down the kite. Lofty had been thrown against the side, and was stuck there with his arms wide, the pipe in his fingers. Then petrol ignited in the fuselage. A river of fire flowed over the metal, pouring down toward the nose, pouring over Lofty's boots. In the glow of flames I could see him staring at me. Just staring with a wild look. And the fire rose around him.

I grabbed my parachute and pulled it toward me. It weighed hundreds of pounds, that bundle of silk. I buckled it on, but couldn't get out of my chair. The fire and the searchlights wheeled round and round in the astrodome. Then there was a flash of light, an incredible wallop of air. And the Lancaster exploded.

I woke up in my dream. I was spinning through bitter-cold air. The ground below me was on fire—not solid earth, but a sea of flames. I felt weightless, as though I was floating.

It was Percy who woke me. As he struggled from my jacket, his wings slapped against my throat, then against my face. I didn't know if he meant to save me or only to save himself. When he was halfway out, the air caught his wings and his tail, and it snatched him away in a thrashing blur of feathers.

I fell facedown, watching the earth and the flames. Then I tried to run, my legs kicking at the air, and sent myself tumbling head over heels.

I pulled the rip cord. I thumped my fist against the parachute. The silk erupted from the case, wrapping all around me, spilling up behind. It wrenched me onto my back, and I looked up at the stars and the stream of bombers marching through the searchlights and the smoke. Then it rolled me over toward the earth, and rolled me over again.

Cords zapped across my cheeks and across my arms. Then the chute snapped open and the harness dug into my thighs, and it pulled me right out of my boots. I watched them fall as I floated upright above Berlin, in the sweeping of the searchlights, like Captain Marvel below a multicolored cape.

I drifted along on the wind, scudding above the city. I wondered if Percy was near me, if he would flutter down to sit once more on my shoulder. And then, when he didn't, I wondered what would happen when he got home and found no one waiting at the loft. Someone would find him, I thought; someone would think to go looking. Or maybe Percy would home straight to the mess.

The parachute was huge and round and white above me. The leading edge fluttered in a silent wind; the shrouds stretched down and met at my shoulders. I turned slow circles, looking down past the toes of my socks to the fires of Berlin. I swung from side to side, and the searchlights washed over me and passed along. I saw the Lancaster hit the ground, or the main part of it at least; I was pretty sure it was ours. There was a flash of light as the bombs exploded. And in that instant they all just disappeared: poor stupid Buzz; little Ratty, who had got his last wish; Will the poet, Simon the gadna; and Lofty, with his secret still clutched in his hand.

All alone, I floated into the blackness. With no sense

of falling, no sense of movement, I drifted through the void that belonged to Donny Lee and a thousand others. I was afraid to look around in case I saw him there, or a host of airmen sailing with me, all white-faced or burned to crisps. Between the heaven and the stars I swung below the chute, flying through the world of the dead.

EPILOGUE

I SPENT THE REST of the war, and the rest of my boyhood, in a prison camp. With its rows of wire fences, its wooden huts and sandy ground, it was like an enormous pigeon loft crowded with men and boys who had once been fliers.

We had lived in the sky, in that limitless world of moonlight and clouds, and to be suddenly caged in was too much for some. I thought at first it would be just fine, it would be jim-dandy to be locked in there, to be locked out of a world at war. But soon I was spending my days pressed against the wire, staring out at trees and hills. Through two winters and two springs I wore a trench through the sandy ground, from my hut to the wire.

Now and then the great Flying Fortresses thundered overhead. They didn't even bother with camouflage paint anymore. Their aluminum skins shone like silver as they stretched their cloudy trails across the sky. It was heartbreaking to watch them, and the fighters that followed—like little sparks of sunlight. I came to understand the surly bonds of earth. They bound me down as the months crawled by.

But it wasn't the sky that I longed for. I didn't think that I would ever again climb into an airplane. I ached for the North Woods, for the cry of the wolf and the bursting of deer from the undergrowth.

In 1945 we were freed by American soldiers. We rode a train through ruined cities and flattened villages, past fields full of craters and rubble. A soldier beside me, watching through the window, said, "We sure liberated the hell out of this place."

The war was over when I arrived in England again, and though I looked everywhere for Bert—from Land's End to the Scottish Highlands—I found no trace of the old pigeoneer. In the hills of Yorkshire I found a deserted runway and the rubble of a pigeon loft. In London I sat by the bronze lions in Trafalgar Square. But the pigeons only saddened me, and the whirring of their wings brought sweat to my hands and a knock to my heart.

The things that I had seen and done never faded from my mind. The sight of a full moon, the smell of clover, the sound of a laugh like Ratty's, would bring everything back in an instant. Every now and then I dreamed I was falling, and I woke in a sweat, kicking at the blankets.

There was nothing left for me in England, and I went home to Canada in the spring of 1947. It was the forest that called me, the great stretch of the Canadian Shield, with its red rock, its jack pines and leaping rivers. But I went at it slowly. I bought a train ticket only as far as Toronto.

Yesterday I climbed aboard and headed west. I huddled by a window as we clacked through little villages, through farmland and fields. The farther I went, the more the sky grew thick and stormy. When the sun went down, and there was only darkness around me—and the shaking of the train—I felt that I was flying. And last night, for the first time in many, many months, I dreamed the same old dream of spinning round and round, of the earth below me full of fire.

I woke screaming. I flung away my blanket, and it tangled in my arms. For a moment, amid the rumble of thunder and flash of lightning, I thought it was Percy beating his wings at my face. I woke the others in the railway car; I shocked them from their sleep. And their startled voices sent me back to a burning, spinning Lanc.

Even now, in the brightness of noon, they look toward me, wondering—I suppose—about my air force uniform and the deep lines in my face.

Lake Ontario sparkles on our left; the land on our right is green and flat. We're getting close to the city now. I don't know how long I'll stay, or exactly what I'll do. But someday I'll carry on to the west, and home to Kakabeka.

The train rocks over a switch. The wheels click and clack. The engine sounds its whistle up ahead, and the sound sends me off again in my mind. I travel half the world, in the middle of a war, to a lonely airfield among the hills of Yorkshire.

AUTHOR'S NOTE

Just about everyone who grew up in southern Alberta remembers the Nanton bomber. Seventy feet long, a hundred across the wings, it sat beside the highway near the little town of Nanton, as though its crew had landed there one day and walked away across the fields. It was a big Lancaster with four great engines, with a turret in its tail and a turret on its back, and a pair of rudders mounted on a rear wing that was wider than the road.

It was forty miles from our Calgary home, and it's been almost that many years since I saw it last. But I remember the smell of the Nanton bomber, the yellowness of the glass, and a hollow feeling that seemed to pass from the thing into me. I remember climbing through it, sitting where the pilot had sat, crouching where the gunner had crouched.

In another direction, to the east of our home, there was a landing strip where people gathered every summer for an air show. We went there one year to see another Lancaster, one that actually flew. I can still hear the engines, still see the size of it as it growled across the prairie sky, across the sun, flying for the very last time. When it landed it was shipped away to be a statue somewhere.

It was no wonder that I grew up with a fascination for the wartime aircraft and their pilots. There was so much drama in the air war, so many tales of heroism. There was Guy Gibson flying his great Lancaster along the top of the Möhne dam, drawing fire from the gun towers as the next pilot went in with his fabulous bouncing bomb. There was Charles Mynarski, who battled to free his rear gunner from a burning Lancaster as the flames leapt up and scorched away his clothes and his parachute. There was Douglas Bader, who stomped around his fighter base on two tin legs after a flying accident cost him his real ones.

Years and years later, hoping to find that boyish excitement again, I started planning a story about the air war, about the night fliers of Bomber Command. I read the same books all over again, and whatever new ones I could find. One of the first was *Boys, Bombs and Brussels Sprouts,* by J. Douglas Harvey, a Canadian pilot. I followed him through his days in Halifax bombers, to his first flight in a Lancaster. And the next sentence came as quite a surprise:

"Perhaps the strangest change was the absence of our pigeon, which we had always carried in the Halifax."

It seemed bizarre to me. In its day, the Halifax stood at the peak of aeronautical design. The seven members of its crew could find their way on the blackest night to bomb any city within nearly a thousand miles of England. They could defend themselves along the route; they could talk to England by wireless. Everything they might need, they took along, like the old explorers on the seas. That they depended, in the end, on something as quaint as a homing pigeon seemed silly somehow, and pathetic. It was as though you could strip apart the space shuttles of today, and find at the heart of them little windup rubber motors.

I went back to the books in a different way, looking only for mentions of pigeons. There wasn't very much. It was as though the airmen had forgotten about the birds, or hadn't thought of them as important enough to write about.

But the pigeons saved lives. They carried messages from bombers forced down in the English Channel and the North Sea, from others that landed on fields and lonely moors. The most heroic pigeons were awarded medals for bravery.

One of those was White Vision, who flew in an RAF flying boat.

In October 1943 the flying boat ditched in the North Sea, sixty miles from its base. It came down at 8:20 in the morning, but the weather was so poor that no other aircraft could be sent out to look for it. At five o'clock that afternoon, White Vision homed to his loft. He had flown into headwinds of twenty-five miles an hour, through mist and rain so thick that he couldn't see farther than a hundred yards. But he brought his message with the location of the downed aircraft, and the entire crew was rescued.

White Vision was awarded the Dickin Medal, a presentation given only to animals. Bearing the words "For Gallantry" and "We Also Serve," it was known as the animals' Victoria Cross. Of the fifty-three recipients, thirty-one were pigeons.

In 1943, when this story takes place, the squadrons of Bomber Command and Coastal Command had their own pigeon lofts, and specially trained crews to run them. The pigeoneers were usually fanciers who had kept their own birds in peacetime, and were taught their new duties by the Army Pigeon Service. Their birds flew in every type of bomber until the Lancaster was introduced. *B for Buster* would actually have carried two pigeons, with the navigator probably looking after one of them.

The aircrews often joked about the birds, and the chances of snacking on pigeon if flying rations dwindled. J. Douglas Harvey says, "We never thought of the pigeon except for those times when we were waiting to climb aboard for a flight; and once we got under way we seldom remembered it until the next raid."

That take-them-for-granted attitude, though understandable for men going off to high and lonely battlefields, might explain why the pigeoneers had to wait fifty-five years beyond the war to receive any recognition for their work. It wasn't until 2000 that a representative of the Army Pigeon Service placed a wreath at the Cenotaph in London.

That first wreath was placed by Mr. Jack Porter, an Army Pigeon Service pigeoneer during the war. Over eighty now, he still helps out at pigeon races, though he had to give up his own loft because of lung problems that came to bother many pigeoneers. Mr. Porter kindly helped me with the research for this book, answering questions about lofts and pigeons and pigeoneers. From him, more than any other source, I learned the importance of the job he'd had, and the seriousness of his work. For the sake of this story, Bert—my pigeoneer—is an outcast and a bit of a failure at everything else, a dirty and slovenly man. That is perhaps the most fictional part of this book. In truth, the pigeoneer was a dedicated professional, volunteering for his role out of an interest in and a love for pigeons. Though nearly overwhelmed with paperwork, he kept his birds with great care and fondness.

Throughout the war, pigeons carried messages for the army, the navy, and the air force. They parachuted into France with British spies, and brought back messages that couldn't be safely sent by radio. They even carried messages for journalists. Articles in the wartime papers were sometimes headed "VIA PIGEON."

In Bomber Command, there were several pigeons that flew fifty ops, some that flew more than a hundred. One of those, a Dickin Medal winner called Cologne, made its way home several times by itself, from aircraft that had been forced to land in England. On June 29, 1943, its last aircraft was lost over Germany. But Cologne still returned, seventeen days later, with a broken breastbone and other injuries.

Some pigeons do have the eye-sign. Fanciers have written whole books describing the colors and glints in the eyes of great racers and homers. Others say the marks mean nothing, but they don't argue that the halos and the stars are there.

And pigeons really can fly as fast as Percy. The Army Pigeon

Service trained its birds for speed, and clocked more than one at seventy miles an hour. A Halifax bomber, with its wheels and flaps down, would stall at about eighty-five miles an hour. There wasn't a great deal of difference in speed between a very fast pigeon and a very slow bomber.

Over time, technology replaced the birds. As Bomber Command squadrons converted to Lancasters, with advanced radio systems, the birds became redundant. The birds were somehow removed, but their fate is unknown. Though I doubt very much that any commanding officer feasted on his feathery crew, it's almost certain that others did. While many of the birds belonged to private fanciers, others were bred especially for the air force. Mr. Porter says those birds were destroyed when Lancasters arrived. J. Douglas Harvey says the birds were officially retired. "If you ordered chicken in a restaurant," he says, "you knew it was pigeon that was served, and a question often flicked across my mind: was a fellow crew member now making the supreme sacrifice?"

It seems to me that it was a terrible fate the pigeons met.

To the Germans, the crews of Bomber Command were known as *Terrorfliegen,* the Terror Fliers. The destruction that was brought to European cities by the nighttime raids is difficult to grasp from the numbers in casualty lists. But it was immense, and horrific.

As Allied armies advanced through Europe in 1945, pictures of the flattened cities appeared, and a great dismay and horror rose at what had been done. Churches and monasteries, castles and museums, old bridges and harbors and homes, all lay in heaps of rubble, and it seemed a shameful way to have fought a war. Then in the first months of peace, German war leaders were tried as criminals. Some were sentenced to be hanged or imprisoned for ordering aerial assaults on English cities.

The airmen of Bomber Command, who had brought far greater

destruction to German cities, were—in a way—tarred with the same brush. Campaign medals were issued to soldiers and sailors, but not to the bombers—once heroes and now villains. The same people who had cheered the airmen on their nightly way to Germany suddenly condemned them for what they had done. And over the years, the criticism of Bomber Command only grew stronger. Bomber Harris, today, is often cast as a cold-blooded man who delighted in slaughtering German civilians.

The truth isn't so simple. At the beginning of the war, British bombers worked in the daylight, taking great care to avoid harming civilians. But aircraft losses were so high that night bombing became the only option. And bombing at night was not very accurate. Of the first ones to try it, fewer than one aircraft in ten came within five miles of its target.

Early in 1942 the British government put Harris in control of Bomber Command, with the instructions to target German cities, and especially civilians. By killing workers in their homes, the government hoped to destroy or delay the major German industries. It called this process de-housing.

Harris had the duty of announcing the shift in tactics. In his first public broadcasts he said Germany could now expect to receive what it handed out in the bombings of Rotterdam, London, and Warsaw, but on a scale far greater and more deadly. "They have sown the wind," he said. "And now they are going to reap the whirlwind."

Harris was popular among the aircrew of Bomber Command. He did what he could to make their lives safer and longer. For the fliers themselves, there was no question of right or wrong. They dodged flak and searchlights and fighters to hit back at an enemy that was doing its best to kill them. There wasn't a British soldier on the ground in all of Europe, but night after night the fliers climbed into their bombers and took the war to Germany.

They suffered for it terribly. Their casualties were higher than in any other branch of the service. Of the 125,000 men who flew with Bomber Command, 55,500 were killed. Thousands more were wounded or captured, and an airman beginning his thirty-op tour had no logical hope that he would ever complete it.

They were all volunteers. For the most part they were teenagers, or men so newly out of their teens that they were still really boys. They fought in the darkness, in bitter cold, where the air was too thin to breathe. They came home to empty chairs and empty beds, where their friends had been just hours before. Of course they were terrified.

"The fear of flying operations was a constant with most aircrew," says Harvey. "Faced with what they considered impossible odds, many aircrew simply quit. It was rare for an entire crew to quit but nearly every crew had one member pack it in." Harvey had two.

Lack of Moral Fiber. That was the fate awaiting airmen who quit, the label that Bomber Command put on those who refused to fly, whether it was before their first op or long after their twentieth. Punishment was swift, and so terrible in the eyes of the airmen that, for many, the fear of being branded LMF was greater than the terrors of ops. I imagine it often took a great deal of courage for a man to be called a coward.

GLOSSARY

Airscrew—the propeller unit on an aircraft, made up of a hub and separate propeller blades.

Bind—a favorite word of Bomber Command aircrew. Binders are the ground brakes on the aircraft wheels. In airmen's slang, something depressing or troubling is a bind. But bind can also mean bored: if something bores you utterly, it binds you rigid.

Bomber Command—the structure set up to control and manage the aircraft and crews of the Royal Air Force, and the "colonial" crews of the Empire. Airmen from the United States fly under their own, separate organization, unless—like Ratty—they have volunteered for Bomber Command.

Bomber Harris—Air Marshal Arthur Harris, Commander-in-Chief of Bomber Command.

Bowser—a fuel tanker that is towed from bomber to bomber. The sergeant in charge of it is known as the bowser king.

CO—commanding officer.

Clag—cloud, tending to be thick. In its oldest sense, the word refers to the clotted bits cut or combed from a sheep's fleece.

Darkies—"Darky" is the code word for a system of emergency navigation. A lost aircraft can call "Darky," and searchlights on the ground will be aimed by their controllers to guide the bomber to a nearby airfield.

Erk—an abbreviation of the rank of aircraftman: an air mechanic. But for more than half a century before the war, the Royal Navy called its lower-deck ratings erks.

Flaming onions—the tracers of antiaircraft guns.

Gen—reliable information. According to Squadron Leader Ward-Jackson, who wrote a book on RAF slang, it likely comes from the stamp "For General Information" applied to official documents. Pukka Gen is "the real gen," coming from the Hindustani word "pakka," meaning substantial.

Goodwood—the code word for a maximum effort of Bomber Command. Every available aircraft is readied for flight.

High Wycombe—a village in Buckinghamshire. The headquarters of Bomber Command are here, in underground offices.

Jink—to keep an aircraft swerving from side to side.

Mae West—a life jacket, worn on top of flying clothes. Its shape and bulk give airmen a slight similarity to the buxom movie star.

Mag drop—an abbreviation of "magneto drop." Magnetos power the spark plugs. If one isn't working properly, an engine test results in a drop in revolutions.

Mickey Mouse—the bombardier's instrument panel.

Nissen—the British equivalent of a Quonset hut.

Prang—to land heavily or crash. The word approximates the sound of a collapsing aircraft.

Second dickey—an extra, "oddball" pilot.

Sprogs—inexperienced aircrew. Ward-Jackson says the word originated at a training school, where a student airman confused sprockets and cogs, and defined a toothed wheel as a sprog.

Stooge—to fly about aimlessly.

Synchronizing—The four engines of a Halifax bomber have to be brought "into sync" by adjustments of the engine speed and the propeller pitch. Properly synchronized, they make a steady, throaty sound.

Tracer—a gun round or shell designed to glow as it moves through the air. Tracers allow a machine gunner to see where he's firing, but allow others to see where he's firing *from.*

WAAF—Women's Auxiliary Air Force, or any of its members.

Wimpies—airmen's slang for Wellington bombers.

Wop—an abbreviation for Wireless Operator. Wops who are trained in air gunnery are WAGs.

Wop May—a Canadian pilot in World War I. He was being pursued by the Red Baron when the baron was shot down. Wop May returned home to Edmonton after the war, bought an old Jenny, and started his own tiny airline.

Yellow Peril—a training aircraft, named for its distinctive color—and dangerous behavior.

ACKNOWLEDGMENTS

I would like to thank the following people for their help with the research and writing of this book. If I mentioned everyone who offered assistance and advice, the list would fill many pages. But these people in particular helped me imagine what it might have been like to be a boy in 1943, living and flying with Bomber Command.

Jack Porter, a wartime corporal with the Army Pigeon Service in North Africa, now living in Stalmine, Blackpool, England, for all his kind help in understanding the world of wartime pigeons and pigeoneers.

Bill Foote, a Halifax pilot in World War II, now retired in Alnmouth, Northumberland, for his wonderful explanations and recollections of an aircrew's role in Bomber Command, and for showing me, as far as possible, what it must have been like to fly a Halifax.

Guy Jefferson, MBE, a thirty-four-year veteran with the RAF in radar and radio, now of the Yorkshire Air Museum (in Elvington, York), for details of wartime airfields, runways, and flares.

The Yorkshire Air Museum, for providing the names of Guy Jefferson and Bill Foote.

Mrs. Marjorie Southern and Ms. Pat Southern, of Altrincham, Cheshire, for sharing the story of their husband and father, Thomas Edwin Southern, a member of an RAF crew rescued through the efforts of the pigeon White Vision.

Mr. Peter Elliott, senior keeper in the Department of Research and Information Services at the Royal Air Force Museum in Hendon. Also Joanne Ratcliffe, office administrator, Department of

Research and Information Services, for technical information on the Halifax and the air force in general.

Tim Stankus, archivist at the Royal Signals Museum in Blandford Camp, Blandford Forum, Dorset, for information about pigeons in the war.

Mary Godwin, curator and archivist at the Museum of Submarine Telegraphy, Cable & Wireless Porthcurno Trust in Porthcurno, Penzance, for information about the role of pigeons in the war.

Derek Partridge, Freshfield, Formby, Lancashire, of the Animals in War Memorial Fund, for contact information.

Margaret Taylor, information officer for the Royal British Legion in London, for contact information.

Stephen Hayter, executive director of the Commonwealth Air Training Plan Museum in Brandon Manitoba, for information on the training plan.

RAF pilot Alan Stuart, of the Flying Training Command, now living in Langley, British Columbia, for his help with flying details.

RCAF navigator Bill Lowther, of Vancouver, for assistance in understanding the role of a wartime navigator.

Peter Bryant, general manager of the Royal Pigeon Racing Association, in the United Kingdom, and David Higgins, region secretary, RPRA, for information about racing pigeons.

Deone Roberts, sport development manager with the American Racing Pigeon Union Inc. in Oklahoma City, Oklahoma, for information on racing pigeons.

Christopher Hunt of the Imperial War Museum in London, for details of pigeons in wartime.

Liliane Reid Lafleur, library technician at the Hartland Molson Library of the Canadian War Museum in Otttawa, for reference and library materials.

Ian Leslie, library assistant at the Canadian Aviation Museum in Ottawa, for information about pigeons in the war.

J. Kevin Ash, a former bush pilot and flying instructor now living in Prince Rupert, British Columbia, for flying lessons by long-distance telephone.

Bruce Wishart, for his suggestions, criticisms, and sympathetic ear.

Raymond Lawrence, my father, for his wartime memories and careful critiquing.

Kathleen Larkin, research librarian at the Prince Rupert Public Library, for absolutely everything. Without her help, advice, and encouragement, this book might not have been written.

ABOUT THE AUTHOR

IAIN LAWRENCE studied journalism in Vancouver, British Columbia, and worked for small newspapers in the northern part of the province. He settled on the coast, living first in the port city of Prince Rupert and now on the Gulf Islands. An avid sailor, he wrote two nonfiction books about his travels along the coast before turning to children's novels. *B for Buster* reveals his interest in flying, which he developed during his school days. But none of his schemes worked out, from his grade two plan for linoleum wings that would help him fly from his garage roof, to his later hope of becoming a bush pilot. During high school he joined a skydiving club near Toronto and made fifteen parachute jumps. On his last jump, he landed on an electric cattle fence. After that, he went north to work in a logging camp not far from Kakabeka Falls.

Iain Lawrence is the author of six other novels for young readers: the acclaimed High Seas Trilogy: *The Wreckers* (an Edgar Allan Poe Award nominee), *The Smugglers,* and *The Buccaneers; Ghost Boy,* a *Publishers Weekly* Best Book of the Year, a *School Library Journal* Best Book of the Year, an ALA Best Book for Young Adults, and an ALA Notable Book; *Lord of the Nutcracker Men,* a *Publishers Weekly* Best Book of the Year and a *School Library Journal* Best Book of the Year; and *The Lightkeeper's Daughter,* an ALA Top Ten Best Book for Young Adults.